"Gayle Bran[...] [...]n her fiction, and characterist[...] [...]intelligent look at xenophobia [...] [...]th her trademark flair for story[...]

—*Seattle Post-Intelligencer*

"Walt Whitman couldn't have asked for a slyer, funnier, savvier envoy than Gayle Brandeis to carry his 'Song of Myself' into our day and age."

—ABBY FRUCHT, author of *Polly's Ghost*

"The personal and the political collide in Gayle Brandeis's complex and witty novel. Like the flashlight Flan shines into storage lockers, *Self Storage* illuminates the way we define our loved ones, our neighbors, and ourselves."

—AMANDA EYRE WARD, author of *Forgive Me*

"Lyrical and winsome."

—*Pages*

"Peppered with wry wit and Walt Whitman, *Self Storage* is a skillfully told treasure-hunter's tale of compassion, coming of age, and, most important, transforming the life you've got into the life you want. In the American tradition of songs of oneself, Gayle Brandeis has written for her characters a standout song of personal growth accelerated by social awakening."

—MARIA DAHVANA HEADLEY, author of *The Year of Yes*

"Brandeis masterfully combines dangerous situations with laugh-out-loud humor in a story that is as unique as its heroine. The author expertly imbues the novel with great depth of feeling."

—*Romantic Times*

"Gayle Brandeis's marvelous novel is a rare thing: a story of love, marriage, and friendship that stirs our most tender emotions without manipulation or bathos."

—AYELET WALDMAN, author of *Love and Other Impossible Pursuits*

"Brandeis hasn't written a typical post-9/11 novel filled with rhetoric and assumptions. Instead, she presents something that we need more of today—a willingness to try to understand those who are different [from] us and a commitment to doing what's right."

—*Feminist Review*

"Beautifully written and warmed with wit, *Self Storage* is a bold, brave meditation on both the family and the whole family of man."

—CAROLINE LEAVITT, author of *Girls in Trouble*

"Deftly plotted and engagingly told, Gayle Brandeis's novel is a suspenseful, thought-provoking, and inspiring exploration of what it means to be a sensitive and thougthful human being living in George W. Bush's America."

—ADAM LANGER, author of *The Washington Story*

"Ms. Brandeis writes about parenthood with insouciance that seems lived."

—*The New York Times*

"A novel that seamlessly blends social and political consciousness in an engaging narrative, truly one of the best books I have read all year."

—Largeheartedboy.com

"A must-read . . . The story is vivid and rich, the plot twists and turns, the characters are quirky and deep."

—Armchair Interviews

# SELF STORAGE

# SELF STORAGE

A NOVEL

## Gayle Brandeis

BALLANTINE BOOKS  NEW YORK

2008 Ballantine Books Trade Paperback Edition

Copyright © 2007 by Gayle Brandeis
Reading group guide copyright © 2008 by Random House, Inc.

Published in the United States by Ballantine Books, an imprint of
The Random House Publishing Group, a division of Random House, Inc., New York.

BALLANTINE and colophon are registered trademarks of Random House, Inc.
RANDOM HOUSE READER'S CIRCLE and colophon are trademarks
of Random House, Inc.

Originally published in hardcover in the United States by Ballantine Books,
an imprint of The Random House Publishing Group, a division
of Random House, Inc., in 2007.

Grateful acknowledgement is made to Alfred A. Knopf and The Wallace
Literary Agency, Inc., for permission to reprint an excerpt from "I see the sign
and tremble" from *Available Light* by Marge Piercy, copyright © 1986, 1988
by Marge Piercy and Middlemarsh, Inc. First appeared in *Images*,
vol. 12, number 1, 1986. Reprinted by permission of Alfred A. Knopf,
a division of Random House, Inc., and The Wallace Literary Agency.

LIBRARY OF CONGRESS CATALOGING-IN-PUBLICATION DATA
Brandeis, Gayle.
Self storage : a novel / Gayle Brandeis.
p.   cm.
ISBN 978-0-345-49261-6
1. Self-actualization (Psychology)—Fiction.   2. Auctions—Fiction.
3. Whitman, Walt, 1819–1892—Fiction.   I. Title.
PS3602.R345S45   2007
813'.6—dc22        2006042937

Printed in the United States of America
www.randomhousereaderscircle.com

246897531

Book design by Fearn Cutler de Vicq

*In loving memory of Jack Cotter*

I first saw that sign off the MidCape highway and thought
I dreamed it in two a.m. fatigue bleary as drunkenness;
then in a dying city on a rusty steamer table
of street, there it was offering
convenience, preservation and power at once:
    Self Storage.
Who would have guessed it?

൮

Sometimes I find no self in me
but a hungry multitude demanding the use
of my body. Self-storage? Is that all
poems are?

We are four-fifths water
and when we die, what remains after the fluids
dry but a stain and the many colored grits
of the ashes, like a puzzle that won't assemble?

Not the wornout wardrobe of self, a knockdown rummage
sale of smelly lusts and stains of fear and meals
dribbled and holes burned for little stars of flesh
to sparkle through. Only what we did, what we made
and what we botched: that shines on
eventually through all the red shifts of distance,
the shape of the constellation our best
and worst acts finally reveal to others,
not to us, buffeted in the center of the explosion
we call our lives.

—Marge Piercy, from "I see the sign and tremble"

# part one

Unscrew the locks from the doors!
Unscrew the doors themselves from their jambs!

*I celebrate myself.*

Sorry. I just can't do it.

Walt Whitman starts "Song of Myself," the greatest poem in the world, with those three words. I wish I could follow his lead, start the same way, but I can't. The words sound tinny in my own voice—arrogant, wrong. Maybe someday I'll be able to say "I celebrate myself" freely, even joyfully, like he does, but I'm not there yet.

Whitman's book saved my life. *Leaves of Grass* saved my ass. If it wasn't for that book, I might be in jail right now. If it wasn't for that book, I wouldn't be writing this one.

I have to admit, it's a bit intimidating to write under Whitman's long and illustrious shadow. I suppose I could try to picture him in his underwear. It worked for Marcia Brady when she gave her big speech (not that Whitman was in the audience at Westdale High). I have an advantage: I've already seen Whitman naked. A series of photos by Thomas Eakins from the early 1880s—"Old man, seven photographs." Whitman's name isn't mentioned, but I can tell it's him. Others have thought so, too. He was pretty cute for a sixty-something-year-old. I love how his belly pouches out just a little, the way my daughter Nori's does over her diaper. I love the way he cocks one hip to the side—a little peevish, a little saucy. I love seeing him stripped bare.

I guess I have to strip myself bare here. I have to unload all that happened these last few months. If I write it down, there's a chance I'll begin to understand it.

One image keeps coming back to me. An image of Sodaba, my neighbor from Afghanistan, hunched inside the storage locker. The front of her burqa was flipped up off her face; it hung down the back of her head like a nun's habit. She was turned slightly away from me; tendrils of hair were plastered against the side of her neck. The wide plane of her left cheek was slick with sweat. That was the first time, the only time, I saw any part of her face. I never learned the true shape of her lips or nose, the full scope of her eyes—just that wet expanse of skin before she realized I was there and pulled the veil back down. The skin of her cheek looked so smooth. It gives me chills to think about it now.

But that's not where I want to start.

I want to go back to my normal life, before her life collided with mine. Back when I had more simple things to worry about—my kids' lunches, my husband's TV addiction, the auctions I attended each week.

The auctions. Of course. I could celebrate my self-storage auctions. That is something I think I could do.

This is how the auctions work.

You get one minute with a flashlight.

The auctioneer breaks open the padlock with a blowtorch or bolt cutters, and you get one minute to stand in the doorway of the storage locker. One minute to peer inside and decide whether the wrinkled black trash bags, the taped cardboard boxes, the bicycle parts and beach chairs and afghans that reveal themselves in your mote-filled path of light, are worth your while.

You learn to trust your intuition. You learn to listen to that ping inside your gut that tells you to bid. You learn to look for the subtle clues—the shopping bags with a Beverly Hills address, the boxes marked FRAGILE with a sharp black marker. You learn to avoid certain smells—mold and mildew are no good; you'll probably end up with a bunch of old sweatshirts and socks that someone put in the wash but never bothered to dry properly, just left them to rot in plastic sacks. You develop a sixth sense for the smell of jewelry, the smell of electronics. TVs emit a hot, charged smell, even if they haven't been turned on for years, while diamonds smell blue, like sweet cold water.

You try to remember that you're bidding on someone else's misfortune. Someone who couldn't pay for their storage locker, who let it lapse into lien. You try to remember that you are benefiting from someone's sadness, someone's failure, that the money you'll gain from this merchandise will come from someone else's loss. You try to remember that there was a self who first put these items in storage, a self who planned to take them all back one day, a self who will miss these photo albums and brittle swim fins and frames filled with dried beans. But you push this all aside when the auctioneer says "Bidding will start at one dollar," and your own self muscles its way to the front, and your own hand flies into the air.

I lifted my chin. Just the slightest tick. A few centimeters at the most. A small tilt of the head, a concurrent yet subtle lift of the brow. I wanted to see how small I could make my movement and still be noticed by the auctioneer. The auctioneer standing on a step stool in his Hawaiian print golf shirt and cargo shorts, the auctioneer with his Ray-Bans and poofy hair, saying "TendoIheartententengoingoncegoingtwice . . . ," his mouth looking too solid to go so fast. Then he said "*Sold* to Flan Parker for ten dollars," and I felt like I had been granted superpowers.

Early in my auction career, I waved both arms to bid. Soon I shifted to one flailing arm. Then one calm arm. Then a single hand. Then a finger. Then the chin. I thought maybe I would get to the point where the auctioneer would notice my pupils dilating, and that would be that.

I fanned myself with the auction list and gave my two-year-old daughter a sip of water. I wished I had been granted superpowers to keep us cool. The year 2002 was one of the hottest on record so far. Even the palm trees seemed to be drooping in the hundred-degree early-June weather. Everything at EZ Self Storage seemed to be drooping, not necessarily because of the intense Riverside heat. It was an older self-storage complex, and the owners hadn't done much to spruce it up over the years. Like most self-storage establishments, it consisted of row upon row of low, rectangular buildings fronted with a series of garage doors. The walls were all unpainted cinder block, gray and crumbly-looking; the roll-up doors had probably been bright yellow at some point, but now were dinged and hammered into a dull, bruised shade. The asphalt on the ground was cracked and pitted, shot through with weeds. I wondered who would want to store their stuff in such a decrepit place.

I looked into the unit I had won. I couldn't wait to find out what was inside one particular JCPenney's bag. The plastic sack looked blocky, like it was full of transistor radios. Possibly bricks of gold.

*Stuff'd with the stuff that is coarse and stuff'd with the stuff that is fine.*

"Good work," said Mr. Chen-the-elder, a dapper junk-shop owner and fellow bidder. He patted me on the shoulder and ruffled Nori's white-blond hair. The auctioneer folded up his step stool and put his clipboard under one arm, his red three-foot-long bolt cutters under the other. The crowd of eight or so of us rambled after him to the next garage door, the last unit of the day, a ten-by-fifteen, most likely out of my league. I just went for the "Flan lots," as my auction cronies had dubbed them. No big-ticket items, just modest assortments of boxes and bags, things I could easily carry to the car myself while pushing Nori's stroller. I was usually able to get them for the opening bid. Most of the bidders weren't interested in the small stuff—they wanted the furniture, the appliances, the big-money pieces; most of them were dealers with pawnshops or stalls in antiques stores. My yard sales were small potatoes. The lots full of antiques could start at over $100 and could go to several hundred, cash only, but they were still a steal. People generally earned back at least twice what they paid in auction once they sold the goods; sometimes they earned back ten times the amount. Sometimes more.

The lot on the block was full of instruments—a drum kit with AMENDZ written on the front of the bass drum in electrical tape, a couple of guitars plastered with stickers, a stand-up bass, a saxophone, all set up like the band had just left to get their requisite groupie blow jobs. A few beer bottles and a couple of towels were scattered over the concrete floor. The storage unit had obviously been a rehearsal space. How could a band let all their instruments go into lien? Maybe everyone died in a Central American bus crash; maybe their wives had nagged them into giving up their rock 'n' roll dreams.

Nori struggled to get out of her stroller. I had augmented the buckle with a complicated knotting of twine to thwart her escape attempts. Nori had become quite the little Houdini lately; it was getting harder to restrain her.

"Tigars, Mama!" She pointed to the guitars. I tried to hush her; the auction was about to start. I wasn't very successful—she screamed at the injustice of being trapped in her small canvas seat. The auctioneer raised his speeding voice.

Mr. Chen-the-younger, a slightly shabbier version of his father, lifted a finger when the bidding reached $250. Yolanda Garcia gave her bouffant-fluffed head a quick tilt to the right when it got to $375. Soon after, Norman, the crusty old swap-meet man, shouted "Right here" over Nori's cries of protest, lifting both of his veiny hands.

"*Sold* to Norman for $425," the auctioneer bellowed. "Good going, everyone." He shot Nori a slightly reproachful glance. "I'll meet y'all in the office for payment."

It was an easy transaction for me—ten bucks for at least a dozen bags and boxes. I couldn't wait to bring them home and crack them open.

.   .   .

My favorite part of the whole auction experience was the moment right before I found out what I had won. The moment when I was sitting on the floor of our second-bedroom-turned-storage-auction-storage-room in my overalls and red Converse sneakers, my short blond hair thick with other people's dust. The moment when I was holding my X-Acto knife over a cardboard box, ready to take the plunge.

I found few things more satisfying than slitting tape with an X-Acto knife. That first pop of the seal, the way the tape snapped and curled beneath the blade, the fusty exhale in its wake. I loved it. I could have slit tape and pried open boxes all day. That moment right before you knew what was in the box—that was the best moment. *That's* what I celebrated. Anything was possible.

I never did find out what was in all the JCPenney's bags. After I paid up and started loading stuff into Booty, the trailer hitched behind Beulah, my old blue Datsun, a woman came up to me, frantic. She was wearing a faded sundress and house slippers. Her hair was a mess. She had probably just woken up.

"Hey, that's my stuff," she said.

"No, it's not," I told her. I was drenched with sweat; it was probably 120 degrees inside that locker. "It's mine. I just bought it."

She started to cry. "I was going to settle the account," she said. "I got here too late."

"How much did you owe?" I asked.

"Three hundred dollars," she told me. The way she said it made it sound like a million dollars. I knew how huge $300 could feel. "All my pictures and crap are in there."

"Tell you what," I said, thinking fast. "You give me a hundred dollars, and I'll let you have your things." I tried to sound charitable. I didn't tell her I had bought everything for one tenth the price.

"Thank you!" She threw her arms around me. I felt like such a schmuck. I could have let her have it for a lot less. I could have let her have it for free.

I helped her carry her stuff, the stuff that was briefly mine, to her seventies-era Oldsmobile. I caught a brief glimpse into the blocky bag that had piqued my interest. It was filled with what appeared to be shoe boxes. Little ones. A baby was asleep in the backseat, strapped into an old chrome-framed car seat, snot dried on his face. I felt even worse about taking the woman's money, but I didn't give it back. It was the easiest money I ever made.

"You're a shrewd business woman, Flan," Yolanda said to me after the woman drove off.

"Nah," I said, "I'm just a jerk."

She was loading boxes into her trailer. One box, marked ART & ECT, caught my eye.

"Hey, will you sell me that box for ninety bucks?" I asked her.

"This box?" She picked it up and looked at it as if she had missed something.

"I don't want to go home without a box," I told her. I also realized I didn't want to go home with that woman's money. My conscience was a tricky thing, taking a snooze, then sneaking up on me like a thief.

"You're crazy," she said, but she shook my hand, then Nori's, to seal the deal.

·  ·  ·

I strapped the box into the passenger seat and we drove home, the battered EZ SELF STORAGE sign getting smaller and smaller in the rearview mirror until I couldn't see it at all.

⟲ When you see the term "Self Storage" all the time, you can't help but start to think about it. You wonder things like where, exactly, is the self stored? Is it in the heart? The head? The pelvis? Is it something that billows through us like a ghost?

Walt Whitman thought the self was expansive, transcendent, divine; he thought the self was *everything*. I wanted to feel that way, I really did, but I wasn't so sure. My self felt pretty small most of the time.

When I was seven and my mom was near death—pancreatic cancer—my father made me stay in her hospital room. It was horrible. She was in so much pain. I could almost smell the pain emanating from her—a sharp animal stench that cut through the antiseptic air, made the hairs on my arm jut like needles from my skin. My father wouldn't let me leave. My mother's body heaved and bucked under the waffled blanket as if she was going to levitate off the bed. She growled and shrieked and made all kinds of inhuman grunts and trills. I wailed and tried to bolt, but my dad held me tight. "This is your mother," he said. "This could be your last chance to see her alive."

"This. Is. Not. Me," she forced out, her lips cracked, her eyes puffy and pink. I got even more scared then. If that wasn't my mom writhing around, who was it? And where had my real mother gone? The last thing she ever said to me—her hand hard on my wrist, her rabbity eyes locked onto mine—was "Take. Care. Of. Your. Self." I thought of the cultured pearls she kept in a soft cloth bag, the teapot she rubbed with silver polish every month, even though she never went anywhere fancy and none of us drank tea. I thought my self must be some expensive and high-maintenance object like that, something rarely, if ever, used. I wondered where I could find it, what sort of care it might require.

My father was no help in this regard. He had one idea for how he wanted me to be after my mother died: quiet. Make that two: quiet and obedient. Neither of which came naturally to me. He wanted me in a preppy schoolgirl uniform twenty-four hours a day. I rebelled. I tried on different skins. Sports-girl skin with striped tube socks and a ponytail and softball jersey. Sullen-girl skin with lots and lots of black. Hippie-girl skin with peasant blouses and worn Levis and bare feet. Hard-rock-girl skin with acid wash and big perms and boots with pointy heels. Nothing too original, I admit. I chameleoned my way through school, picking up the different hairstyles of friends, the different musical and alcoholic tastes of boyfriends, molding myself into their chosen image, a mirror they could look into and see themselves more clearly, not me.

I found Whitman when I was a senior in high school. I pulled *Leaves of Grass* off the shelf—an ancient edition covered with mustard-yellow cloth. I thought it might be a campy old tract about marijuana, although it would be surprising to find such a thing in our house. My parents didn't have that kind of humor. Our bookshelves were sparse, a few technical manuals and

*Reader's Digest*–condensed novels shoved between tissue boxes and geodes and wooden boxes filled with shells from Lake Erie. My own nightstand, on the other hand, was always overflowing with library books. I loved the smell of them, the flutter of their pages against my fingers. *Leaves of Grass* felt different from any other book I had touched—there was a heft to it, a weight, even though it was a fairly slender volume. When I saw my mother's maiden name looped onto the inside front cover in her once familiar handwriting, I felt like someone had kicked the air out of my lungs. I flipped through the book, breathing in the scent of my mother's past, her life before my father, before me. The entire section of "Song of Myself," pages and pages of long-winded verse, was underlined with dark, glossy pencil. My mother had really pushed the lead into the paper. It had even broken through in a few places. I ran my fingertip over the thin, yellowed pages, the narrow-ridged grooves that bulged like veins on the opposite sides. Maybe this was the self she had wanted me to take care of.

I have to admit I found Whitman a little embarrassing at first, a little rhapsodic for my pseudojaded taste (a recently acquired trait, via my boyfriend Rob), but I was intrigued. I liked that he said *I believe in the flesh and its appetites.* I liked how he corroborated my new stoner experience (also courtesy of Rob) . . . *considering a curl of smoke or a hair on the back of my hand as curious as any revelation.* I liked the line *With music strong I come.* Sex, drugs, and rock 'n' roll, Whitman style. I liked how, whatever mood I was in, I could open the book and new rooms would open inside me.

I followed my mother's advice. I've taken good care of the book, kept it safe in the folds of my underwear drawer. Whether I've taken good care of my own self is another question entirely.

. . .

My husband, Shae, was studying—or at least supposed to be studying—the Self. Selfhood. Virtual selfhood. Original self-hood. I was so jealous.

One day, I vowed, I would be back in school and I'd study the self, myself. I wanted to study "Song of Myself," look into what Whitman was really doing with it. I already knew a lot of his omnivorous lines, as he called them, by heart. I wanted to under-stand them in a better, deeper way. I still do.

I tried to share Whitman with Shae, but he was incredibly analytical about everything, and not in an English-major kind of way, which I would have liked—more in a way that deflated any Whitman-related conversation (and it's pretty hard to deflate Whitman). I've shared a few lines with the kids, too, but they're more interested in poems that rhyme—Dr. Seuss, Shel Silver-stein. As much as I loved to read, *Leaves of Grass* was pretty much the only nonchildren's book I was able to squeeze into my life. I picked it up whenever I could, taking sips of poetry between auc-tions and meals and diaper changes and lullabies. The lines chanted through me even when I was far from the book. Whit-man was my therapist, my priest, my touchstone.

One of the new security guards waved me into the leafy oasis of Student Family Housing. I was always glad to drive back home. The large complex was kind of like a self-storage setup, itself—similar houses with different lives behind each door. It used to be army property, housing for married servicemen, be-

fore the University of California, Riverside campus was built in
the 1950s.

There were two hundred or so small plaster houses in the
complex—duplex and single-family, some with peaked wooden
roofs, some flat—all of them sturdy but showing their age. The
thick walls muted the Riverside heat to some extent, and the
curved streets were thankfully shady, draped over with oak and
pepper trees. Some of the houses faced the road; others, like ours,
were set back, arranged around courtyards. Our street, Avocado,
curved by itself at the rear of the complex like the tail end of a
nautilus. Guards had been posted to all the street entrances after
the September 11 attacks the year before; I can't say their presence
made me feel any more safe—the guys let pretty much anyone
in—but they didn't make the place feel any less cozy, either. They
had become part of the community. A few of them even brought
their kids to our playground on their days off.

I loved the gnarled lemon tree outside the kitchen door, the
pair of tall, pointy cypress—my son called them Dr. Seuss
trees—out back. I loved our tiny house, overtaken with my auction stuff as it was. I loved the secondhand feel of the neighborhood. Everyone lived in old houses, pushed old strollers, drove
old cars. Even the plants were raggedy and woody—bug-bitten
rosebushes, papery puffs of bougainvillea, palms that dropped
shriveled orange dates.

Whenever someone shiny showed up in the neighborhood—
someone with polished nails or a new sedan or Baby Bjorn—
they were treated, however unfairly, with suspicion. They didn't
tend to stay long. The shiny people could usually afford to rent a
condo or a house with a pool. The people who stayed here for
years ended up looking like the houses themselves—some peel-
ing plaster, some splintering wood, a good solid foundation. We

all wore jeans that were too tight, or too loose, or too light, or too small-pocketed or too high-waisted to be hip; our tank top straps too wide; our bodies too mushy, but I liked it that way. I liked clothing the neighborhood, furthering our untrendy world.

I deposited Nori next to Shae on the couch, gave my six-year-old-son, Noodle, a kiss, and carried the ART & ECT box into the auction room. The room stuffed to the gills with piles of linens, stacks of plates, bags of clothes. The room so full of random, loosely organized stuff it was almost impossible to walk through it. The little trails I had left between piles were disappearing as the piles slowly gave in to gravity and spilled over. My crazy room. The only place where I could breathe without my children's breath rushing into my mouth.

I sat down on the floor, in the little rectangle of space I had carved out to do my unpacking and sorting. The school-grade linoleum that covered the floor of every room in the house was cool through my overalls. I sat for a while, eyes closed, relishing my time as a solitary body.

My anticipation was building. What could be inside the box? Stolen Rembrandts? Black velvet toreadors? Noodle ran into the room just when I was about to dig in. I should have locked the door. I didn't like having the kids around when I was yielding sharp blades, unloading potential hazards. Once an emaciated but still alive rattlesnake was in one of my boxes, once a bunch of syringes, some full. I knew dead bodies were found in lockers every once in a while—cut up, wrapped in plastic, stuffed into freezers or hope chests or Samsonite.

"What is it, Noodle?" He was wearing one of Shae's tie-dyed shirts, with, I could tell, nothing underneath. His long blond hair, the hair that often caused people to mistake him for a girl, was wild and uncombed. My little hippie.

"Nori's outside!"

"Can't your dad get her?"

"Shake's sleeping."

Everyone called Shae Shake but me. My name was Flan, short for Flannery, and I figured one dairy product name in the family was enough. We all ended up with food names, somehow. We didn't plan it that way—we've never cared all that much about food. Noodle was really Newton—a family name with its own figgy connotations. Shae couldn't bring himself to say no to his grandmother, who wanted us to give our son that name, and I couldn't bring myself to call my baby "Newton." He became Noodle almost immediately. We named Nori after my mother, Nora. We didn't think about the sushi connection until she was a couple of weeks old. It made sense, though; it was probably inevitable. We weren't a very balanced meal—two desserts, a helping of carbohydrates, and some seaweed—but then, what family is?

Noodle tugged at one of my overall buttons. "Mama, she's going to go in the street!"

I dropped my X-Acto knife and chased him outside.

My best friend, Pia, was across the courtyard, holding Nori, clad only in a diaper, on her broad hip. Pia was a doctoral candidate in cellular biology. Her family was from the Philippines. She wore a floral T-shirt and khaki shorts I recognized from one of my auction boxes. I felt a small kick of pride. It was always a treat to see the urban planning scholar from Ghana wearing a Tweety T-shirt I had folded, to know the English major from India walking by probably had red underwear beneath her sari. Student Family Housing was a wonderfully international community. In our courtyard alone, there were also families from Wales, from Guatemala, from Afghanistan. Our blond family was an anomaly.

"Look who I found playing with my hose." Pia handed me a dripping Nori. The front of her body was slippery and cold; her curls were plastered dark against her head. Her diaper felt like a squishy melon. She squirmed in my arms, wanting to get down.

"Thanks, Pia," I sighed.

"Not a problem." One of my other favorite things: Pia's voice. And Pia's long coarse black hair, her large no-nonsense body. "Listen, I'm making a big pot of ziti tonight. If you could throw together a salad, I think Isobel's making bread."

I was routinely assigned some sort of easy side dish during these shared meals. My neighbors quickly learned that even though we all had food names, I wasn't much of a cook. Usually they asked me to bring a bowl of fruit or a pot of rice or some cherry tomatoes from the community garden. Our neighbors shared food from their home countries every once in a while, but more often than not, big pots of pasta reigned on the picnic tables.

The couple from Afghanistan, who lived two doors down from us, never participated. I wished they would—I was very curious about the dusky-spicy smells that wafted from their kitchen. I was even more curious about the woman, who wore a full burqa. I had never talked with her, had never even made eye contact—I didn't know if it was even possible to make eye contact through the mesh window in her veil. The couple kept to themselves. A large American flag hung outside their front door, but I'm pretty sure it was more of a "leave us alone" gesture than a patriotic one. Their duplex had been egged twice since September 11. Once I saw the woman standing in the window while we were eating outside. *She hides handsome and richly drest aft the blinds of the window.* I waved, but she immediately pulled her blinds shut.

Nori wriggled out of my arms and bolted across the yard, her waterlogged diaper starting to sag. Noodle's shoelaces flapped as he followed close behind.

"Stay where I can see you," I said, just as they disappeared around the corner of the duplex. Pia touched my arm and went back to her gardening.

Our front door rasped open and Shae stepped onto our tiny front porch looking bleary and disoriented, running a hand through his long hair. When I first met Shae, his hair was lush, a wavy cascade of maple syrup, shot through with gold. Seven years later, it was still long and wavy, but it had thinned out a lot. His forehead was more prominent, too. His hair used to make him look like a rock star; over time, it made him look like an aging biker, a speed freak.

I had chopped off most of my hair the year before. I was getting tired of Nori yanking on it while she nursed. Now it looked kind of like surfer dude hair, clumps sticking out in all directions. Pia deemed it pixie hair. I kept trying to convince Shae to join me in short-hair-dom, but he wouldn't hear of it.

"What's up?" he asked, his voice groggy.

"You were supposed to be watching the kids."

"I *was* watching them."

"Through your eyelids? Nori got outside, Shae."

"I thought the door was locked. . . ."

The kids reappeared, giggly and breathless. Nori's diaper had fallen off. Noodle was holding a bird-of-paradise stalk like a jousting pole, poking his sister in the butt with the pointy orange flower.

"I'm biting you! I'm biting you!" he said. She squealed happily until she saw me.

"He bite me," she sobbed with gusto and ran into my arms. "He bite me!"

I mouthed "Bite me" to Shae over the top of Nori's musty, damp head. I gave him a snarl that I hoped looked half-playful, half-vicious. He sighed and went back inside, leaving me alone, once again, with the kids.

What can I say about Shae? He was busy working, or at least claiming to work, on his dissertation, "Hands on the Joystick: Televisual Abstractionism and the Postnarrative Origins of Virtual Selfhood." He was getting more and more distracted, more and more abstracted, all the time. His work was centered around the theories of Jean Baudrillard, who believed that simulations of reality were just as real as "real" reality. Shae's whole dissertation hung on those bony French shoulders, but as far as I could tell, his research consisted primarily of watching soap operas, stacking library books in front of the couch, napping, playing video games, and occasionally smoking pot. Every time I came upon him furiously typing, it turned out he was playing Doom. "I have to experience virtual reality if I'm going to write about it," he said. Baudrillard would be so proud. I wanted to trust that he knew what he was doing, but I was beginning to feel as if I had a virtual husband.

·  ·  ·

I met Shae when I was twenty-one; he was twenty-nine. I was working at a place called Grounded, a coffeehouse with a yoga studio in the basement. We served all organic coffee, but it was still full of caffeine, so the yogis in their tight, flared, black pants and colorful Hindu tank tops swung wildly between states of mania and blissed-out calm. The power yoga class was the most popular on the roster; I could almost feel the frantic steam of coffee-fueled asanas rising through the floorboards.

As a barista, I didn't venture downstairs too often, but every once in a while, if I was acting cranky, my boss ordered me to take a restorative yoga class. All the workers had to wear yoga pants and purple Grounded T-shirts, so it was easy to slip into a session. The shirt featured a stick-figure woman doing the tree pose, hoisting a cup of coffee over her head with both hands. It was the logo of the place, and it drove me crazy. I always imagined the cup tipping, the coffee spilling, scalding the woman's scalp. I suggested that an image of a person in classic, cross-legged meditation, holding the coffee cup in her lap, might be more appropriate, but my boss wouldn't listen. I think the terms "centered" and "self-centered" had gotten jumbled up in her brain.

I didn't really like yoga classes. Yoga is supposed to be non-competitive, but I could tell people were sizing each other up, plus my body couldn't figure out basic poses like triangle and down dog. The only good thing about restorative yoga classes was the extended *sivasana* time, corpse pose. It was like getting paid to take a nice little nap in the middle of a workday. Not that I was getting paid that well. My boss thought free yoga classes more than made up for the fact that she paid her workers seven bucks an hour. I considered quitting, but the hours fit with my school schedule, and it was easier to keep working than to find another job.

I was taking a couple of classes at Riverside Community College, saving money so I could move to Oregon. I had been accepted to Reed College, but hadn't been offered any scholarships, so I was biding my time, rooming with a couple of coworkers in a tiny downtown apartment, socking away what I could, knocking some core requirements—math, science, all the boring stuff—off my list. I couldn't wait to get up to the rain and green of the Pacific Northwest, away from the smoggy brown Riverside summers. I wanted to live in a place where I could wear colorful knit scarves, a place where my hiking boots would sink into rich thick mud. A place where I'd be able to focus on my true love: books. I was a voracious reader, but I wanted to become more discerning. Judy Blume and Rumi took up equal space on my shelves. I grabbed whatever called to me at the library and eagerly sought book recommendations from friends, but I didn't know what I really should be reading, how I should be reading it. My high school teachers hadn't been much help; they just had us work with humdrum textbooks and grammar sheets in class. I asked one English teacher about *Leaves of Grass,* but he blushed and said I was too young for Whitman. I couldn't wait for professors with elbow patches and bifocals to point me in the right direction. Maybe I'd become a professor myself someday. Or a librarian. A book reviewer. Something that had to do with Whitman, with words. Then Shae walked into my life. A lot of guys at Grounded had long hair, but Shae was different. He didn't have that beatific yoga look. He was a little pasty, a little paunchy, a little preoccupied-looking under that glorious mane of hair. It was a look that appealed to me. He wasn't wearing a tweed jacket, but I could practically smell the university on him. He barely glanced my way when he ordered a large coffee.

"You consider yourself grounded?" He pointed to my T-shirt. I had been beaming *look at me, look at me* as I rung up his order.

I leaned across the polished wooden counter and said, "No, I can come out and play any time I want." I gave him a smile that almost knocked him over.

I think I fell for Shae because he lived in his head. Most of the guys I met at Grounded were too touchy-feely and sensitive; most of the guys I met at Riverside Community College were all body, body, body. They only seemed to be in school because their parents wanted them to be, plus it was a way to meet girls and avoid entering the job market for a couple of years. They didn't care about learning. I wanted someone to talk to, really talk to about ideas. Shae was great for that. And I figured I could tease him into his body, tease him into opening his heart. The body part was easy. I was pregnant with Noodle five months after we met. I was torn about the pregnancy—I didn't want anything to get in the way of my going to Reed, not even Shae, who I imagined would follow me up there eventually—but he convinced me that when he was done with his dissertation, I could go to school anywhere I wanted. We would take turns, he said, kissing my belly. He was so sweet about it, so earnest, so thrilled about the baby. How could I say no?

Shae was crashed on the couch when the kids and I came back inside. *Days of Our Lives* was on, blasting from seven TV sets, the ones I hadn't sold yet at yard sales, stacked against the wall in a blocky pyramid. Shae tried to convince me his soap opera fixation was related to his studies, but I was pretty sure it was something he had picked up from his grandmother Ada, who raised him after his parents died in a car crash when he was three. That was another thing that connected us, losing parents early on. Shae said he had always wanted to have babies young; I was glad to give him the family he hadn't known as a boy. Not a family marred by tragedy. Not the soap opera family that Shae shared with Ada. The soap operas were always on when we visited her rest home in Alta Dena; she and Shae talked about the characters as if they were related by blood.

Shae's favorite was *One Life to Live.* Sometimes I wanted to shake him and say "This is your one life to live and you're blowing it." I didn't understand how he could fritter away precious study hours when I would kill to be in school. He didn't watch *The Young and the Restless,* but that's how I felt—young, restless. Restless, at least. Maybe not so young. I was almost twenty-eight. *Twenty-eight years of womanly life, and all so lonesome.* (It wasn't as bad as Whitman made it sound. Not always, at least.) I could feel my studies drifting farther and farther away. I looked into some online humanities programs, but they were ultraexpensive, plus I didn't know how I'd be able to find the time to focus on the work. The kids didn't afford me much computer time; I could barely keep on top of my eBay transactions as it was. Once Shae was done with school and settled into a teaching position, he said, we'd be able to afford child care. And he'd watch the kids while I studied. The way things were going, though, I worried the kids would be in college themselves before I'd have my own chance.

A woman was in hysterics on the screens, her face greenish in three, gray in a couple, pink in one, orange in another.

"Shae, what's that character's birthday?" I asked him.

"October nineteenth," he said.

"And what's your daughter's birthday?"

He was silent. The woman's hysteria turned up a notch.

"May third?" he asked. He didn't dare look at me.

"May second," I said. "You suck, Shae."

"I was close," he said. He picked up a notebook and pen and wrote something down.

I sighed. "You let Nori get out."

"Sorry, Flan." He kept scribbling. "You know Nori's escape velocity."

"Escape velocity" was a term Shae borrowed from Baudrillard; it had to do, I think, with how we run from the real world to the virtual one of cell phones and computers and the like. I used to love when Shae told me about Baudrillard's theories. I loved how his name was pronounced—Bau-dree-aard; I felt very sophisticated saying it out loud. Now Baudrillard felt like a dinner guest who had stayed in our house way too long.

"Nori's a real girl, not a virtual one," I told Shae before I went into the kitchen to see what sort of salad I could throw together. I knew it would be cathartic to tear a head of lettuce to shreds.

The evening air was just starting to cool when everyone converged in the courtyard, arms full of bowls, plates, and silverware.

I put my mauled and overdressed bowl of greens on the grayish picnic table. Pia set her pot of ziti beside it. It was no ordinary pot of ziti. It looked—forgive me, Pia—like a pot of vomit, but it smelled great.

"Peanut sauce?" I asked her.

"With mango," she winked at me. Every once in a while, Pia had the urge to experiment with food. Sometimes the experiments were sublime. Sometimes they were just plain weird. When she stuck to Filipino food, it was always fabulous. Even the blood stew.

I wondered what the Afghani couple was having for dinner. It smelled like lamb, onions. Something savory. Something syrupy and sweet with it, too—a sauce of sour cherries, maybe.

Isobel set down a baking dish of corn bread studded with shrimp. Isobel was an economics fellow from Guatemala. She was short and squat, but she exuded the energy of an Amazon; I can't say she was pretty, but there was something smoky and seductive about her. She had beautiful eyes.

"That smells like sex," Nigel, a chemistry major from Wales with a foppy head of dark hair, leaned over Isobel's pan of bread as he set a platter of mushrooms and a six-pack of Corona on the table. The two of them were always flirting.

"That looks like sex." She pointed to the mushrooms. She was right—they were a messy, glistening tangle. I felt as if someone had plucked a guitar string that ran down the center of my body and ended, buzzing, between my legs.

"Is Jorge working tonight?" Nigel asked, trying to sound casual. His wife, an anthropology student, was off doing Ph.D. research in the Basque region of Spain. Jorge, Isobel's husband, had a master's in engineering, but the degree didn't translate in America. The only job he could find was at a canning factory, swing shift.

"Wouldn't you like to know." Isobel hid a smile as she scooped a spoonful of mushrooms onto her plate.

Pia and I raised our eyebrows at each other.

"The party has begun." Nigel smiled at Isobel as he began to distribute bottles.

"So, what's everyone working on today?" I asked after we did the obligatory clinking. I wanted a vicarious shot of academe. Non-Baudrillard academe, that is.

"I plead the fifth," said Isobel, to my disappointment. "This is the one time of day I don't have to think about that."

"Hear! Hear!" Pia took a big swig of beer.

"Come on, you guys," I said.

Nigel began talking animatedly about something involving borons that I tried to follow, but I was immediately lost. At least his accent was nice to listen to.

"I cleaned up some labia today," said Michael, Pia's husband, when Nigel was done. Pia cuffed him on the arm.

"It's my job," he said. Michael was tech support for a porn site. It allowed him to work at home while Pia was at the lab. "The jpegs were all wonky."

"Children are present, might I remind you," said Pia.

"Labia is an anatomical term," said Michael. "We don't need to hide it from them."

The kids weren't paying any attention. They were fully engrossed in their bowls of ziti. I think Pia laced it with some sort of junior smack.

"Did you put coconut milk in this?" I asked her, spooning up another helping. It was incredible, the red peppers and mango bright and fresh in the creamy, nutty sauce.

"Yeah. And some sesame oil."

Shae came outside.

"Shake!" the table called out collectively. He didn't always join us during these meals; I often had to put together a plate for him and bring it to the couch or the computer, wherever he was currently sacked out.

"Hi guys," he said and scooched in next to me on the picnic bench. He had just showered. He smelled sweet, steam still rising from his skin; I could feel my festering anger melt away. All I wanted to do was touch him. It had been way too long since we had seriously touched. I bit into a hunk of corn bread and understood why Nigel said it smelled like sex. The little shrimps packed a fleshy funk. I squeezed Shae's knee under the table. He slid an arm behind my waist, leaned toward me, whispered "Sorry about before." I hoped we would find some time alone together that night.

Nigel handed Shae a beer. I took a second one. Shae and I clinked bottles; the sharp clack sent a hopeful reverberation through my body. People talked about financial aid woes, what was going to be on TV that night, the war in Afghanistan, but I barely heard them. I watched the candles drip down onto the table, watched the kids slide around on the acorn-covered grass after they had finished eating, watched an owl take to the air as the sun started to set, and thought about what Shae and I would do to each other after we got the kids to bed. Baudrillard may have thought that we all wanted to escape reality, but I wanted to get right into the messy heart of it. I popped open another bottle of beer and tried to be patient.

Nori drifted off to sleep after just a couple of minutes of nursing—the three Spider-Man bowls full of ziti had knocked her out. I went out to the living room to read Noodle his bedtime story, and found Shae sound asleep on the couch. I kissed him on the lips to try to rouse him; his lips just flattened under mine. Then they parted, and I was hopeful for a second until he snored into my mouth. His breath tasted like shrimp. I knew that was as sexy as things were going to get.

I hadn't realized how tipsy I was until I stood up, dizzy, my anger reignited. Noodle was sitting on the floor with his book.

"You wanna come in the auction room?" I asked him. "I need to open a box."

"Really?" Noodle had never been allowed in for the opening of boxes before.

"It will be our secret." I touched a finger to his lips, then quickly removed it when I felt a little charge shiver down my body.

He dropped his book and followed me into the room. I ripped my X-Acto knife through the tape that sealed the ART & ECT box. I felt as if I was going to fall into the box and keep falling.

"What do you think it is?" I asked Noodle before I opened the flaps.

"I think the art is going to be shiny, but I don't think we should open it," he said.

"Why not?"

"I think the ect is ectoplasm." He hunched his small shoulders.

"Where in the world did you learn that word?"

"*Ghostbusters.* Ectoplasm is ghost goo. I saw it at Ravi's house, Mama. I don't think we should let it out."

"I think we'll be okay." Even the word "goo" stirred me. I took a deep breath.

Noodle crouched behind my back; I could feel him scrunch his eyes tight against my overalls and brace himself for whatever I was about to unleash.

"Look, Noodle, no ghosts." The only thing that wafted from the box was the scent of kindergarten. The smell knocked the horniness out of my system. Noodle cautiously ventured out from behind me to take a look. ART turned out to be a few pieces of construction paper swirled with cracked tempera paint; ECT was some stone paperweights, an apron advertising a hot sauce company, Dalmation-spotted oven mitts, and a folder filled with operating instructions for electric tweezers, a foot bath, and a popcorn maker shaped like a UFO.

I lifted a stiff painting from the box. Flecks of blue and orange and green fell onto my overalls, the linoleum, Noodle's feet. A large colorful face stared up at us, arms jutting where the ears should be, legs poking out where the neck should be.

"Dan, age 4, first painting, 8/22/90" was written at the bottom with ballpoint pen.

"Dan must be sixteen now," I told Noodle. I put the painting on the floor to start a Return pile. I knew Dan's mother would be happy to get that painting back.

At the start of every auction, the auctioneer exhorted us to return the "personals" to the office after we had gone through the lockers—photographs, letters, important documents. The office made an effort to reunite delinquent renters with items that held obvious financial or sentimental value. I sometimes tried to find the renters' contact information so I could mail them their possessions myself. I knew a lot of people wouldn't want to set foot in the office where they owed money, even if it meant they could get their birth certificates back.

"Dan is sad, Mama," said Noodle. He leaned over the pile of art. His tie-dye shirt rose up; his little penis dangled free, pointed at the floor like a baby's finger.

"Why do you say that?"

"Because he kept getting older."

"And why did that make him sad?"

"Because he already did his first painting and now it's all going to be old."

I wrapped my arms around him. "You're always going to be my baby. You know that, right?"

"I'm your old baby now," he said.

"Yep," I said. "You're my wrinkly old white-haired baby." I kissed his cheek, and to my surprise, he began to cry. Misery rose from his body and blasted into mine.

"I don't want anything to happen to us, Mama." He shook against me. Did he have a premonition something was going to happen? How could he have known?

"Me neither, sweetheart," I said. I patted his head, my own head swimming. I hated to think about anything happening to my kids; I couldn't let myself do it. I scanned the room to see what to include in my next yard sale.

Objects were safe. Objects didn't promise to break my heart.


People were already milling around our front door when I started to drag blankets and boxes out at six-thirty in the morning. If I didn't start at the crack of dawn, I lost a lot of business. Word had spread beyond our neighborhood; veteran Riverside yard-salers often made my house part of their weekend rounds. They didn't have any trouble getting into the complex, but sometimes they plied the guards with doughnuts or coffee anyway. Every once in a while, a guard gave one of the shoppers a few dollars to look for a necklace for his girlfriend, a couple of cereal bowls for his new apartment.

Shae was still passed out on the couch. I had a bit of a hangover, so the cool air felt good on my face; I dreaded the heat that would come with the sun. I set the blankets—the fuzzy, fake-fur kind emblazoned with Raiders logos and sunset scenes and the like—on the acorn-studded grass, under the shade of the corky oak tree. One blanket was for women's clothes; one was for kids' clothes; one was for men's clothes and tools (for some reason, there usually weren't a whole lot of men's clothes); one was for accessories—belts, purses, hats, jewelry; one blanket was for kitchenware; one was for tchotchkes—figurines and decorative tins and assorted doodads; one was for linens; one was for toys; one for books; one for miscellanies that didn't fit in anywhere else. Pretty much every item was fifty cents, except the heavy-duty things like furniture and electronics or the collectibles I hadn't managed to sell on eBay.

I had considered selling all of my auction lots online, but I would miss my yard sales too much. I loved hanging out with my neighbors. Plus it would be a pain to have to take pictures of every single item, to write a description, and upload it all onto eBay. It was hard enough to spend a few minutes at my computer without the kids pulling at me. And that's not even to mention all the packaging and trips to the post office that would be involved. I saved that hassle for the stuff that could really bring in the bucks—nice jewelry, trendy kitsch. I enjoyed watching the prices go up on my eBay page as people bid—it wasn't quite the same sweaty energy of a self-storage auction, but things could get quite heated if there were dueling bidders in the final seconds. I loved thinking of people all over the world hunched over their computers, holding their breath, waiting to see if they won the things I dangled before their eyes.

The nice thing about yard sales was I could see people's eyes; I could see the flickers of anticipation and excitement there. The sheen of satisfaction when they found just what they wanted. The crackle of disappointment when they came up empty-handed.

I set my cigar box full of quarters on my little metal TV tray, unfolded my chair, and my third-world-style mall was open for business. *I have stores plenty and to spare.*

"How are you able to do this every week?" A woman asked as I added up her items in my notebook.

I put her 2T shorts and sippy cup and paper towel rack and Christmas plate and David Cassidy eight-track into a wrinkled plastic bag from Stater Brothers. "If I told you," I said, "I'd have to kill you."

She grabbed her son and left as soon as I handed her her change. She didn't seem to realize that I was joking.

I first found out about the auctions from a family on Grape Street who had started having yard sales every weekend. Noodle was a baby; we got most of his baby clothes there, most of his toys, most of our mismatched plates and silverware.

"How can you have so many yard sales?" I finally asked the mom, a tall woman with a long salt-and-pepper ponytail and intense blue eyes. "Don't you run out of stuff?"

"It's a secret." She winked at me. An inordinate amount of gum flashed when she smiled.

The next weekend, I went to pick up some extra towels—Noodle was going through a major spit-up phase. I asked the woman again: "Where do you get all this stuff?" None of the items laid out on the lawn had been there the week before.

"Magic," the woman said with her horsy mouth, and pocketed my three dollars.

The following weekend, I went back to look for a bathmat (I

found one, decorated with sea creatures, barely used). I opened
my arms to encompass the kitchen canisters and rolling pins and
macramé plant holders.

"What the fuck?" I asked.

A smile danced across the woman's face. She looked around
to make sure no one was watching, then whispered "Follow me,"
jerking a shoulder to her house.

I lugged Noodle's stroller up the front steps and trailed her
inside. Her entire living room, aside from a couch and a narrow
pathway, was filled with boxes. The air was stuffy; it smelled of
mothballs and dust. My throat started to close up immediately;
my eyes began to water.

"Are you moving?" I asked, through a sneeze.

"As a matter of fact, I am," she said. "But not all these boxes
are mine. I mean, they are now. But they weren't always."

She laughed in a way that made me wonder whether it had
been a good idea to go inside some strange woman's house with
my baby. I hoped we wouldn't end up sealed inside one of her
crates.

"I don't follow," I said and sneezed again.

"Auctions," she whispered.

I thought she said "Achoo" to mimic my sneeze.

"Excuse me?" I said.

She looked around again to make sure no one was watching
and said, a little louder, "Self. Storage. Auctions."

I had no idea what she was talking about.

"You know those self-storage places you see off the freeway?"
she asked. I nodded. "When people don't pay, they auction off
the stuff. For cheap. And then you sell it and make a huge profit."

"So that's where your yard-sale stuff comes from?"

She pointed to her nose and whispered "Bingo."

*Who is this kook?* I wondered, but I was intrigued.

"I'm only telling you because I'm moving," she said. "If I wasn't moving, I wouldn't say a word. I wouldn't want the competition. There are too many of us in the mix already. But I'm out of here. I'm moving to Frisco. You can take my slot."

"How did you find out about it?"

"A family who used to live here was in the circuit," she said. "When they moved, they passed it on to me."

She plucked a newspaper from the arm of her sofa. The pages rattled and ruffled under her fingers. She opened them to a page full of small print.

"Look for these." She pointed to the Public Notices. "The lien sales. Business and Professions Code 21700. They'll tell you all you need to know."

She was right. And, following her lead, I didn't pass the auction information on to anyone else in the complex. I didn't want competition over Flan lots. I didn't want competition in the neighborhood. I had the yard-sale market cornered. I was the Godmother of Student Family Housing.

Pia knew, of course; she was part of the family. She came with me to my first auction to make sure the place wasn't full of creeps who would take advantage of me. I found a box of flan mix in the first locker I won, buried in a bag of weird pantry items. Caramel custard glistened on a white dish beneath the brown and orange letters.

I held it up for Pia to see. I could feel the bag of powder shift inside the box.

"It was meant to be," she said. Pia always tells it like it is.

I kept the flan box on the windowsill of my auction room at home until the ants found it. Then I cut off the front of the box and tacked it to the door. The edges were nibbled by silverfish, but I kept it up there anyway; it reminded me I was on the right track.

"You didn't tell me you had a Filipino blouse in your stash." Pia lifted a see-through shirt embroidered with tan flowers. The whole thing looked as if it had been soaked in a tub of tea.

"I didn't know that's what it was." I probably couldn't identify a third of the items that passed through my hands.

"Just for that, you're going to give me this for free," she said. She slipped it on. It looked bulky and wrong with her teapot-patterned T-shirt underneath, but I knew it would be beautiful over a tank top, or the one fancy bra Pia owned.

"It's yours," I told her. She fingered the thready flowers. Already the shirt had grown on her, the reverse of a snake shedding its skin. I don't think clothes can make the person, but I think they can help you see that person. When I saw Pia in that shirt, I could picture her at home with her family, surrounded by banana trees. If she had been naked, I wouldn't have been able to see her life as clearly.

When my mother died, my father asked me to choose the dress she would be buried in. I remember standing in front of her closet, dazed, looking at all the clothes that her body would no longer slip into, all the clothes that would no longer hold her beating heart; they were just limp pieces of cloth now, empty, still smelling of perfume, hair spray, her own warm smell. I finally picked what I thought was the prettiest dress—red and Victorian-looking, covered with tiny gray flowers—and handed it to my father. He smushed it into a ball and brought it to the mortuary.

The funeral was open casket. My mom looked beautiful, but I could barely stand to look at her in that box. I could almost hear her saying *This. Is. Not. Me.* through her thin closed lips. I wished I believed in Heaven, but I didn't. My real mom had disappeared.

Our neighbor Claire, one of my mom's best friends, gasped when she stepped up to pay her respects. "Oh my God," she said. Many people said that when they looked in the coffin. Then she added: "That's my dress."

"What are you talking about, Claire?" my father asked. He was dazed, himself.

"Nora borrowed that dress from me about a year ago," she said.

My father glared at me. I knew I had made a horrible mistake.

"I said she could keep it as long as she wanted . . . ," Claire trailed off. She started to laugh and cry at the same time, which scared me. Later, when my mom was buried, I heard Claire whisper "Bye, Laura Ashley."

"My mom's name is Nora," I whispered back, and Claire started to laugh and cry again.


Pia came over later, wearing the blouse over a blue camisole. It looked gorgeous.

"Do you think the person who used to wear that shirt is still inside it?" I asked her.

"*I'm* inside it." Pia swigged a glass of wine.

"No, I mean, do you think part of a person stays inside their clothes after they give them away?"

"It all comes out in the wash, sweetheart," she said. "Every bit of DNA."

I wasn't talking about DNA, but Pia's mind was much more literal than my own. It was probably an easier way to live.

"Do you think our neighbor would be a different person if she didn't wear her burqa?" I asked.

"Obviously," said Pia. "She wouldn't wear it if it wasn't who she was as a person."

"Do you think she *wants* to wear it or she *has* to wear it?" I asked. I was endlessly curious about the woman. I wonder if that's why our lives collided later; maybe my curiosity acted like a magnet, pulling her into my orbit. Maybe nothing would have happened if I hadn't been so intrigued.

"I don't know." Pia poured more wine into my glass. It glowed like a cup full of light. "Do you like to wear those overalls, or do you have to wear them?"

"It's not the same thing," I said, but I looked down at my red Converse high-tops and wondered if I had set my own trap.

Sometimes I felt a bit trapped in Riverside. Don't get me wrong—I liked Riverside. It was like a bigger version of Student Family Housing. Worn in, a little ragged, but not without its charms. I just had the sense that my real life was waiting for me somewhere else.

Riverside sits in a valley halfway between L.A. and Palm Springs, and doesn't have the glitter of either place. It technically should be desert, but thanks to irrigation, even the brown, rocky areas are scattered with green, including every type of palm tree imaginable—the short squat ones that look like pineapples, the ones that look like they're wearing shaggy hula skirts, the ones that are so tall and skinny they arch over like lowercase "r's" in the wind.

Riverside was derided on all the cool radio stations, called the armpit of southern California. News stories never hesitated to name it the meth lab capital of the world. But those reporters didn't know the Riverside I knew. The Riverside of restored Craftsman bungalows and crumbling Spanish haciendas, of fifties ranch-style homes and brand-new salmon-colored housing tracts. The Riverside of tacquerias and mini-malls and street fairs and roads lined with magnolia and eucalyptus trees. The Riverside of gorgeous clear winters when you can see all the way to the snowy tips of the San Bernardino Mountains. The Riverside where the navel orange was born; the Riverside with the best smog-enriched sunsets you could ever hope to take in—electric swaths of apricot and lavender.

I first came to Riverside right after my high school graduation, three years before I met Shae. My boyfriend back then was a musician; he wanted to head to L.A. to seek his fortune as a head banger. He wasn't very good; I wasn't holding my breath for any record contracts. But I couldn't wait to leave Cleveland, to leave my father, to head for unimaginably exotic California.

We drove cross-country in his primer-splotched Dodge pickup truck, all our stuff crammed under a tarp in the back. *Leaves of Grass* was back there, wrapped in an old half slip, tucked in the inside zippered pocket of a duffel bag. With each passing state, the landscape felt bigger and grander and the cab of the truck felt smaller and stuffier. When we stopped at a Taco Bell in Riverside for lunch on the final leg of the trip, I couldn't bring myself to get back in the truck. I couldn't bring myself to spend any more time with my boyfriend's clove cigarettes and the way he clicked his tongue piercing against his teeth. I slipped my duffels out from under the tarp, left a note ending "C Ya" on the passenger seat, and headed down University Avenue. I walked toward the big yellow "C" carved into the side of the Box Springs Mountains behind the UC campus, moving from one C to another, toward whatever life had in store for me.

Those mountains were directly behind our neighborhood in Student Family Housing. If I looked out the bedroom window, I could see their stony flanks glowing in the moonlight. Our bedroom was literally a bed room. All four of us slept there. My old futon was splayed on the floor, along with the crib mattress that Nori sometimes slept on (no box spring, no frame), and a twin mattress (ditto) that Noodle sometimes slept on, each bed covered with a rotating assortment of clashing, often decades old, cartoon-themed sheets from my auction boxes. We often ended up in bizarre configurations—the average morning found me partly on the crib mattress, partly on the futon, partly on the floor, Shae curled on the twin, Noodle stretched out at the foot of the futon, Nori's little body splayed across the rest of the bed like a giant pink starfish.

The kids loved running around the room in their socks, jumping on the springy mattresses, launching themselves onto the firmer landing pad of the futon. They had more fun on those beds than Shae and I did. The futon hadn't seen much action since they were born. The couch was another story. And the living room floor. And the bathtub. You have to be creative when you have little time and little bed space to work with. But since Shae started getting more and more distracted by his dissertation, none of the surfaces in the house were getting much play.

·   ·   ·

I loved watching the Box Spring Mountains change. Sometimes they looked purple at dusk; sometimes, if it was cloudy, they looked gray, the large rocks embedded there radiant and sandy, like they were glowing from the inside. In the winter, after the rains, the hills were green, the rocks white; in the summer, when you could see them through the smog, everything was brown. There were a few trails leading up to the C, leading up to the radio towers that blink their red lights at the very top of the range. We hiked up twice—once when I was pregnant, and once with a kid strapped to each of our backs. It was a disaster both times—my allergies went bonkers, plus when I was pregnant, the height and exertion made me queasy, and when the kids were with us, Noodle was scared of the lizards doing push-ups on the rocks and Nori's diaper leaked all over my back. I much preferred to look at the Box Spring Mountains through the window of our box spring–less bedroom, the C flashing like a beacon, reminding me—sometimes as a blessing, sometimes as a curse—"See, see, see where you are?"

I normally didn't go to auctions outside of Riverside. Every once in a while I went to Moreno Valley or Corona or Colton, towns close enough so I could get home in time to pick Noodle up from school. But it was summer and I could bring him with me and Nori, expand our purview. So I decided to go to Fontana.

·   ·   ·

We found Your Self Storage on a dusty road lined with eucalyptus trees, sandwiched between a goat farm and an auto parts yard. The freshly painted roll-up doors and roofs of the storage units looked mockingly bright against the dingy landscape. Someone else must have felt the same way—the first "S" on the raised-letter sign had been hit by a rock. Most of the letter was shattered—it made the sign appear to say YOUR ELF STORAGE.

"I guess I'll have to store you here," I told the kids. "My little elf-children." Nori shrieked with laughter, but Noodle looked stricken, as if I might really leave him behind.

I didn't recognize any of the cars, mostly huge SUV-pickup monsters, parked along the sides of the road. This was a whole other auction community. The Garcias and the Misters Chen and Norman and the rest of the gang were not going to be here, that was pretty clear.

I parked my car near the chain-link fence and watched goats stick their wet noses through the diamonds of wire.

Nori was so excited I could barely clip her into her stroller. She immediately began to work at the twine, crying out to the goats as if they could save her. Noodle was thrilled, too, but he tore himself away from the animals and dutifully slipped our bottles of water into his backpack. I learned early on that water was a crucial part of auction preparedness, especially on hot smoggy days.

When I signed in at the registration desk inside the office, the receptionist, an older woman wearing a Rancho Cucamonga Quakes baseball cap, glared at me.

"What?" I asked.

"This isn't a place for kids," she said.

"Yes it is," piped up Noodle. "We saw goats outside! Baby goats are kids. And we saw them! Outside!"

I could still smell their gamy breath in my hair.

"Ghost," echoed Nori, still fumbling with the buckle. A line of drool hung down from her mouth to her lap.

"And this is Elf Storage," Noodle said. "And elves are kids, too." He looked at me for corroboration.

The woman was not amused.

"Do we have to leave?" I asked her. "We came all the way from Riverside."

"Just don't let them out of your sight," she said. "We can't have kids running around the complex."

"I can handle that," I said just as Nori broke free from her stroller and knocked over a plant stand. Noodle righted it, and picked up the crumbs of dirt that had fallen to the floor as Nori ran around the small reception area.

"Auction starts in five minutes," the woman said. "Keep those kids in line."

The Fontana auction crowd wasn't very friendly. No one made eye contact with me. No one made comments, good or bad, about the kids. They kept their eyes glued on the auctioneer, on the storage lockers.

The first few lots were out of my league—huge entertainment centers and sectional sofas and motorcycles. Towering bureaus and old refrigerators. A unit stuffed with so many boxes, poor Booty would never be able to haul them all away. The prices were outrageous—$700, $1,200. I never would have guessed Fontana, which I had always heard was a grungy rural burn-out mecca, to be a big-money town; maybe these people, mostly men, in their pressed jeans and short-sleeved dress shirts and cell phones clipped to their belt buckles, had driven in from L.A.

The auctioneer stood beside the next unit. It was one of the biggest in the place, twenty by fifteen. I almost didn't watch as he opened the lock with his bolt cutters, as he started to roll up the shiny purple door, but something pinged inside my belly. I pushed my way to the front of the crowd, Nori on my shoulders, Noodle hanging on to a belt loop in the back of my overalls, the stroller clunking and hopping as he pulled it behind him with one hand.

The purple door whooshed up to the ceiling. Everyone leaned forward to see what was inside. The combined heat of the day and the closeness of the bodies made me feel dizzy. I held on to Nori's legs with one hand to steady us both. I was about to beam my flashlight into the dim cave when I realized there was no need. The sun had sent a shaft of light at just the right moment, just the right angle, to illuminate the contents of the locker. There was a single box in the middle of the floor. A single, solitary box—no markings, no labels—inside all that space. It glowed in the spotlight of sun. My heart started to race. I wanted it. It was irrational how much I wanted it. I wanted it more than any auction lot I had ever seen. I took a deep breath and could smell the sweet blue of diamonds, the nacreous tang of pearls, the grassy sugar of emeralds, the carbonated clarity of desire.

The crowd began to murmur.

"They wouldn't rent a big unit if the stuff weren't valuable," I heard someone whisper.

"Maybe it's a severed head," said someone else.


The bidding started. Three people, including me, wanted the box. The price kept going up, and I kept raising my hand. I couldn't stop myself. I had never bid beyond $50 before; now I was agreeing to $150, $200. One of the bidders dropped out at $225.

If this had been Riverside, the regulars would have called this a Flan lot right away. They would have let me snag it for the opening bid. But my main competitor, a man with gold cuff links and aviator sunglasses, didn't know a Flan lot from a bowl of caramel custard. He kept raising his hand, and I kept raising mine. My kids, for once, were perfectly still and silent; it was as if my own breath-holding had plunged them into some sort of animated suspension. My adversary dropped out at $330 and the box was mine.

Three hundred and thirty dollars was a lot of money. A month's worth of groceries, not to mention way more than I made at my average yard sale. It was not something to throw around lightly. I had never lost money on an auction before. I hoped the box was full of treasure I'd be able to parlay into more cash.

When it was time to pay and haul the lots off, several buyers milled around my unit.

"Are you gonna open it here?" the guy with the aviator sunglasses asked.

I had planned to—with one box, it would be easy as pie to go through it on site—but I changed my mind. My box-opening time was my yoga, my time to relax. It was sacred. "Sorry," I told him.

I strapped Nori back into her stroller, wended the twine around an extra turn. I squatted to pick up the box, using my knees, as I had learned, not my back. The box was disappointingly light. It flew up to my shoulders with no effort. I was worried it would keep on rising, like a helium balloon, and disappear.

"Three hundred and thirty dollars for an empty box," the man laughed and shook his head. "Hell, I'm glad you won it, not me." He walked away, cocky and bowlegged. I wanted to tackle him to the ground, but I restrained myself.

"Is it empty, Mama?" Noodle asked, worried. He took the box from my hands and, like a pint-size strongman, lifted it easily up over his head.

The box jostled quietly on the passenger seat the whole ride home; nothing rattled inside of it, no clunk of metal, no ring of crystal, no soft rustling of newspaper or bubble wrap or Styrofoam. I wondered how I was going to tell Shae I had just spent $330 on an empty box. I wondered how we were going to get through the month. I had a couple of eBay auctions ending soon. Maybe the bidding would spike up at the last minute and save me.

Shae was sacked out on the couch when we got home, his hand buried in a bag of cheese puffs. His eyes were tellingly red. The stack of library books had grown taller on the floor, but none of the spines had been cracked. None of the pages were coated with orange powder from his fingers. The only thing tinged with orange was the remote control. A soap opera woman in a blue bridesmaid dress was having some sort of conniption fit. Shae said "Hey" when he heard us come in, but he didn't take his eyes off the seven screens. I had tried to encourage him to just turn on the one with the best reception, but he insisted on all seven. He said if he only had one screen on, the other six stared at him blankly and made him nervous.

"Daddy, we saw ghosts." Nori jumped on his lap. "And one of them eated a flower!"

"Cool, baby girl," said Shae. He tilted the bag of cheese puffs so she could grab some. Noodle sat down next to them. His face immediately slackened into TV-watching mode.

"I'll be in the auction room," I said as I walked past with the box. I couldn't bring myself to tell Shae what I had paid for it. "Don't let Nori get outside."

"I won't," said Noodle.

I closed the door of the second bedroom behind me; I fell into corpse pose and let the coolness of the linoleum seep into my body.

The box sat next to me, full of emptiness.

How could I have spent so much on a single box?

Was this my karma for taking one hundred dollars from the woman whose lot I won for ten?

I sat back up and grabbed my X-Acto knife. My usual box-opening fizz was gone, replaced by a dull throb of dread. I closed my eyes and dragged the knife across the filament tape. With each pop of the slender fibers, I felt I was slitting the tendons of my own wrist.

I half-expected spirits to swirl out of the box, à la Pandora. Angry ghosts, maybe the ectoplasm Noodle was so scared of. Instead, a vaguely floral smell drifted up, a surprisingly clean smell. I slipped my fingers into the gap between the cardboard flaps, and slowly, cautiously, spread them open.

The inside of the box was painted with swirls of color—purple and silver and orange and green. I thought I could see things in the serpentine of swoops—a sun, a half-melted face, a pear, an owl, a spoon—but I wasn't sure if the artist put them there or if I was just finding stories in the clouds. It was such a vibrant riot. If I unfolded the box and framed the cardboard, maybe it would be worth something. A woman in San Bernardino had recently bought a painting for five bucks at a thrift store; it ended up being a Jackson Pollock, worth millions. I shined my flashlight inside to see if anyone had signed the box.

The beam lit upon a scrap of blue paper, half-tucked into one of the bottom folds of the box. I tugged it out, losing a corner of it in the process. The paper was hand-made, a thick slab, like a hunk of blue oatmeal flecked with dried flowers and copper thread. A single word was written on it, in gold ink, in thick swoopy letters: YES.

The word caught me off guard. It felt like a karate chop to the throat.

I flipped the paper over. It said, also in gold ink, but with thinner lettering: "If found, please return to me at the blue house on Mount Baldy. Many thanks, Julia."

I was supposed to return the box? Maybe this Julia would re-imburse me for some of the auction money. I headed over to my auction-room computer to do a Google search on "Julia," "Mount Baldy," "blue house," "art," when the doorknob began to rattle.

"Mama?" It was Noodle, now knocking frantically. I had locked the door this time. "Nori got outside!"


The word "Yes" clunked through me as I ran past my passed-out husband, as I grabbed Nori before she ambled into the street, as I carried her back inside, as I attempted to reason with her, as I glared at Shae until he woke up and retreated to his computer in the kitchen.

I probably wouldn't have admitted this to anyone, but I didn't have a lot of Yes in my life. I had a lot of Yeah. A lot of good stuff—my kids; Pia; my neighborhood; my neighborhood meals; my opening of boxes; my occasional, though increasingly infrequent, fumblings with my husband. But not a lot that made me light up. A low flame, maybe. A dull glow. The word "yeah" sounded like a yawn, a sigh. Not a sizzle. "Yes" was garlic thrown in hot oil. "Yes" was waves hissing onto the shore, Pop Rocks crackling in the mouth. Maybe a "Yes" was waiting for me somewhere. Maybe this Julia had an answer, a key. I went on the computer and learned, to my relief, that the bidding on one of my eBay auctions—an original Star Wars Play-Doh set—had inched up over $200. I couldn't find anything online about the artist, though. I'd just have to drive up to Mount Baldy, I decided, and see if I could find her myself.

# part two

In vain objects stand leagues off
and assume manifold shapes.

I was a nervous wreck driving up the mountain. I hadn't driven on steep twisty roads in years; having the kids in the car made everything seem even more dangerous and terrifying. Every time I turned a corner, I was sure a car was going to come barreling around from the other direction and plow into us head-on. Every time our car was on the outside edge of the road, near the drop-off, near a railing, I was sure we were going to go over the edge.

The ride didn't have its normally soporific effect on Nori, probably because of all the twists and turns and my propensity to stomp on the brakes when things got hairy. The kids were being noisy, which made me even more anxious. They screamed when we went through the tunnels; they shrieked with every hairpin turn—Nori with joy, Noodle with fear thinly disguised as joy. I was tempted to turn around and go home but the word "Yes" kept me plowing forward.

Mount Baldy Road wended past lodges and trout pools and campgrounds until it ended in the parking lot for the ski lift. The lift operated all year long; in the summer, it took hikers and mountain bikers up to the trails. We got out of the car to stretch our legs and catch our bearings. The air was so clean, it almost hurt my lungs. Manzanita and pine trees towered over us.

"Can we go up there, Mama?" Noodle pointed at the ski lift, which shocked me. Heights terrified him.

"Up, Mama, up dare!" Nori jumped toward the feet dangling above our heads.

"Are you sure?" I asked. "Wouldn't you rather run around? We've been sitting down so long."

"Please?" Noodle's eyes grew wide. Nori followed suit with a plaintive "Pwease?"

I glanced at the price list. Kids under six were free.

"Okay, but only if you don't tell them you're six," I whispered to Noodle. Noodle took great pride in being six. Five was a baby; six was a big boy. This could be a problem.

He nodded solemnly. He had seen the list, too.

We got our tickets and went over to the loading area. The chairlift seats were higher than I had anticipated; they zoomed around the corner and to the loading station at a speedy clip. They barely stopped to let people on. It seemed as if I would have to hold both kids, stand on tiptoe, and jump backwards to get on. We stood off to the side, intimidated.

I considered getting a refund, but then an employee, a high school girl in a navy polo shirt and tan shorts, offered to help us. She said she'd hoist Noodle onto the lift if I helped Nori.

When the next chair swung around, she put Noodle on. Then Nori jumped out of my arms and ran away, giggling. I chased after her, and the chair holding Noodle took off. The safety bar hadn't been pulled down. I wanted to yell, but I was too stunned. I watched him go higher and higher, farther and farther away, my throat shrinking as he grew smaller. I couldn't seem to move my limbs. I finally grabbed Nori and held her so tightly, she screamed. Of course Noodle was shrieking his head off, too. My blood prickled back to life.

"Can you stop it?" I asked the girl, who looked as frantic as I felt.

"He's too far up," she said.

"Can you bring him down backwards?"

She shook her head.

"His safety bar isn't down." I had visions of him plummeting off the lift, falling onto the pine trees and rocks below.

"Pull the bar down," the girl and I started to call up to him. Nori joined in, yelling "Pada bada, Noodie!" We could see him do it. The bar looked thin as a paperclip from where we stood. I was grateful Noodle was the one up there, not Nori. At least Noodle would be cautious. Nori would have jumped out by now.

"I'll radio the people on top and tell them to hold him until you get there," the girl said. She helped us onto the next seat. I was so shaky, I could barely move. I kept my arms around Nori like a vice grip. Noodle was about twelve seats ahead of us. He cranked his head back so he could keep his eye on us the whole way up.

"We'll meet you at the top," I shouted. "It'll be okay!" I wasn't sure if he could hear me, or if I believed the words myself.


We finally got to the top. A worker there was trying to entertain Noodle with funny faces, but it wasn't working. Noodle looked pale, disengaged, oblivious to the man's crossed eyes. As soon as I stumbled off the lift, Noodle grabbed on to me and started to sob.

"I thought I was going to fall," he cried. "I thought I was going to die forever."

I hadn't budgeted for a meal out, but it seemed like some soup and melted cheese would calm us all down. We went to the restaurant by the top of the lift. Noodle barely touched his burger, but Nori happily tore her grilled cheese sandwich apart and ate the scraps. With all the grilled cheese we ate at home on non-communal-meal nights, I was surprised that's what she wanted; maybe it was the only thing Nori knew. Just like escaping is what she knew. And worrying is what Noodle knew. And vegging is what Shae knew. And exhaustion is what I knew. It was hard to imagine life any other way.

I looked out the large windows at the pine trees, the saturated sky. I took some deep breaths, ate some onion rings, and tried to convince myself we could find new ways of being in the world.

When it was time to leave, Noodle didn't want to get back on the lift.

"We'll be together this time," I tried to reassure him. And we were, even though it took us a few tries to get on the seat. This time it was nice, despite the fact that my stomach flew up into my mouth a few times when I pictured Nori sliding out from under the safety bar, and Noodle freaked out every time one of us swung our legs and the seat began to sway.

I was able to appreciate the scenery a bit more on the way down. We could see for miles, gorgeous hillsides covered with trees, dotted with houses. The kind of foresty green landscape I'd always felt drawn to. The visibility would have been better if it hadn't been a smoggy day. The haze lay like a blanket beneath us, covering the lower elevations. Other mountaintops shot through it, tips of icebergs in a gray sea. Supposedly on a clear day, you can see all the way to Catalina Island. The view was beautiful even with the disturbing number of dead trees, victims of recent droughts and the resulting bark beetle proliferation. We spotted a couple of deer. The air smelled resinous, wonderful. Noodle, still shaken, noticed a hawk perched on top of a pine. Then, the coup de grâce, Nori pointed a finger and said "Da bue." And there, nestled within a stand of trees, was a small cabin painted an electric shade of blue.

Both kids fell asleep in the car almost immediately; all the drama had worn them out. I drove through the curvy, residential sections of Mount Baldy Village feeling reckless. There were no big drop-offs to worry about, the kids were quiet, and adrenaline was coursing through my veins again.

The blue house seemed to have disappeared. Maybe it had been some sort of shared hallucination. We passed brown cabins, stone cottages, dark green A-frames. I turned down a couple of roads marked "Private," a little nervous that someone would come barreling out of a cabin with a shotgun to see who was chugging up their drive, but the only signs of life were squirrels and chipmunks that narrowly missed my tires.

Then a car zoomed past in the other direction. It was painted like the inside of the auction box, swirls of color everywhere. The roof was studded with what appeared to be marbles. It had to be Julia. I did a hasty U-turn, driving off the road into a trough of pine needles. Noodle woke up with a start, gave a little yell, then drifted back off to sleep as I gave chase.

I felt like an action hero, a girl detective, zooming around corners, on the trail. I lost track of the car for a couple of minutes, then caught some kaleidoscopic flashes between the trees. I turned onto a dirt road that wasn't marked "Private"; it didn't look like a road at all, just a narrow, tire-troughed, leaf-glutted path. Branches smacked at the windshield like a demented carwash, leaving a couple of scratches on Beulah's glass. I felt as if I were driving down that punishing path for hours. Then it opened into a small clearing. There, tucked away inside some trees, sat the blue house. A woman with a shock of bright blue hair—Julia, I presumed—was sitting on the front step as if she were waiting for me.

The kids were still asleep. I left the windows open a crack and got out of the car, carrying the box with me.

Julia wore overalls similar to mine, covered with splotches of paint. She wore Converse shoes, too, although hers were white sneakers, not red high-tops; they were also spattered with color. I wondered if maybe she was me in a parallel world, my artistic doppelgänger. Smoke curled around her head.

"Which one is it?" she asked, grinding her cigarette into the step.

"Excuse me?" I walked toward her.

"Which one is it?" She looked tired. "Yes or No?"

"In the box?"

Julia nodded.

"Yes. It says Yes." From a distance, I thought Julia was young, in her twenties, but as I got closer, I saw that she was more likely in her fifties, her angular face etched with a web of fine lines beneath her Technicolor hair.

Her shoulders sagged. "Shit," she said. "I knew it. Fuck!"

I placed the box at her feet. She opened it, pulled out the slip of paper, snorted, and dropped it. It fluttered back down into the box, twirling like a winged maple seed. If the paper had said "No," would I have been as compelled to find her? I doubted it.

I glanced back to the car to see if the kids were still sleeping.

"Yes to what, if you don't mind my asking."

"You know the Zen Center?" she asked.

I nodded; I had seen a sign for it near the ski lift.

"I guess I'm going to be a nun there," she said.

"A Zen nun?" I had never heard of such a thing. I had been around plenty of Zen posers at Grounded, but never a Zen nun.

"Yeah." She lit a new cigarette and took a deep drag. "I'm going to give up my art and be a fucking Zen nun."

"You can't." The words flew out before I knew what I was saying.

"And why not?" she asked calmly, blowing smoke out of the corner of her mouth.

"Your art is so good." I didn't understand how she could let storage units, fate, determine her future like that. Maybe it was a Zen practice in itself.

Julia threw the cigarette, barely smoked, on the ground, sending sparks flying over dead pine needles. I hoped they wouldn't burst into flame. She ground the butt out with her sneaker, stood up, and stretched. She wore a stained men's undershirt under her overalls. When she lifted her arms, the shirt slid aside and I could see a glimpse of a droopy breast. Some sort of tattooed sun radiated across her sternum.

"Those your kids?"

I nodded, wondering if she was going to say something about me leaving them in the car, but she just said "Cute."

"You're a hard woman to find," I told her.

"That's precisely the point," she smiled wryly.

I had a sudden flash of envy for her solitude, her little house draped with wind chimes and bird feeders and strange ornaments made out of bottle caps. Her aloneness.

Noodle started to scream for me. It wasn't long before Nori was screaming, too.

"Excuse me," I said. I raced over to the car and unhooked my rumpled, panicky kids.

"You found the blue house?" Noodle tried to sound excited, but his chin was trembly, his eyes teary.

"Isn't it cool?"

"Bue," said Nori groggily. I caught a whiff of her diaper, which desperately needed to be changed. I grabbed her and the diaper bag and trudged over to the blue house. Julia had gone inside, leaving the door open. Nori wriggled out of my arms and raced into the house, Noodle close behind her.

Julia was in her narrow, cluttered kitchen, setting a teapot on her tiny stove, also painted in swirls of color. So was the fridge, a rounded model from the fifties. Plants, ladles, pots, and assorted baubles and winged creatures hung from ceiling hooks around the room. Everything was well above my head, but I felt the need to duck. The kids disappeared into another part of the house and began to hoot like barn owls.

"Come in, why don't you?" Julia's voice was tinged with sarcasm.

"I hope you don't mind."

"Mi casa and all that," she said. She rummaged through a drawer until she extracted a red-and-white-striped tin of tea. "Kids should like peppermint," she said. "I don't think they'd like my normal brew." She held up a bag of what looked like twigs and chips of bark.

"Peppermint sounds good," I told her. Something crashed in the background. I held my breath. The kids were suddenly very quiet.

Julia opened a long, thin box of cookies as if nothing had happened. Her self-possession was unnerving.

"I'll go see what they're up to," I said.

They had been jumping on a daybed—possibly Julia's bed,

since I wasn't sure there was enough space for a bedroom inside the small cabin. Multicolored pillows were strewn over the floor. A purple glass vase had shattered on the ground; the long stems of calla lilies it had contained were scattered like a game of giant pickup sticks.

"Oh no," I said, mortified. "You guys! What have you done?"

"I didn't mean . . . ," Noodle started. They both looked guilty.

"Don't worry about it." Julia came into the room, holding a plate of hard-looking cookies. She set it on a low side table and began to scoop up pieces of glass. "This would be great for mosaics," she said. "Not that I'm going to do any more of them."

*Do more mosaics,* I tried to tell her telepathically. I couldn't understand how she could give up something she was so good at.

"I can repay you for the vase." I bent down to help her. She waved me away.

"Are you a troll?" asked Noodle.

"Are you a girl?" Julia asked back, drily.

Noodle's face crumpled.

"He means those dolls with the hair." I wrapped one arm around Noodle and pulled my other hand over my head to outline a big tuft. "He has one with blue hair at home."

"I'm not going to have this much longer." She shook her blue thatch in our direction as she continued to pick up shards.

"You have to cut it off?"

Julia grabbed an empty flower pot and dumped her handful of glass into it. Little bits stuck to her skin, sugaring her palm.

"Yessiree, Bub." She wiped her hand on her overalls, leaving a trail of glitter.

"All of it."

"Yep. Want to do it for me?"

"You don't have to do it in any sort of ritual way?"

"Nope. I just have to get rid of it. I'm going to be a baldy on Mount Baldy." Her laugh rang right through me.

I thought about all the times I had offered to cut Shae's hair. It would probably feel good to run clippers over someone's head. "Sure, why not?" I told her.

Julia dragged a chair into the kitchen. She grabbed electric clippers out of a drawer filled with spatulas, vegetable peelers, paintbrushes, tampons, and at least one yo-yo. I wondered if all her drawers were equally jumbled. The answer, as far as I could tell, was yes: Julia pulled some plastic sheeting from another drawer that also contained, from what I could see, a glass jar full of buttons, a bag of trail mix, some scissors, a rubber cat toy shaped like a hot dog, and huge rolls of duct tape. It looked like the contents of a box I might win at an auction. I wondered how many people had drawers like this, and simply shook them into cardboard boxes before they moved.

Julia lay the sheeting on the ground and put the chair on top of it. She wrapped another sheet of plastic around her neck, then sat down and handed me the shears. "Go for it," she said. "The outlet is next to the sink."

I suddenly felt shy and weird, as if she was handing me some sort of sex toy and wanted me to get her off.

"Are you sure?" I asked. Cutting a virtual stranger's hair seemed too intimate all of a sudden. I could still feel the heat from Julia's hand on the metal handle.

"Shave me, baby," she said. That didn't help matters.

An erotic jolt went through my limbs when I pressed the plug into the outlet. I felt my face redden. The clipper began to whir. I took a deep breath. The kids watched from the doorway.

"Where would you like me to start?"

"Anywhere. It's all coming off, right?"

I touched the edge of the clippers to the nape of her neck. My hand jerked; the blade dug into Julia's skin and drew blood. Two red dots welled, like a vampire bite.

"Ow!" she shouted. Her hand flew back as if to swat a mosquito. She touched the cut, then licked the blood off her finger. "Damn."

"Sorry," I told her. "Do you want me to keep going?"

"Just be careful."

I gently eased the blades into the back of her hair, glided them up the contour of her skull. Blue hairs flew into the air in their wake. *This is the press of a bashful hand . . . this is the float and odor of hair.* I remembered when my high school boyfriend hit a pheasant with his truck on our way out of Cleveland; feathers exploded into the air like earth-toned fireworks. Now blue hair was everywhere, on the floor, on Julia's shoulders, in my pockets, in my mouth. When Julia was left with a blue crewcut, I switched the blade for a closer shave. Each sweep of the clippers revealed new swaths of scalp. The skin was tinged blue in places, like the USDA stamp on chicken at the grocery store. The shape of her increasingly bare head struck me as poignant, as if she were sick, fragile as an eggshell. It made her look mortal.

When Julia went off to the bathroom to inspect her shorn head, Noodle shyly sidled up to me and said, "Can you cut mine, too, Mama?"

"Really?" My heart did a mini-plummet. I loved his blond never-cut-in-his-life hair.

He nodded, sucking in his lip.

"But your hair is so beautiful." I ran my fingers through the silky, tangled strands.

"I want to look like a boy." I could tell he was trying to make his voice sound firm.

"I wanna look like a boy, too, Mama," Nori piped up.

"Not today, love girl," I told her. There was no way I was slicing off those golden curls. I turned to Noodle. "Hop on the chair."

"Don't make me bald." He ducked forward, already anticipating the bite of the blade.

"Don't worry, sweetie." I turned on the clippers and watched my angelic, timeless-looking child turn into a modern boy, inch by inch.


Noodle, trailed by Nori, ran to the bathroom to look at himself just as Julia was coming out.

The floor was covered with blue and white-blond hair. I wished I had kept the very first lock that had fallen from Noodle's head. I grabbed a pinch from the sheeting instead, and slipped it into my pocket, some of Julia's mixed in.

"I hope you didn't want me to keep your hair separate," I said as she stepped back into the kitchen.

"Nah, I was just going to put it outside for the birds."

I imagined looking up into a tree and seeing a blue nest.

"What do you think?" I asked. She looked much older without the blue hair. I couldn't mistake her for someone in her twenties, now. Her whole body seemed to have shrunken into something more compact, more vulnerable. Her overalls sagged on her body in a way they hadn't before.

"Your boy looks good."

"He looks grown up."

*The boy I love, the same becomes a man.*

I felt as if I was going to cry.

"You missed a couple of spots." She showed me some stubble behind her ears.

"Sit down." I changed the blades and cleaned up the overlooked bits. It felt good to rub the shears over a bald head, smooth and easy. I didn't realize I had put my other hand on Julia's shoulder until she reached up and covered it with her own. The front of my body leaned against the back of her body. I could feel the rise and fall of inhale, exhale, inhale, exhale, but I wasn't sure if it was Julia's breath or my own. I hadn't felt that close to another body, another grown-up body, for a long time. I took the clippers off her head, but they were still whirring in the air. Julia turned to face me; her eyes were filled.

I wondered if this fifty-something almost-nun was going to kiss me. Much to my surprise, I kind of wanted her to. I could feel my lips soften in anticipation. Then Noodle walked back into the room, his face gleaming and serious with pride. His stride had taken on a new energy, more confident, more *male*. I pulled away from Julia, thinning the tug between us. The front of my body felt instantly cool. I turned off the clippers.

"Hey there, little man," I said. He beamed shyly back at me.

"Mama, when you gonna cut my hairs?" Nori popped up in front of her brother. She had a soggy cookie in each hand.

"Not today, sugar beet," I told her.

Julia's eyes were closed. She was breathing deeply. Meditating, I guessed. Trying to center herself again, too.

"Well, I guess we should be going," I said. "It's a long drive back—I don't want to hit traffic."

Julia didn't open her eyes, but she nodded.

"Good luck with everything," I said. A little half-smile passed over Julia's face.

I felt funny leaving while her eyes were closed, but thought it would be even weirder to stay. I gathered up the kids and ushered them out of the room. As we were closing the door behind us, I heard Julia jump up. I wanted to keep walking, to get away before I felt tempted to kiss her again, but she called, "Wait!"

I turned around and there she was, holding the cardboard box.

"It's yours," she said. Without her hair, her eyes looked much bigger.

"Thank you." I didn't know what else to say.

"You, too." Julia ran her palm over her newly smooth head.

"We should go." I glanced into the box and saw the word YES flickering in the shadows.

"You don't have to do what the box tells you to do," I told her. "You should do what makes you say Yes inside." I didn't know I was going to say that. It just popped out of my mouth. It felt like something I would have overheard at Grounded. It felt like something Whitman might have said. I blushed. Julia touched my shoulder, smiled at our shoes, and walked back to her house.

After I helped the kids into Beulah, I caught a whiff from Nori's pants and realized I had never changed her diaper. Nori's poor little bum. I felt horrible about it, but I didn't want to do the dirty work in front of Julia's house. I was worried I would be pulled back inside those blue walls. I barreled down the driveway, branches smacking and scratching Beulah in the face. I changed Nori in the parking lot of a little market in Mount Baldy Village; I had to practically chisel the poop off her butt. Noodle watched, his face twisted in disgust. I tossed the diaper in a Dumpster, Noodle breathed a sigh of relief, and we began our twisty, turny drive back down the hill.

I was acutely aware of people's hair on the way home. I saw men, women, children in other cars and wanted to run my fingers through their hair—brown hair, red hair, black hair, gray hair, curly hair, frizzy hair, lanky hair, dried-out hair, hair of every length and style. I wanted to stand behind each of them and cut all their hair off, watch the shapes of their skulls emerge, feel their backs breathe against my rib cage. A pang darted through me when I thought of all their human heads, all their human skeletons that would one day be stripped of hair and skin, gone. I watched my kids sleep in the backseat and thought my heart might rip open.

When I pulled into my parking spot, the burqa woman walked by. I was consumed with an urge to pull off her veil, to see what her hair looked like, to unclasp it—for I was sure it was bound up in some way—and let it cascade down her back, into my hands. The woman glanced my way, and, as if reading my mind, hurried to her house.

Shae was at the computer—actually writing, it seemed—when we came into the kitchen. I walked toward him, dying to dig my hands into his hair. He quickly shut down the window, as if he didn't want me to see what he had been working on.

"What happened to you?" he asked Noodle.

"Mama cut my hair," he said proudly. His neck had never looked so long before.

"Hmmm," said Shae. He seemed unsure what to make of it. I saw Noodle's confidence waver.

"He looks so grown up, doesn't he?" I said.

"My little man," Shae said, ruffling Noodle's hair. Noodle smiled and ran out of the kitchen, Nori right behind him.

I stepped behind Shae. "Let me cut your hair, baby," I whispered into his ear. It felt like the most erotic, most profound thing I could say to him. I wanted to melt into his back, but he stiffened in his chair.

"No way, Flan," he said. He stood up so fast the top of his head clanged against my chin. For a second, I saw stars.

Maybe I couldn't cut Shae's hair, but I could yank the husks off some corn. Pia had asked me to pick a few ears from her patch at the community garden. She was going to make black bean burgers to go with it. I gathered up the kids and walked over to the dusty clearing near the corner of Avocado and Utah.

That spring, each family had been given the chance to care for a small plot carved out in the dirt. We weren't sure we were going to get one, but Pia helped me and the kids get started in April. Our carrots never got any bigger than withered little fingers, and the basil was eaten up by some kind of pest, but we had some luck with our tomatoes, and way too much luck with the zucchini. By early June, we couldn't give the squash away fast enough. We let a few of the veggies keep growing on the vine; they ended up obscene, almost as long and hefty as baseball bats. The kids loved checking the plants' progress, measuring the squash in relation to their feet, then their arms, then their legs. Now, at the end of June, one was gaining on the length of Nori's body.

The stalks of Pia's corn were papery and dry next to the lush abundance of the rest of her crops. The corn silk poofing out from the husks looked like monks' top knots. I ran my hands over the damp strands and thought of Julia. I decided to open up the painted box and tack it to the wall of my auction room.

When we got back to the house, I set the grubby kids on the kitchen floor so they could shuck the corn, with a paper grocery bag for the husks and a plate for the cleaned ears. I had planned to shuck, myself, but felt compelled to log on to Shae's kitchen computer instead. I hoped he wouldn't mind; I usually only used my computer in the auction room. I had a burning desire to look up the Zen Center website and to see what Julia's life would be like there.

The practice was very regimented—wake up at 3:00 a.m., chant at 3:30, meditate at 4:15, have breakfast at 6:30, do work practice (cooking, sewing, plumbing, office work, etc.) at 8:00, have lunch at noon, more work practice at 2:00, dinner at 5:45, meditate at 7:00, retire at 9:00. The monks online all wore black robes, but not all of them were bald. None of the women were bald. Why had Julia asked me to shave her head if it wasn't required?

When I finally looked up, corn silk was everywhere. The slippery strands covered the floor in an even jumble; they hugged the legs of the dinette chairs, were plastered against the metal sink cabinets, and thoroughly woven into Nori's hair, which looked like corn silk to begin with. Her bath was going to be a particular challenge tonight.

Shae ambled into the kitchen and frowned at all the corn silk.

He was the life I've chosen for myself. His schooling. His distractions. The family we created together. I had to remind myself that he was what I had wanted, who I had chosen.

"Do you need your computer?" I asked him. A monk standing under a pine tree stared out from the monitor; the sleeves of his robes draped down toward the snowy ground. His glasses looked anachronistic on his gaunt, beatific face. I wondered if Shae would ask me what I was looking at. I wondered what I would tell him.

"Not yet," he said. "I'm marinating." If he marinated much longer, all the meat would fall off his bones. I wanted to be sympathetic. I knew how much pressure he was under; I could hear the strain in his voice. He wasn't always like this. He used to be excited about his work. About me. I tried to be patient with him, but I could feel the meat starting to fall off my own bones. When had we slipped into this holding pattern?

I got up from the dinette chair. I picked my way across the narrow room, around the kids, between the corn silk strands. I stood in front of him, my husband. I put my face against the front of his T-shirt and breathed him in.

"What do you need, Shae?" I asked. "I want to help you if I can. Just tell me what you need."

"I need time, Flan." He rested his chin on the top of my head. His breath felt nice, warm, on my scalp. His voice was weary. "That's all. Time. Can you give me some time, please?"

I wrapped my arms around him. I knew that was the one thing I couldn't give him. Corn, I could give him. Love, I could try to give him. A quiet house every once in a while. But I didn't have any control over the clock. I could feel the minutes, the hours, the years skidding away from both of us.

"I could give you a *good* time," I whispered into his shirt. He kissed the top of my head.

"That's not what I need right now, babe," he sighed. "As Baudrillard says, seduction is opposed to production." He kissed my hair again and headed back for the couch.

The anger I had been tamping down bubbled into my throat. I was tempted to yell "What about what *I* need?" but I thought I would sound too much like one of his soap operas. I wanted to say "Fuck your precious Baudrillard," or "You're not being productive, anyway, you asshole." Instead, I barked "We need to clean up this mess," making both kids jump. I bent down and helped them collect one sticky strand of vegetable hair after another. It was tedious work. If I could have given that endless, thankless time to Shae, I would have, gladly.

To stave off my looming funk, I decided to do an experiment. I wanted to find out what made me say Yes inside. A very Whitmanesque quest, it seemed to me. I kept reading the line *You must habit yourself to the dazzle of the light and of every moment of your life.* I decided that in every lot I won, I would find one object, one thing, that dazzled me.

At the next auction, I found my Yes in a pair of roller skates. They were men's roller skates, probably from the seventies; the sneaker-kind—blue-suede-ish running shoes with yellow stripes, yellow wheels, yellow toe-stops. They were poking out from underneath a Member's Only jacket in the back of the unit. I was excited; I loved to roller skate when I was little. I hadn't skated in years. I slipped the skates on even before I started hauling the rest of the stuff—a mix of boxes and garbage bags and loose clothes, and one of those backless chairs that you kneel on that used to be insanely popular—to the trailer.

The skates were way too big, at least three sizes. I laced them up as tight as I could and stumble-glided down the bumpy asphalt, hoping they would stay on my feet, hoping Nori's stroller would keep me upright, hoping I wouldn't pull both of us down to our doom as Noodle ran behind to catch up. Nori squealed with joy every time we hit a bump or I lost my balance and the stroller swayed to the side. Mr. and Mr. Chen clapped and waved when I skated by the unit they had won; the Garcias cheered us on, too. We got thumbs-up and hoots from just about everyone we passed. Norman just shook his head as we went past his trailer, probably because I almost crashed into him while he was carrying a large glass lamp shade.

Back at home, I pulled four pairs of socks over each foot, balled another sock into each of the roller skate toes, and did some tentative cruising around on the courtyard sidewalks. The paths were cracked and pitted; I kept tripping, much to the delight of my kids. I ripped a hole in the knee of my overalls, scraped up the skin on my kneecap. I kind of hoped it would scab. I hadn't had a scab in years, not a good pickable one.

I tried to imagine the guy who wore the skates before. Most of the stuff in his unit was seventies ephemera—phallic bottles of Pierre Cardin cologne, vests dripping with fringe, striped shirts with big collars, Adidas sneakers, short green athletic shorts with white piping, a Pet Rock in its original box. Lots of vintage things that I'd be able to sell on eBay for good money. He was probably in his twenties when he wore this stuff, which would make him in his fifties now. I wondered if he ever roller skated anymore, if he was even alive. A lot of times, units go into lien because payment stops with the renter's heartbeat.

I could give this guy some new life. I imagined my feet morphing into his feet, my toes growing longer and hairier, my legs growing more muscled and furry, my chest flattening, broadening into a hirsute male chest, a mustache prickling under my nose, the hair on my head coiled in a dark perm. I imagined skating around, checking out the ladies under the disco ball; gold chains would smack against my clavicle, my package prominent in my polyester slacks while I bopped and wove to the Hustle.

Whitman was a master at imagining himself in other skins. *I am large,* he said. *I contain multitudes.* He could see himself as a soldier, a slave, a mother giving birth, a blade of grass. That didn't come as easily for me—I'd always felt stuck in my own body, my own point of view—but with these roller skates, I got a little glimpse into the largeness he knew so well.

I slowly became steadier on his feet, my feet, didn't have to wave my arms around as much, didn't fall down quite as often. I learned to anticipate certain cracks on the pavement, learned to avoid certain uneven corners. It wasn't long before I could race from one end of the sidewalk to the other without wobbling much.

"Can I try?" Pia asked when I sat down to catch my breath.

"You'll need socks," I said. She was just wearing huaraches.

"My feet will be too hot," she said.

I slipped the skates off without untying them and handed them to Pia.

"They're way too big," I tried to warn her.

"I'll be fine." Pia thrust her feet, still in their sandals, into the skates. She stood and took two tiny steps forward. She didn't glide; she just tried to walk as if she were wearing regular shoes. Her feet slipped out from under her and she landed with a loud smack on her bum.

"Are you okay?" I jumped up. She obviously wasn't, but she kept her voice in its normal cool tone.

"Get a bag of peas from my freezer," she said. "And some ibuprofen—you know where it is, by the stove."

"You should have worn socks," I muttered and raced to the house.

When I returned, Noodle, Nori, and Ravi were all sitting on Pia's lap. Nori was leaning over Pia's broad leg and spinning one of the skate wheels round and round while Pia grimaced.

"Off, you guys," I said, and the kids scooted away. I gave Pia her peas, her pills, and a glass of water. I knelt down and slipped the skates off her feet. The sandals came off with them. The sight of Pia's yellowed toenails filled me with affection.

"This is how roller derby queens must feel." She pressed the frozen vegetables to her tailbone.

"Maybe that's what I should be, a roller derby queen." There are so many things to be in the world. Roller derby queendom was definitely a profession I had never considered. Sailing over a smooth wooden floor and knocking people down would probably be cathartic. Something to aspire to. I wished I could find out what I was good at, what I was best at. It made me crazy that Julia knew what she was best at, and she was going to throw it all away.

"Do roller derbies still even exist?" Pia asked. She put the ibuprofen in her mouth and threw her head back to swallow them.

"I hope so."

"Me, too." She took a big swig of water. We sat together on the sidewalk and watched the kids in their own roller-less derby, running around in circles.

I slipped the skates back onto my multisocked feet and raced around some more, imagining myself in blue satin shorts and knee pads, a helmet painted with flames strapped to my head, tube socks pulled up to my knees. My tank top would be emblazoned with something cheesy like Flantasy, or maybe Flantastic, in big loopy airbrushed letters. I would grow my hair out and feather it. The guy who once owned these skates would love me.

I was skating with my arms over my head in imagined victory when the burqa woman stepped out of her house. I wanted to skate up to her, sweep her into my arms, and do one of those death spirals ice skating pairs do at the Olympics. She would look amazing on roller skates, the black fabric rippling in the breeze. I almost crashed into her as she turned around the bend.

"Sorry," I said.

I caught a whiff of her body, sweaty and dusky, as she jumped away from me. She kept walking as if I weren't there. Neither of us had any inkling of the duet we'd perform in the not-too-distant future. How could we have?

Noodle once told me he thought the burqa woman looked like a black ghost; he was scared of her, always turned his head away when she came outside. This time, I felt as if *I* were the ghost, a pale specter who had momentarily startled her, then disappeared.


A couple of days later, Pia and I were lying on a blanket in the courtyard, listlessly rolling acorns back and forth between us while the kids played. Nori ran up to the porch of the Afghani couple screaming "I get you!" to Noodle, who was hiding in the bushes. I jumped up and raced over to them.

"Nori, shush," I said. I didn't want the couple to think they were under attack. Someone had drawn a swastika on their sidewalk with chalk not too long before, and the man had a cut on his cheek that was slow to heal; I could only imagine its source. Luckily, it appeared they weren't home. Their mailbox was full. Some kind of water sprayed down from a mimosa tree next to their porch—it almost felt like rain.

As I grabbed Nori, I peeked at their names on a pink envelope marked "Urgent" (most likely from a collection agency; I know this from way too much experience)—Raminullah and Sodaba Suleiman. I was glad to know their names. Suleiman had a nice ring to it. I whispered it to myself a few times, let the name roll over my tongue. *Hello, Mr. and Mrs. Suleiman,* I imagined myself saying. *Good morning, Mr. and Mrs. Suleiman.* I wondered if they would be happy to be acknowledged, or if they would look at me as if I had taken something from them.

Later in the day, I took the kids to the little café on campus for ice cream. I saw the woman, Sodaba, swimming in the outdoor pool behind the sports center. She wore her full burqa in the water. The black fabric looked incredibly heavy wet, but she managed to keep plowing forward. Maybe she had a special swimming burqa that wasn't as cumbersome as the one she wore around the neighborhood. I didn't know how she could survive the Riverside summers in such an oppressive-looking thing.

I wondered if her husband knew she was in the pool, if he had given his consent. I sort of hoped she had done it without his permission. She looked like an oil spill in the water, or a giant sea mammal. I could see the determination in her body as she lifted one sleeved arm, then the other. Her feet were bare. They looked utterly naked, almost erotic.

"Ice ceam!" Nori yelled from her doubly enforced stroller.

"Yeah, Mama, we were going to get ice cream, not go swimming," Noodle echoed. We occasionally went to public swim sessions at the pool, but it always ended up an exercise in frustration. Neither of the kids could swim, and there wasn't a shallow end to speak of, so I had to hold both of them in the water. It was never much fun, even though I always hoped it would be.

Sodaba reached the end of the lap lane and turned, the burqa swaying all around her like a dark exotic anemone.

*Where are you off to, lady? for I see you,*
*You splash in the water there, yet stay stock still in your room.*

When we got home, I combed the newspaper for the Public Notices. They were wily, sometimes appearing in Sports, sometimes in Business, sometimes in the Local section, sometimes in Classifieds. Sometimes they didn't appear at all. Sometimes the ones that did appear didn't list any storage auctions, just fictitious name-and-debt statements and citations to appear in court.

When I finally found them (in the Living section), a newly familiar name jumped out from a list of delinquent renters: Raminullah Suleiman. I lifted my magnifying glass, then lowered it, watched the ink break into points of black, then coalesce again into compact letters. I wondered if I should show it to the Suleimans—maybe they weren't aware they had fallen behind on their payments—but I didn't want to embarrass them. I knew I had to do something, though. The fact that I had just learned their last name seemed to mean that I was *supposed* to find it in the paper, that I was destined to help them. I would rescue their stuff. I would even let them store it in my house if they didn't have room. Then they would know we didn't mean them any ill will.

Pia offered to watch the kids while I went to the auction. She was normally at the lab in the early part of the day, but she had to be home to wait for a phone call from her brother in the Philippines. I was excited; it was like I had uncovered some master plan. Plus, I had never been to an auction alone. The prospect of that was a thrill in itself.

The auction was on the other side of town, near the Galleria, the largest mall in Riverside. I had never been to Tyler Storage before. It was a newer business; the cinder block was painted an orangey color, the doors and roofs and trim turquoise. It gave the place a kind of faux-Southwestern, new-housing-development feel; so did the landscaping throughout the complex—lots of cactus and succulents. Not my style, but I was happy to be there; even in the heat, I felt refreshed, unencumbered. The auctioneer brought a box of doughnuts for the bidders, and I was so giddy I ate three of them.

I knew from the ad that the Suleimans' storage unit was number 238; names and lot numbers were always published in the paper. I passed on a couple of prime "Flan lots" as I waited for the auctioneer to get to the right one. My auction colleagues looked at me expectantly as each modest unit came up on the block, but I told them "Not today. You go ahead." Once I was out of the running, there was a bidding frenzy. Those Flan lots went for a lot more money than I had ever paid for them. Yolanda winked at me after she nudged a unit up fifty bucks, and I felt a rush of gratitude. That never happened when I bid on my piddly treasures.

"Where are the children?" Mr. Chen-the-elder asked me between auctions.

"At home," I said. "I'm free today."

He smiled and gave me a thumbs-up. He gestured to his

son and said, "He's forty-three and he still doesn't leave me alone." Mr. Chen-the-younger shook his fist at his father, then laughed.

The auctioneer finally got to unit 238. It was a big one—twenty by fifteen. I wasn't expecting it to be that large. I took a deep breath.

"This is mine," I told my cronies. "This is what I came for today."

"Good luck," said Yolanda. Crusty old Norman grunted in my direction. My heart started to jump.

I hoped there would be enough room in Booty for whatever hid behind the ribbed metal door.

⟨✴⟩ I had imagined the storage unit would look like a harem den, covered with Persian rugs, elaborately carved lanterns sending out small diamonds of light, the ceiling draped with scarves in all shades of red. I half-expected to see large satin floor pillows decorated with gold thread, metal teapots with long curved spouts on low round tables, a hookah hunched like an octopus in the corner. I thought the air would be filled with incense and dusty spices and nasal-sounding music.

Such rooms might exist in Afghanistan, but maybe not. They might be a Hollywoodized, completely stereotypical, vision of the Middle East, for all I knew. I was unfamiliar with the real Afghanistan, other than what I saw on the news, and that was mostly rubble. Still, I was a little disappointed when the door rolled up and it was just a normal storage unit filled with normal everyday things. And I mean filled. There was a lot of stuff. More than I had ever bid on before. I was right to have worried about Booty. This would surely take more than one trip.

I tilted my chin for the opening bid of $75. No one challenged me, even though a locker that big would usually go for a few hundred bucks.

"Are you sure no one else wants to bid?" the auctioneer asked, looking at us in amazement. "This is a pretty sweet lot."

"Let Flan have it," said Mr. Chen-the-elder. The rest of my auction friends called out their assent. I felt like a celebrity.

"Well, then." The auctioneer winked at me, banging his bolt cutters against the wall for emphasis. "Sold to Flan for seventy-five smackeroos."

Here is what I found inside: two ice blue La-Z-Boy recliners; a crib, disassembled; bags of crib linens printed with fluffy cartoon lambs; a dresser/changing table; a couple of rolled-up rugs (of the Kmart ilk, not Persian); a medium-size Wurlitzer organ; an open box of fancy china plates; lots of women's clothing (mostly silk and polyester; no burqas; a pink bra, which surprised me; pink panties); some men's clothes (mostly polyester); a brass chandelier; a couple of floor lamps (the $6 utilitarian Ikea variety); boxes of baby clothes (mostly white; some yellow; a few mint green); economy-size packs of newborn diapers; many pairs of shoes (including some improbably jeweled sandals); and one closed, unmarked, cardboard cube after another. The closest thing to my fantasy was the word "genie" on the Diaper Genie box.

It looked like the aftermath of a baby shower, as if the guests had finished their Jordan almonds and drawing-a-baby-on-top-of-their-head party games, as if they had packed up the streamers and balloons and cake and left everything else behind. Obviously there had been a baby. Obviously something had happened. I felt awful. What was I supposed to do? I couldn't bring the Suleimans these things. I decided to keep all the stuff at my house until I knew what to do with it. I hoped I would have enough space. My auction room was already stuffed to the gills.

"You expecting, Mama?" Yolanda touched the front of my overalls after she had checked out her own lots.

"Hell, no." I knew my overalls were baggy, but I didn't think they made me look like I had a bun in the oven.

"Then why get all this baby crap?" she asked.

"It's my neighbor's stuff," I told her. "I didn't want them to lose it."

"They gonna pay you?" she asked.

"They don't have to." I hadn't even thought about that.

"Not a good business move, Miss Flan," she said, clicking her long nails against her belt. Yolanda was taking some business courses at night. "A good-neighbor move—I'll give you that— but not a good business move."

Mr. and Mr. Chen and Yolanda's burly husband, Rafael, helped me wrestle the recliners and the organ into Booty. The trailer wasn't big enough to carry everything. We decided I should run the first load home, then come back for the rest. Mr. Chen-the-younger came with me to help get the big stuff off the back of the trailer. It seemed funny to have him in my neighborhood, to have someone from my auction world enter my courtyard world. No one was around—Pia had probably taken the kids to the park; Shae was maybe, hopefully, at the library—so my two worlds didn't intersect as much as they could have.

Mr. Chen liked the neighborhood a lot.

"My father and I have been in the same apartment for twenty

years." He looked around at the green lawns, the flowers ringing Pia's house. "Second floor. My father grows vegetables in little pots on the terrace; he would love a garden. . . ."

"We have a community garden here," I said and he lit up.

"How do we get in?"

"You have to sign up for school first," I told him. "This housing is for students and their families only."

He got a faraway look on his face and said, "You know, I always did want to study astrophysics. Or perhaps the musical theater." And then this slightly gaunt but remarkably strong, middle-aged, oily-haired, Chinese-American man stretched his fingers out into jazz hands. He started shifting jauntily side to side, knees bent, and launched into a few bars of "Oh we got trouble, right here in River City." I was tempted to kiss him. I could almost taste the garlic stuck between his long front teeth, feel the few fine hairs striping his upper lip. Why did I want to kiss anyone I was alone with for five minutes? Whitman probably wanted to kiss everyone, too. He probably even let himself do it. I bit my bottom lip to give my mouth something to focus on. *Wanting kisses for all the red fruit I find.*

We left everything behind my house, under the Dr. Seuss trees, because I couldn't take the time to lug it all inside; Tyler Storage had a strict out-by-one-p.m. policy, and we had to rush back so I could clear out the rest of the unit. Mr. Chen-the-younger sang the whole drive back.

It honestly never occurred to me that the Suleimans would find their stuff stowed in my backyard; they lived on the opposite side of the courtyard, and, as far as I knew, didn't have reason to walk behind my house. I never imagined that people would start picking through the Suleimans' stuff as if I were having a week-day sale. But that's just what happened. When I got back from the storage place with the second load—without the Music Man this time—my backyard was full of people. People opening drawers and boxes, riffling through clothes, sitting on the chairs, plunking on the soundless organ. And Raminullah Suleiman barreling over, screaming at the top of his lungs.

"What is this?" he bellowed, arms flailing. "Why are you touching my things?! Why do you have my things?!"

The small crowd froze as he continued to scream. Then people scattered, saying things like "We didn't know, man," and "Chill out, dude" and staring at him in terror. As if he had a grenade in his hand or dynamite strapped to his chest.

*Out from the crowd steps the marksman and takes his position and levels his piece.*

"Mr. Suleiman." I walked up to him, my hand extended. He seethed at me, didn't move to shake my hand. "Forgive me. I was just trying to help." I lowered my palm to my side.

"Help what? How did you get all of this?" His lips, ringed with a bristly mustache and beard, were chapped and snarly, but beautiful. His teeth were small. His breath smelled of lunch meat. I probably should have been scared. Isn't that who the news told us to be scared of, angry Middle Eastern men? Isn't that who all those color-coded alerts were supposed to warn us about? All I could think about, though, was kissing him. His tongue would be thick with mayonnaise. Warm. I tried to shake the sensation from my head. Maybe Whitman had corrupted my thoughts.

"I saw your name in the paper."

"What lies are they telling about me now?" The gash on his cheek was still wet. It looked like it might be infected.

"Your name was listed in the public notices." I kept my voice calm. "I go to storage unit auctions—it's what I do. I bid on units that people have stopped paying for. I saw your name and bid on your unit so I could give your things back to you. I didn't want you to lose them."

I watched rage sweep across his face, then turn into confusion, then pain, then rage again. Should I have been afraid? I felt more hapless than anything. And I found myself wondering: Did Sodaba like to kiss that face? Did she like to feel her cheek pressing against his bristles? How often did she lift her veil to touch her lips to his?

"These are things we already lost!" he yelled and stormed off.

I put my hand to my mouth. Only then did I feel a cramp of fear, but it had nothing to do with Raminullah.


I couldn't bring myself to sell the Suleimans' belongings. I couldn't bring myself to throw them away, either. I got into Beulah and drove to Store-U, the closest storage place to campus, so I could rent a locker. It was the first time I had rented one myself. As I signed the contract, I thought of all the people who had signed similar contracts in good faith, never imagining their stuff would end up in my auction room, on my lawn, in other people's homes. I wondered how long I would continue to pay for this unit, how long I would store the Suleimans' past in my name.

Later that day, Pia, Michael, Shae, and I loaded everything back onto Booty and brought it over to the unit. It felt good to work side by side with Shae, to feel his arms and legs moving next to mine. We were able to take everything in one trip. I think that was Michael's doing—with his computer programmer brain, he arranged everything like a puzzle, boxes and furniture all neatly dovetailed.

The walls at Store-U were metal prefab, not cinder block like most of the older complexes. The inside of the unit smelled like a new metal lunchbox, a hot metal lunchbox. We were the first customers to rent the locker. It was reassuring to know that other histories, the ghosts of other people's lives, weren't haunting the space. It was going to be haunted enough as it was. The Suleimans' grief rose out of their boxes, filled the small room.

"I feel like such a jerk," I said to Shae that night. Both the kids were asleep. I lay on the couch, spent; Shae sat on the floor, his head resting against my hip. David Letterman's face glowed from the seven screens against the wall. I still hadn't convinced Shae to watch only one set.

Shae rubbed the back of his head against me. "You did what you thought was right, Flan."

"Those poor people," I said. "We're so lucky our kids were born healthy."

He turned and kissed my belly through my overalls.

"Thanks for helping me today," I said.

"No problem," he said. "It was fun." He kissed the bib of my overalls, between my breasts.

"No," I said. "*This* is fun." I could feel him smile against my clothes.

He pulled himself up onto the couch, draped his weight over me.

"What about Baudrillard?" I asked.

"Screw Baudrillard," he said. How long had I wanted to hear him say that?

"I'd rather you screw me . . . ," I said as I dipped my foot down, ran it along his leg.

His lips were just about to touch mine when Noodle started to scream.

"Maybe he'll go back to sleep by himself," Shae whispered, but the screaming grew louder.

I slid out from under Shae, kissed his prickly chin, and went to check on our son. He was having one of his occasional night terrors—shrieking and screeching in his sleep, never waking up all the way. He woke Nori up, though, and her screams trumped his. Calming them back down, helping their sweaty bodies relax into the sheets, took longer than I would have liked. By the time I walked back into the living room, eager to finish what we had started, Craig Kilborn's face was on all the screens and Shae was sound asleep.

I woke up late the next morning. Shae wasn't home; at least he had remembered to lock the door behind him when he left. The kids were watching TV—cartoons on three screens, *Sesame Street* on the rest—and eating Kix directly out of the box. The cereal was scattered all around them like pale porous BBs.

"We have to get ready to go to an auction," I told them.

Nori tossed a handful of cereal at me and ran into the bathroom.

"Nori," I cajoled, too groggy to do anything else.

"Do we have to?" Noodle whined, his eyes still glued to the TVs. Snuffleupagus and George Jetson were competing for his attention. I didn't stand a chance.

"If you want to keep eating, we have to," I said.

He grudgingly got up, crushed Kix stuck to his pajama bottoms. Nori opened the bathroom door after a lot of wheedling and let me dress her. We were all in a fairly dark mood when we got to Moreno Mini Self Storage, a shabby place off the 60 freeway.

Witnessing Raminullah's pain had let some genie of sadness out of the bottle for me. Now I saw sadness everywhere. It wafted out of every unit at the Moreno auction. I could smell it, like a haze of body odor. I saw a battered plastic truck in one unit and imagined that the boy who once played with it was now nineteen, and in trouble. His mother could no longer afford to pay for the storage unit because she had spent all her money on lawyers' fees and bail. I saw a bedroom set in another unit and saw the last moments of a marriage play out in my head—the yelling, the storming out, the crying into the mattress. I saw a bedpan in another unit, the sadness of long illness. I thought of all the patients in my mom's hospital ward, *sacs merely floating with open mouths for food to slip in.*

I could feel the sadness of my auction compadres—the sadness of Mr. Chen-the-younger and his squelched dreams, the sadness of the Garcias' never-ending quest for cash, the deep sadness of Norman that I couldn't begin to fathom.

Sadness adhered to each molecule of dust; sadness weighed me down as I chased after Nori and tried to keep Noodle, sponge that he was, from picking up more of my gloomy energy by osmosis.

*That life is a suck and a sell, and nothing remains at the end but threadbare crape and tears.*

I wasn't sure I'd be able to find anything at that auction that made me say Yes, but I was committed to trying. I thought of Walt Whitman. He wouldn't give up on a chance for momentary bliss, no matter how down he felt. After I won a locker that held a few neatly sealed boxes, no hint of the contents inside, I decided to try an experiment. I closed my eyes and pointed to a box, then drew a little star on the cardboard so I'd know which one to dig into first when we got home. If I could find a Yes inside that random box—no, make that in the first thing I drew from that random box—I could find it anywhere.

At home, I closed my eyes and pulled out a little makeup case, a sleek plastic one, the kind you get for free when you buy jillions of dollars' worth of department store cosmetics. I felt a surge of panic.

I am not comfortable with makeup. My mom didn't wear any; she had a stash of it in her dresser, but I never saw her put it on. I had a disastrous but thankfully brief blue-eyeliner-and-white-lipstick phase in high school, and then a short heavy metal, heavy makeup sojourn, but that was it. I really didn't want to wear these cosmetics, which, despite the nice bag, looked old and cruddy and were probably full of someone else's germs, but I reminded myself that it was part of the experiment.

"Tell me about the people who owned this stuff," I said to Noodle as I psyched myself up.

Noodle peered into the little bag, looked inside the unpacked cardboard boxes at the high-heeled shoes and satiny dresses. He stuck his hand into the slippery fabric and pulled out a small blue booklet.

"It's you, Mama," he said, after he opened it up. "It's you if you looked like a girl."

I snatched the book from him. It was a passport, the blue vinyl cool in my hand. The woman in the photo *did* kind of look like me, at least the large eyes, the thin lips, the upturned nose. Everything else was different. She had long, wavy auburn hair; she wore an elegant emerald green blouse, a necklace made of large amber chunks. Her makeup appeared to be professionally applied. She was radiant with health and money. If Julia was my artistic doppelgänger, this woman was my glamorous doppelgänger. Her name was Samantha Walker. She lived in Palos Verdes at the time the passport was issued. It would be valid until 2004.

I flipped to the back of the passport to look at all the stamps inked onto the pages—Czechoslovakia, France, Morocco, Argentina. My mind filled with cobblestone roads, arched doorways, spice markets heady with scent. If I couldn't travel the world the way I had once longed to, at least my fashion-plate body double could. Once I tracked her down and returned her passport, at least. I wondered if she knew her passport was missing. Had it fallen into the bag by accident, or had she put it there on purpose? Had she left her identity behind and stepped into a new life? The pages were dusted with eye shadow and blush, the edges powdery, like butterfly wings.

"What do you think Samantha Walker did in Argentina?" I asked Noodle. I felt drab, washed out, compared to her. Surely she had a degree. Surely she knew just what books to read, just how to talk about them.

"She got married," he said, looking at the fancy dresses.

"Nah, she wouldn't do anything that boring," I said. "I think she learned the tango. Or maybe she was a spy. . . ." I pictured myself in her shoes and clothes, putting on dark sunglasses, walking confidently, stealthily, up the marble stairs of an embassy with a satchel full of secrets.

"You should make your hair like that, Mama." Noodle looked at her picture. He crossed his arms over the top of his head.

"Do you miss your long hair, sweetheart?" I asked him.

He shook his head but tears sprang into his eyes.

"It will grow back," I said. I noticed him eyeing the sleek bag. "Do you want to wear some makeup?"

I saw a spark of interest as he shrugged and lowered his arms.

"I'll just put a little lipstick on you, okay?" I hoped he wouldn't have to tell a therapist about this someday.

He closed his eyes and tilted his chin up, puckered his lips. I opened a tube of lipstick. It was a brownish shade, the color of dried blood, cracked and old-looking. The tip was smashed in. I wiped it on a tissue, rubbed the crusty end of it until it appeared to be fresher, then touched it to Noodle's wet mouth. It slid across without leaving much color behind, just a few crumbles. He smacked his lips together a couple of times and the color streaked and clumped; it made him look wounded. A shiver traveled down my arms.

"I'm sorry, Noodle," I said. His lips felt tender to the touch, like segments of Mandarin orange, as I started to clean them. "This wasn't a very good idea." Noodle looked relieved by the news.


I was still determined to find a Yes in the makeup. After I washed Noodle's mouth, I played with the spicy powders, the unguents, the tubes and compacts and brushes and bruised-looking pads. I tried not to think about germs. I tried to imagine these things touching Samantha Walker's lips, her cheeks, her delicate eyelids. I imagined I was touching her this way, cheek to cheek, eye to eye, lip to lip; I imagined my face becoming her face, color by added color.

By the time Shae walked into the bathroom, I was wearing eyeliner, mascara, green eye shadow, three kinds of blusher striped on my cheeks, brick-colored lip liner and a plummy shade of lipstick, all on top of an anemic-looking foundation. I was wearing a yellow satin ball gown, fishnet stockings, an ivory pump on one foot and a purple and green stiletto on the other. I'm sure Samantha Walker would be mortified, but Noodle loved the outfit.

"What's all this?" Shae asked.

"Just playing dress up," I told him.

"Not a good look for you," he said, but his lips rose in a half-smile as he unzipped his jeans to pee. I was so starved for his attention—it makes me sad to admit this—I considered that enough of a Yes.

I didn't have any proper makeup remover, so my attempts to wipe everything off were pretty half-assed. Once my face was sort of clean, I pinned the passport, open to the photo, on the door of my auction room, right above the cardboard cutout of my name.

Whitman said *In all people I see myself—none more and not one a barleycorn less.* In this Samantha Walker, though, I saw myself quite a few barleycorns more. Whenever I looked at her, I remembered that I could travel someday, that I was a citizen of the world, too.

Flecks of mascara drifted into my eyes all night. By morning, they were red and irritated, still rimmed and smudged with liner. My face had broken out into small white bumps. I looked like Samantha Walker's strung-out sister.

I put on some sunglasses, took the kids to the park, and plunked myself down under a tree. I hoped no one would talk to me, but a mom from Cherry Street sat down right next to me on the grass.

"Did you hear about that crazy Arab on Avocado?" she asked as she put a hippo-printed sun hat on her daughter. An expensive, shiny-person hat. She wasn't long for the neighborhood.

"That was at my house," I told her. I watched Nori disappear behind a slide as Noodle hesitantly approached the swings. Gray bees liked to tunnel in the sand beneath the swing set; no matter how many times the entomologists among us told him they wouldn't sting, he was nervous around them.

"Really? You must have been terrified." She pulled her daughter's pants back to check inside her diaper.

"Not really."

"I heard he was insane. I heard he threatened to bomb the Child Development Center."

"What?!" I jumped up from my spot under the shade of the pepper tree. Little pink pepper berries skittered around my feet.

"Do you think he's a terrorist?" the woman asked as she let go of her daughter's elastic waistband. It snapped lightly against the girl's skin.

I wondered if the woman was the one who had scrawled "Terrorists live here" in green chalk in front of the Suleimans' house. I kind of doubted it—she looked like she would have much neater penmanship—but I could picture her urging someone else on.

"People were messing with his stuff. He had every right to be upset." I stepped on some pepper berries; their sharp tang filled the air.

"He shouldn't be allowed to have an outburst like that," she said.

"Why? Because he's from Afghanistan?!"

"He better watch his back." She slathered sunscreen over her daughter's arms. "His days here are numbered."

"He never said anything about a bomb." Maybe it was my own regret over what happened, but I felt deeply protective of the Suleimans. How dare she threaten a man who had already been through so much.

"My friend lodged a complaint," she said. "The FBI should be showing up any day now. . . ."

"What the hell?!"

"We need to protect our neighborhood," she said, sitting up straighter. As if her spine could be a barrier against all bad things.

"He's part of this neighborhood."

"I see what's happening here, and it needs to stop," she said.

I was so mad, I ran up to Noodle and pulled him from the swing he had finally worked up the courage to claim.

"Hey, guess what?" I yelled, Noodle rigid in my arms, Nori running toward us. "*I'm* having an outburst. Are you gonna call the FBI on me? Am I a threat to the neighborhood now?" The woman grabbed her UV-protected daughter and stormed off. The gray bees buzzed around my ankles. I kicked the sand and watched them roil.

*What living and buried speech is always vibrating here . . . what howls restrained by decorum . . .*

On the morning of September 11, I had been in my pajamas helping the kids brush their teeth when Pia barged into our tiny bathroom, knocking the door against my side. Shae had left the house unlocked again.

"What's up?" I asked, rubbing my arm.

"Oh, honey." She tipped her head against the wall. "I don't even know where to begin. You better turn on the TV."

I told the kids to spit and followed Pia into the living room. I had never seen her so rattled before. When I flicked on just one TV set, she said, "Turn them all on. There could be different information on different channels."

I don't know what I was expecting, but it wasn't the Twin Towers collapsing on all seven screens. It looked like a whole city was crumbling at once.

"The Pentagon's been hit, too," Pia said, dropping onto the couch.

The kids raced out of the bathroom, their mouths still ringed with foam. They looked so trusting, it just about killed me. How could I protect them with such shaky hands?


It was hard to believe nine months had already passed. Time enough to create a new life, a new world order, but I could still feel the shock of the day under my skin.

When we got home from the park, the kids eerily quiet in the wake of my screaming fit, a folded piece of paper was waiting in my mailbox. I hoped it was from the Suleimans. I had written them a note to apologize for the storage unit fiasco; I hoped they would understand. I had barely seen them since that day. Their blinds were always shut. Their door rarely opened. More chalked epithets had appeared on their sidewalk. More eggs had been thrown at their windows. I was tempted to wash the congealed, fly-attracting mess away, but I didn't want to rattle their windows and scare them. I didn't want my good intentions to blow up in my face again.

The note wasn't from them.

"Dear Mrs. Parker," it said, "It has come to our attention that you have been engaging in illegal retail practices on the premises of Student Family Housing. Riverside zoning laws state that citizens are allowed to have three yard sales per year at their place of residence. You have had that many this month alone. We ask you to cease and desist your yard sales immediately or we will be forced to contact city officials. Thank you for your prompt attention to this matter. Sincerely, Sheila Wickman, Management, Student Family Housing."

Sheila was a big stickler for laws. She often sent out remonstrative flyers to the community with messages like "No cars on the grass" or "Only machine-wrapped treats on Halloween" or "No more than two sheds per household." I had run-ins with her just about every month when I had to tell her our rent would be a few days late.

"Fuck!" I shouted up into the oak tree, scaring a mockingbird away. I never used to be an angry person. I was startled by how much rage was smoldering in me.

"A duck!" Nori yelled from her stroller. My own little mockingbird.

"Fuck a duck!" I yelled.

"Fuckaduckfuckaduckfuckaduck," Nori said, fast as an auctioneer. Maybe I should have been more careful about the words I used around her.

Noodle stared at both of us, scandalized.


I turned around and stomped over to the Student Family Housing offices, Nori's stroller bucking in front of me, Noodle racing to catch up. When we got there, I shook the letter in Sheila's face. Noodle stood by the doorway, pale. He hated when I was angry. Unfortunately it seemed to be happening more and more often.

"What's this all about?" I asked. I hoped I didn't look too washed out, beaten up, from the aftermath of the makeup.

"It's all outlined right there, Flan," she said. She smoothed the ruffle that ran down the front of her beige blouse. Sweat stains radiated from her armpits. A small fan sat on her desk, but the office was still stuffy. "You're violating county law."

"You're not a county official."

"No I am not," she said. "But I act as their liaison. We can't have you breaking zoning laws on campus property."

"Does this have anything to do with what happened with Raminullah Suleiman?"

"It has nothing to do with that." She sat up straighter. Again, the almighty spine.

"Because if it does, I could sue you for discrimination."

Nori pointed an accusatory finger from her stroller.

I swear I could see perspiration spread down Sheila's blouse, like a time-lapse film of the tide. "I assure you that won't be necessary."

"I've been having these sales for years and no one says anything until a Middle Eastern man freaks out on my lawn—and for good reason, I might add. I think that sounds a little suspicious, don't you?"

"You are breaking the law," she said. "Pure and simple."

I had a puzzling desire to touch the slippery beige fabric of Sheila's sleeves. To run my hand over its slickness or grab it and shake her until she couldn't see straight, I wasn't sure. Most likely the latter.

"I'm not the first person to have yard sales here, either. Why haven't you cracked down before now?"

"It's a different era, Flan, and you know it. Your yard sales bring an outside element into the complex."

"The guards let them in," I said.

"I'm going to have to have a talk with those guards," she said.

"This is supposed to be an institution of learning, not a police state." I hoped our friendly guards wouldn't have to start demanding paperwork, lifting rifles.

"I'm going to have to ask you to leave the premises."

If I had been Samantha Walker, Sheila probably would have given me all the time in the world.

"You haven't heard the last of me." My dramatic exit was slightly hampered when the stroller wheels got stuck on the doorjamb.

"Are we going to go to jail, Mama?" Noodle asked, terrified, as the door shut behind us.

"Of course not, Noodle boy." I kissed the top of his head, my lips trembly with adrenaline. I was confounded by how hot the tops of my kids' heads got. It was remarkable their brains didn't boil inside those hot, hot skulls. "If anyone's getting in trouble, it's Sheila."

He seemed satisfied by that answer, but I could feel the heat building under my own scalp.

I let Nori out of her stroller when we got home; she immediately ran up to Pia's garden and dove into the nasturtiums.

"I a ghost, Mama." She tore several flowers out of the ground with her teeth.

"Goat, Nori," Noodle tried to correct her. "Goat, not ghost."

"No, honey!" I ran over to her, legs shaky, and forced her to spit the macerated orange petals into my palm. Nasturtiums are edible, but I didn't want her to get in the habit of eating plants. You never know which ones are poisonous or sprayed with something like DDT. Sheila had actually sent out a flyer saying "No poisonous plants on the grounds!" after a teenage kid almost died trying to get high on local vegetation. The maintenance guys had chopped down all the oleander and trumpet vines on the premises, but it was possible they didn't catch everything.

Pia came outside, looking drained. She was wearing more of my auction clothes—a short-sleeved, button-down shirt with Ping-Pong paddles embroidered along the front, long navy shorts, green slip-on shoes.

"Sorry about your flowers." I showed her my slimy palm.

She waved my concerns away as I rubbed the chewed-up petals into the grass.

"What happened to you?" she asked.

"Just some makeup mayhem." I wanted to rant about my tangle with Sheila, but it didn't feel like the right time, not with her looking low.

"How's your mom doing?" I asked. Her mom had gone into the hospital in Manila a couple of weeks before. Recurrent breast cancer.

"Not good," Pia said. "I don't know why I'm not there already." Pia was scheduled to travel to the Philippines in three weeks. She would have left sooner, but she had some important research to wrap up.

"Can you change your tickets?"

"Not without a hefty fee."

Nori came running up to us, more orange flowers crumpled in her little palm.

"I a ghost, Pia." She tossed the nasturtiums onto Pia's lap.

"We all are, sweetheart," said Pia, her eyes moistening. She kissed Nori's cheek, then mine, and went back into her house.

I was about to go home, too, when Sodaba walked into the courtyard, carrying a heap of oranges in a plastic grocery bag. She had probably picked them from a tree by the park. I walked toward Sodaba, but she started to walk faster. I wondered how she could move that fast within those heavy layers. I called out "Sodaba! Are you okay? I'm so sorry. . . ." She didn't turn around. She kept speeding up until she got to her house. A couple of oranges tumbled out of the bag and rolled down the sidewalk when she fumbled with her key. I picked up a warm orange and pressed it to my lips as she disappeared behind the door, ignoring the lost fruit. The mimosa tree sprayed me with its strange sharp mist.

"Mama, why you kissing dat orange?" Nori came up next to me, flowers stuck in her waistband.

"I'm smelling it," I said, heart walloping. I handed it to her so she could smell it, too.

She bent over the fruit and said "It smells yike TV." She touched her tongue, still covered with orange scraps of petal, to the bumpy rind.

If Shae were there, he would have said something about Baudrillard, a real orange smelling like a virtual screen. He probably wouldn't have given Sodaba a second thought after she closed her door. Not the way I kept giving her second thoughts and third thoughts and more thoughts than I could begin to admit. I lifted another orange from the ground and ripped it open, spilling juice all over my hands.

That Saturday, I woke up early, as usual. I washed my face until all traces of makeup were gone. I dripped some Visine into my eyes. I was about to haul out the blankets when I remembered Sheila's letter. All energy seeped from my arms. What was I going to do without my yard sales? I brewed some coffee and sat on the front step, waiting for the throngs to arrive.

The yard looked small, dwarfed by the oak tree in the predawn light. I didn't see how I could fill it with so much stuff each week. Heat was already teasing the air when the first people showed up.

"Getting a late start?" a mom from Kentucky Street asked. She was there pretty much every week. Her husband was working on his English thesis; they had four kids, all under five years old. Except for her blue eyes, she was colorless as an albino. She had made a lot of colorless purchases over the years, too—bone-colored clothes, Plexiglas lamps and tissue box covers, scuffed clear plastic cups.

"The store is closed," I told her. She looked like she was about to cry.

"What am I going to do?" She sat down next to me. I told her about the swap meet, the good thrift stores in the area.

"We don't have a car," she said. I could only imagine what it would be like to wrestle all of her kids onto a bus.

"Tell you what," I said. "You can come over sometime and look in my storage room. We'll work something out."

She looked at me with such gratitude I felt sheepish.

I wanted to throw open the doors that morning, let everyone in to dig through the piles in the auction room, but there was barely enough room for one person in there. Plus, everyone else in the house was still asleep.

The tamale woman came by after the sun was up. I hadn't seen her in a while. Her husband was working on his teaching credential; she used to come through our neighborhood twice a week, her small cart filled with homemade tamales—green chile, pork, chicken, sweet corn, for just one dollar each. We always looked forward to the sound of her bell.

"No sale today?" she asked. She was an occasional customer, mostly kitchenware and clothes for her daughter.

"They shut me down," I told her.

"They shut me down, too." She shook her head in disbelief. "Said I posed a health risk to the community."

"We never got sick."

"Of course not," she said. "I run a clean operation. I wash my hands and everything. It's not like I put anthrax in the masa."

"Why do you think they're cracking down on us now?"

"They're cracking down on everyone since the attacks," she said. "You gotta wrap yourself in plastic if you want to stay alive these days."

"I hope they're not going to shut down our dinners," Pia said that night. She had made tamale pie in the tamale lady's honor. It wasn't an ordinary tamale pie—it was filled with stewed chicken and raisins, and she had baked some pineapple into the corn-meal crust. Isobel made home-made salsa and a pot of black beans. Nigel sautéed some broccoli rabe with garlic—the kids and I thought it was bitter, but everyone else seemed to like it—

and brought more beer. I could smell mint and potatoes through Sodaba's open window.

"You never know," said Isobel. "What with your Patriot Act and all that." She looked at me and Shae as if we had written it ourselves. I realized we were the only American citizens at the table. "The FBI might swoop in and arrest us all just for talking about it."

"I wouldn't be surprised," said Michael. "America is not going to look like America much longer with the direction your president is headed."

"He's not my president." Shae shook his head.

"Like it or not, he is," said Pia. "Whether you voted for him or not. Whether the Supreme Court appointed him or not. He's your man."

"Don't remind me." Shae took a large bite of tamale pie.

"Say farewell to freedom," Nigel said, lifting his bottle of Newcastle.

"Freedom of speech." Isobel raised her bottle and clinked it against Nigel's. The rest of us clinked our bottles, as well.

"Freedom of the press," I said. More clinking.

"Freedom of assembly," Pia said, looking around the table.

"Here! Here!" everyone raised their voices.

"Say good-bye to all of it," said Nigel, hoisting his bottle high.

I took a swig and said, "It's like the Society for the Suppression of Vice all over again."

"What's that?" asked Pia, some broccoli rabe stuck on one of her front teeth.

"Some group in the eighteen hundreds." I reached across the table and scraped the green speck away. Nigel gasped, but I didn't care. "They called Walt Whitman immoral."

"Wasn't he gay?" asked Nigel. I couldn't tell if he said it sneeringly, or if his accent just made it sound that way.

"He was God," I said.

"So what happened?" Pia tented her hand over her mouth to keep my fingers out.

"He sold a ton more books," I said. "He had been searching for an audience forever—I mean, he published his own books, he wrote his own reviews, tooted his own horn, but he didn't get much attention until he was called immoral." I was glad my Whitman obsession came in handy every once in a while.

"The obscene is more visible than the visible," said Shae. Baudrillard, of course.

"I'm going to have to agree with that," said Michael.

"Too bad controversy won't help your yard sales," Pia jumped in before Michael could start talking about his obscene job.

I pushed my fork into my black beans so they oozed through the tines. "I should get a Web cam. I could sell all my stuff online naked."

"Now there's an interesting idea," said Shae. Did he think I was serious? "A real play on the way objects seduce by appearance. Baudrillard says . . ."

I got up to make dessert before I could hear what Baudrillard had to say about me taking off my clothes for the general wanking public. Couldn't Shae be interested in my body without putting some theory all over it?

I ripped some plums from Pia's tree, brought them into our kitchen and hacked them up. Purple juice spurted from the fruit, staining my fingertips, dotting my wrists, filling the room with a sticky humidity. I threw the wedges into a bowl, grabbed a tub of vanilla ice cream, and stalked back outside.

"You can put the plums on the ice cream," I said, dumping everything on the table.

"Ice ceam!" Nori popped out from behind the Dr. Seuss trees and ran to the table, Noodle and Ravi on her heels.

Nigel plucked a slice of plum from the bowl and slipped it into Isobel's mouth. She acted like it annoyed her, but then she parted her lips for another one. I wanted to mash the fruit against their smug, adulterous faces.

I scooped out some ice cream with my finger and shoved it into my own mouth while Shae continued to spout philosophy. If no one else was going to feed me, I was just going to have to do it myself.

Sodaba and Raminullah walked out their door. They froze on their small porch for a moment, as if hesitant to step into the courtyard with all of us there. When I lifted my hand, they dipped their heads down and quickly disappeared around the back of their house.

"I wonder how they're doing," I said.

"You see all those images on the news of the women in Afghanistan tearing off their burqas," said Isobel. "Why won't she do that here?"

"Don't be fooled by those images," Nigel said, slipping another plum slice into Isobel's mouth. "It's just going to get worse for those women. They're not free. The Taliban is going to be replaced by another repressive regime, mark my words. Women once had great freedom in Afghanistan, but those days are over. Our world is becoming less and less free as we speak."

"But we can still have personal freedom, can't we?" I asked, my fingers numb from the ice cream. "Even under a repressive government, right? No one can take away our imagination." I thought of Whitman. No regime could repress his generous mind. *I am afoot with my vision*, he said. I was sure Sodaba had all sorts of secrets under that veil.

"A bomb can wipe out anyone's imagination pretty damn fast," said Michael.

"Fear tends to dampen the imagination, too," said Shae. "Everyone is too afraid to speak out, to think outside the party line these days. It's the whole 'with us or against us' thing. If you criticize the White House, you're a terrorist."

"That's what your government traffics in, of course," said Pia. "Fear."

"Fear and bombs," said Michael.

"Don't forget oil," said Isobel, her lips stained purple. "There's that pipeline they want to build through Afghanistan. . . ."

"I was all for Bush going into Afghanistan at first," said Nigel, "but he's gone at it the wrong way. He's bombing schools, hospitals, for God's sake. Osama bin Laden is nowhere to be found. It's a bloody mess. And Bush has his sights on Iraq, just you watch."

I watched the kids chase each other with sticks and wondered what sort of world they were going to inherit.

The one bright spot in my life that June was eBay. I did a bang-up job with Mr. Roller Disco's stuff. His fringed vest brought in $38.50. His Pierre Cardin cologne in its original penile bottle netted me $43. I got $287 for his vintage Adidas, and—the pièce de résistance—the original Pet Rock sold for $525. When I boxed everything up before bringing it to the post office, it was as if I were wrapping presents for myself. I felt flush, rich. I wanted to do something good with my spoils.

•   •   •

Pia and I were walking around the courtyard one evening, trying to get some exercise while our kids played with a Nerf boomerang. Pia was quiet, distracted. We passed the Suleimans' house; that weird rain pelted us from the mimosa tree.

"What is that, anyway?" I wiped the tiny drops from my cheek.

"It's my research, you idiot." She slapped me in the arm. I could feel the sting of her hand for a long time. It felt like she was really mad at me.

"I thought you were researching bugs." I knew she was doing something in connection with the entomology and ag departments, but I didn't think it had anything to do with trees.

"That's bug excreta," she said. "That's the glassy winged sharpshooter sucking all the life out of that tree and peeing it at us. The bastards."

"Yuck." I ran from the tree, rubbing the wetness off my arms.

"I thought you knew what I've been working on," she said.

"I did," I said. "But I didn't know those bugs were in our neighborhood. I thought they were only in vineyards or something."

"That's the main problem," she sighed. "Once a sharpshooter gets into the grapes, the whole place is toast." She gestured to the mimosa. "That tree will be dead in a year," she said, and a little shiver went up my spine.

"How is your research going?"

"A biomailer was supposed to come in from Peru a week ago," she said. "Live wasps. My hands are tied until they arrive." I could hear the frustration in her voice. I knew she wanted to be in Manila. Her mom had just been put on a feeding tube and was starting to decline.

"I have some extra money, Pia," I said. "If you want to change your plane ticket, I'd be happy to make up the difference. You wouldn't have to pay me back."

"Flan, I can't leave before the wasps gets here. They're a kind I haven't seen before; they could be the sharpshooters' natural enemy."

Wasps seemed scarier to me than sharpshooters—I'd much rather get rained on than stung—but I trusted she knew what to do with them. "Couldn't you get an assistant to take over for you?"

She looked at me as if I were crazy. "This is *my* research. If I leave now, my career will be screwed, Flan."

"Pia, you only have one mother. . . ."

"You think I don't know that?" she snapped. She had never been as sharp with me before. It cut me to the quick.

"Pia . . ."

"And you haven't talked to your father in, what? Ten years? Do you even know if he's alive? Don't you lecture me about being a dutiful daughter, Flan."

Pia stomped off to her house. I stood out in the courtyard alone, stung. The sky was veined with pink, purple, orange—a glorious sunset, thanks to the smog. The particulates polluting the air could kill you, but they caught the light, made people say things like "ah" and "yes." It was the opposite with me. It seemed whenever I tried to do something nice for people lately, I hurt their feelings instead.


If you take a hot pin and stick it into amber, the smell of million-year-old pine resin floats out at you, fresh and alive. The pinprick of the word "dad" was like that for me—it sent memories streaming, filling the air with old angers. I looked up at the fingernail paring of the moon, and I could see my dad standing out-side our small brick house in Cleveland, training his telescope, as he often did, on the Sea of Tranquility or the Sea of Storms or whatever other sea he could find up there.

"Now *that's* the job I should have had, Flanny," he told me on several occasions. "Naming the seas of the moon." This was after he had a couple of scotches with soda. He was a fairly maudlin drunk, given to tears and purple prose.

His real job wasn't nearly as poetic. He worked at the Goodyear Tire plant as a vibration engineer; he came home every day smelling of hot rubber. A pang of sorrow shot through me when I thought of him alone in that house, his body wearing a crater into the seat of his plaid armchair. I was sure the gray globe of the moon was still on the occasional table beside him, right next to the larger pastel globe of the world.

We both loved those globes. We spent hours turning them, talking about them, quizzing each other on capitals and archipel-agos and the places we would go if we had the means. He wanted to go to Antarctica; I wanted to go to the Amazon. He wanted to go to the Sea of Serenity; I wanted to go to Kuala Lumpur. It was amazing to me that such small objects could represent vast spaces, distant things. Kind of like the pictures of my mom. How could she be contained in those tiny frames?

Over the years, my mom had grown huge in my memory. Not physically big—she had always been a small woman. She had become all-encompassing somehow, atmospheric, like the cloud of fragrant steam after a shower.

I thought of how my dad came into my room when I sobbed, missing her so much I thought I'd stop breathing. He would smooth his thick thumbs over my eyebrows, his vaguely stale, fruity breath stirring the wisps at my hairline, until I fell asleep. I missed him with a sudden terrible twinge. With the eBay money, I thought, I could go visit my dad. Or I could bring my dad out to Riverside. I could dial that old familiar telephone number, the one burned into my brain, the one I used to tuck into boys' pockets, write on boys' palms. I could dial that number and talk to my dad.

My dad. I pictured him preserved in amber, in a sort of resinous suspension since I left, but I knew he must have changed, aged. The thought of it broke my heart. I almost couldn't remember why I hadn't spoken with him for so long.

In the end I decided to treat the family to something fun with the eBay windfall. We chose Disneyland. Or I should say Shae chose Disneyland.

" 'Disneyland is presented as imaginary in order to make us believe that the rest is real,' " he quoted from Baudrilliard, " 'when in fact all of Los Angeles and the America surrounding it are no longer real, but of the order of the hyperreal and of simulation.' " He was flushed. "See, Flan, we have to go. It's perfect for my dissertation."

"We *have* to," echoed Noodle, while Nori jumped up and down chanting "Go! Go! Go!"

We ended up going to Disney's California Adventure instead of the actual prototypical Disneyland. Here's the reason: The Soap Opera Café. We went to Disney's California Adventure for the fucking Soap Opera Café. Of course I didn't realize this until we made a side trip to pick up Ada and her walker at her rest home. I sat in the backseat between the kids, Nori's car seat digging into my side, while Shae and his grandmother rattled on in the front about how excited they were to try the Melodrama Meatloaf, or whatever soap-themed foods were on the menu.

The café, it turned out, was filled with re-created sets from *All My Children, General Hospital,* and—drum roll, please—*One Life to Live.* All the ABC-slash-Disney soaps. Actors performed scenes from the shows while you ate your ten-dollar burgers. Sometimes real actors from the real shows showed up to sign autographs. The guy who played Asa and the woman who played Blair were there that day. Ada had had a crush on Asa for years. She thought they belonged together—Asa and Ada, true love forever. The fact that he had married a dozen or so women on the show didn't matter to her. She didn't care that he had committed all sorts of crimes, including kidnapping and attempted murder and faking his own death.

"It's like we're really in Llanview," Ada gushed, and I guess it was if you looked at one little corner of the restaurant and didn't look at the encroaching sets from the other soaps. I had never seen her this excited. Shae hadn't been this excited in a long time, either. I was glad for that, even if it was for a dumb reason.

While the two of them waited for autographs in the long, long line, I took the kids around the park. There weren't that many attractions for little kids, and Noodle was too nervous to go on most of the ones we did find, so we spent a lot of time on the merry-go-round, sitting on dolphins and sea horses, the peppy music drilling into my brain. We also walked through the tortilla factory several times, getting a fresh warm tortilla for free at the end of the tour. We should have saved our money at the café and filled up on tortillas instead.

Shae and Ada were still in line when we returned; their elation had wilted a little, but they still seemed happy to be there. I left Nori with them so Noodle and I could go on Soarin' Over

California, an attraction Nori was too small to ride. Baudrillard, king of simulation, would flip over it. You sit in a row of elevated chairs, your legs dangling, and zoom toward a huge curved movie screen. It creates the sensation of flying over different parts of California: Yosemite, the ocean, orange groves, complete with puffs of orange-scented air blasted in your face. It's really quite spectacular—gorgeous images, the gut-clutching feel of flight. I would have enjoyed it more if Noodle hadn't been screaming at the top of his lungs. He started to wail as soon as our row of chairs lifted up into the air. It must have given him flashbacks to the ski lift on Mount Baldy.

"I'm going to fall!" We all had sturdy, cushioned, safety bars over our shoulders, across our fronts, but he wouldn't stop shrieking. "I'm slipping out! I'm falling! Mama, make them stop! Make them stop it!"

"They can't stop the ride, honey." The chair swept over a red-wood forest. The scent of pine shot out of the nozzle on the seat-backs in front of us. Part of me wanted to whoop with joy. Another part of me wanted to whup Noodle in the head for ruining my good time. I tried to remind him that we were really only a few feet off the ground, but it didn't help.

After we got off the ride, his legs were shaking so much I had to carry him back to the Soap Opera Café, where I found Shae and Ada sitting at a booth, chattering over their signed eight-by-ten glossies. They barely noticed us lurching toward the table. When they finally looked up, Ada proudly held up one shot of Asa, a serious, half-turned-away from the camera pose, dramatically lit. He looked every inch the patriarch with his wing of pale hair, his tailored suit, his expensive glasses over his prominent nose. The autograph said *To Ada, the love of my life. Yours, Asa Buchanan.*

"He kissed my hand," she sighed. "What a gentleman."

I noticed that Shae's photo from the actress—a slutty pose, if you ask me—was signed *To Shake, with love and kisses, "Blair."* I felt an unexpected stab of jealousy. Why did he tell her his name was Shake? Why did she want to give him kisses? I kissed the top of his head—a big possessive smack, more of a punch than a kiss, just because I could. His hair was dry and crackly against my mouth.

He looked up at me, startled. I raised my eyebrows, a challenge. *You wanna kiss that bimbo? You got me to contend with, bub.*

"Mama," Noodle pulled at my overalls. "Where's Nori?"

"That's a good question," I said, my heart lunging. I tried to keep calm. "Where's Nori, Shae?" How could I have not wondered this already?

Panic contorted Shae's face.

"She was playing under the table . . . ," he started.

I flipped up the tablecloth. All I could see were Ada's veiny shins, her nylon anklets, and orthopedic shoes. No sign of Nori.

"Shae, you idiot," I banged my head on the bottom of the table as I stood up.

"Don't you talk to my grandson like that, Flannery," Ada said. "Shae, are you going to put up with that kind of language?"

"Excuse me, Ada," I said, "but he fucking lost our daughter!"

I ran around the restaurant, frantic, charging between two actors doing their shtick—a fight between an amnesiac and his evil twin.

We all shouted Nori's name. A few people yelled "Nori!," too, but there was no answer (aside from the doofus who called out "Polo!" in return, as if we were playing a swimming pool game). I was about to enlist a security guard when we finally found her, giggling, under a table in the *All My Children* section of the restaurant. I gave her a mammoth hug, then started in with my

"What were you thinking? We were so worried. We thought we'd never find you!" attempt at a lecture. By the time we strapped her into her stroller, she was indignant and screaming back at me.

"You ready to go?" I asked Shae over the din. He looked exhausted; so did Ada, who had hung the plastic bag holding the signed eight-by-ten glossies on the handle of her walker. I was drained myself. Shae lifted Noodle up onto his shoulders, and Noodle fell asleep almost immediately, his body drooping forward over Shae's head. Nori fell asleep in her stroller, which happily limited her escape options.

Shae put a hand on the small of my back, then bent down as much as Noodle's weight would allow, and whispered "I'm sorry, Flan. I should have been watching her more closely." His words soothed my rankled nerves. I leaned against him and we walked, very, very slowly, to the elephantine parking lot, all my children accounted for, at least for the time being.

Nori abruptly stopped nursing shortly after our Disney adventure. Between that and losing my yard sales and feeling guilty about the Suleimans and not talking to Pia, I was a disaster. Maybe the stress made the milk taste bad; maybe Nori could sense my impatience; maybe she was just ready to quit. I was glad I had nursed her until she was two, but I was ready to have my body back. When Noodle went cold turkey—from nursing every three hours to total weaning—I developed such bad mastitis I almost ended up in the hospital. Nori hadn't been nursing much, so I didn't think I would suffer any ill effects, but I ended up more engorged than I had expected, my breasts hard and feverish. Maybe my body knew I didn't plan to have more babies, and wanted one last milky hurrah.

I saw Pia across the courtyard, watering her window box of herbs. I missed her like crazy. I didn't know what to say, so I walked up to her and lifted one side of my shirt, instead. Her eyes opened wide—she knew I wasn't normally so spectacularly stacked. "Cabbage," she said. The air was gamy with basil.

"More like melons," I said.

"No," she said. "Cabbage will help." She led me into her kitchen and pulled a pale green head from the vegetable crisper. "I was going to make lumpia, but this is more important."

"How could anything be more important than your lumpia?" It was such a relief to be in her house.

She peeled off two of the outer leaves. "Take off your bra," she ordered.

My overalls were half off, the front of my shirt flipped over the back of my head, my bra unhooked and dangling under my breasts, when Michael walked into the room. I went to pull my shirt back down, but it got stuck on my hair before it fell over the front of my body.

"Hi Michael," I said, my face beet red.

"Hey Flan," he said. "Don't worry. It's nothing I haven't seen ten zillion times already today."

Pia frowned. She lifted my shirt, tucked it back over my head and fitted a cabbage leaf over each breast. It felt wonderfully cool.

"People would pay good money to see that, you know," said Michael.

"If you get the camera, I'll rip your eyeballs out," said Pia, her voice level, her hands still on my breasts, fitting the leaves to my body. If I kissed Pia, I wondered, what would she do?

.   .   .

The kids came running out of Ravi's bedroom, rumpled and wired. Pia moved her hands away.

"You look like a mermaid," Noodle said, breathless.

I looked down at my cabbage cupped breasts, the leaves ridged like seashells, my overalls draped from my waist like a tail.

"Can you breathe underwater, Mama?" Noodle asked.

"I wish I could, sweetie," I told him. It would be nice to escape the noisy world and float inside that cool blue light. Pia would want to be right there with me, drifting and shimmering, getting away from her research, her worry about her mom. I imagined most of the mothers in Student Family Housing would be glad to join us for a few moments of peace, our hair undulating around us like seaweed.

I thought about Sodaba in the university pool, her burqa a dark jellyfish, her progress slow and steady as a whale's. I imagined her joining all the mothers underwater. I wanted to clothe her in cabbage leaves and a glimmering tail, but I had no idea what her face looked like, her body. I could only picture her as a dark and graceful ink spill, her feet and hands flickering on the periphery, free as fish.


Pia gave me a long painful hug and sent me home with the head of cabbage, telling me to keep it cold, to change the leaves whenever they started to feel warm and limp. She said it helped her immensely when Ravi weaned. The leaves were still under my shirt, forgiving against my skin; my bra was balled into one of my pockets.

When I walked by Shae, he perked up and said, "You smell like St. Patrick's Day." Ada had always made a big deal about St. Patrick's Day; she cooked the whole corned-beef-and-cabbage and soda bread supper, even stirred a liberal spritz of green food coloring into her beer. The green beer I could do, but I always felt a little rueful that I couldn't make him the traditional meal. After my mom died, holidays were low-key in our house. My dad sometimes picked up a HoneyBaked Ham for Easter, but that was the extent of our holiday home-cooking. We had Thanksgiving at Bob Evans Restaurant each year unless someone invited us to their house. I never learned how to prepare a big feast. Shae was understanding about my domestic ineptitude, but I know he missed those dinners. Ada didn't have access to a kitchen in the rest home, and even if she did, her arthritis would make cooking difficult, if not impossible.

The kids ran into the bedroom. I could hear them bouncing on the beds, hopefully exhausting themselves further. I unclipped my overalls and let the bib fall. I pulled one of his hands under my shirt and laid it over a cabbage leaf. I was worried he would resist, but he didn't. He kept his hand there.

"You feel like a Barbie doll," he said. "Like your nipples have been erased."

"They're still there," I said. I peeled away the warm leaf, which had molded itself firmly to my body, and let him discover for himself. My breasts were sore but it felt lovely to have his hand there. It felt marvelous to have him lean over and kiss me.

"You want to check out my latest auction stuff?" I asked.

"Not particularly." He pulled back, looking confused.

"It's a euphemism, you dodo," I said. "It's a door with a lock, remember? We can have some privacy. . . ."

"Ah," he said, recognition dawning. "As a matter of fact, I would like to see your latest acquisitions very much."

I took a fake fur blanket down from the linens pile and set it on the one clear spot of linoleum. It wasn't long enough to accommodate the length of our bodies, but there was enough room for him to sit down with his legs crossed, for me to sit on his lap, my legs wrapped around him. There was enough room for our bodies to connect, Shae totally naked, me with one cabbage leaf still plastered to my skin, my overalls hanging from one ankle, my shoes still on.

We were just pulling on our clothes when there was a frantic knocking on the door.

"Mama," Noodle said. "Nori got outside!"

In the heat of things, I had forgotten to check if the front door was locked. When I stood up, hot fluid poured out of me, pooled into my underwear. I realized we hadn't thought about birth control, either.

I opened the door.

"I went to go pee and I told her to stay on the bed, but she got out."

"Thanks for telling me, Noodle," I ruffled his hair.

"Mama, she might go in the *street*!"

I wondered how many times Noodle had said this. Too many of our conversations seemed like rehearsed dialogue. I was stuck in an endless loop: wake up, deal with kids, play with kids, fend off kids, chase after kids, feed kids, clean kids, have the same conversations with kids, go to sleep, wake up, begin again. And again. And again.

Then Sodaba appeared on my doorstep and the entire script flew out the window.

# part three

What is known I strip away.

ᕙ᷾ᕤ "Come." Sodaba grabbed my arm. "Come."

*I just did,* I wanted to tell her, my body still buzzing.

It didn't strike me at first that anything was wrong. It just struck me that I had never heard Sodaba's voice before. It was surprisingly strong. I would have thought only a whisper, a thin murmur, could get through all that cloth. I could see her irises flash through the mesh rectangle of the veil. They were hazel, flecked with green.

I let her pull me across the courtyard, acorns rolling under our feet. People were gathered around a car parked in one of the spaces along the grass. I realized I hadn't seen Nori yet. I started to feel dizzy.

"Nori?" I asked.

"Come." She kept pulling me forward.

"Nori!" I screamed. "Where is she?"

"Come!" I wondered if she knew any other word in English.

I tried to break away, but her grip was too tight. Both of us ran faster toward the car. It was the Suleimans' car, a forest green Cutlass Ciera, at least ten years old. And, once I pushed past the small crowd gathering, I saw Nori, my sweet baby Nori, under the front bumper. Only her head and shoulders were sticking out.

"Oh my God." I fell to my knees and could see that part of her torso was pinned beneath a tire. "Oh my God."

Noodle was right next to me, a pale ghost. He slumped against me. Nori was pale, too. Her forehead was beaded with sweat. Her lips had a bluish tinge. She didn't appear to be breathing.

"Oh my God, Nori," I choked out. "Is she okay? Is she alive?"

"She's in shock," said Pia. I hadn't even realized she was there. I hadn't realized her hand was on my shoulder. "An ambulance is on its way."

Nori's eyes, which were glassy, lifeless, shifted and looked right into mine. As soon as she saw me, she started to scream. I had never been as happy to hear anything in my life.

"Nori," I smoothed my hand over her curls. "I'm here, sweet-pea. I'm here, my love girl."

"What happened?" Shae knelt beside me. I had no idea if he had been there the whole time, or if he had just arrived. I could smell sex waft out from the loose leg holes of his shorts. It made me nauseous. How could we have been so selfish?

"I'm here, curly head," I said to Nori. "I'm here, seaweed girl."

"I saw it happen," said Pia. "Nori ran into the parking spot just as she was pulling in. She didn't have time to stop. But the car was going very slow."

"I'm here, pumpkin pie," I said. "I'm here, my lovely one."

I had never seen Sodaba drive before, only her husband. Had she taken the car without his permission? Did she even know how to drive? She stood off to the side like a mound of laundry. How could she see where she was going?

I pushed up on the bumper, imagining that super human, super mom strength was going to course through my muscles, that I was going to be able to grunt and lift the tire right off my baby, but the car didn't move an inch. My limbs felt sapped of every ounce of energy. I collapsed back on the ground, next to my shrieking child.

Noodle was clinging to Shae, who looked just as drained as I felt. They were both trying to comfort Nori, too. All of us were. All of us were calling her our sweetheart, our honey bun, our angel face. All of us were hoping our words would slide under the car like butter, coat her body, help grease her way back out.

Sirens whined in the distance then grew progressively, ear-splittingly louder. A fire truck, an ambulance, and a police car all zoomed onto our street, huge and shiny, with their flashing lights and their gleaming bodies; they looked like they didn't belong in our neighborhood. And they didn't. They didn't belong. They shouldn't have been there. Nori shouldn't have been under a car. None of this should have been happening.

Yellow-coated firemen spilled from their truck and rushed the Ciera. One of the fireman slipped a large black square under the car.

"Clear!" he yelled and jumped back.

A pump began to hiss; the square started to inflate. The car rose with it, as if it were light as air. Nori's body was more visible now—what a relief to see her chest again, her belly, her legs, although they were heart-stoppingly still and askew.

"Who can tell me what happened?" a fireman asked, but I couldn't find my voice. It had retreated to some place deep in my throat. Pia took him aside and filled him in.

I watched them brace Nori's neck, strap her body down to a board. Nori, whose body I always had to strap down to keep her from escaping. Nori, who had almost found a way to escape for good. Blood stained the pavement beneath her. I saw it as they lifted her onto a gurney.

*I am the mashed fireman with breastbone broken . . .*
*They have cleared the beams away . . . they tenderly lift me*
    *forth.*

Her blood looked too dark. It should be cotton-candy pink, I thought; it should be lemon yellow, robin's egg blue. Not that brick red. Not that blackish, brackish, scarlet.

I couldn't move. I was made of sand, of salt. Someone—I don't know who—helped me into the ambulance. When I turned around, the courtyard was full of people. Any one of them could have been the person who put their palm on my back, hoisted me up. I don't know if it takes a village to raise a child, but that village certainly turns out when a child is hurt. To help and to gawk, both. *Whatever interests the rest interests me.*

A paramedic closed the ambulance doors; another continued to work on Nori. I tried to watch, but when I saw the pain on Nori's face, I had to look away. Shae and Noodle got progressively smaller through the square window in the back of the ambulance. A policeman cuffed Sodaba's hands behind her back; her head was bent forward, her body a dark bracket against the white summer sky. Good, I thought. I hoped I'd never have to see her burqa again. We were probably going at a fair clip, but it felt like a snail's pace. *The ambulanza slowly passing and trailing its red drip.* Whitman was writing about war in that part of the poem. Well, this became a war, too.

☙ Much of the rest of that day is a blur. The blur of palm trees through the little window of the ambulance; the blur of the emergency room, of paperwork, of bustle, of Nori disappearing

through swinging doors. The blur of Shae arriving at the hospital
with a policeman, the one who had questioned him, the one who
would question me. The blur of telling him we had been having
sex. The blur of trying to explain that we hadn't had sex in a long
time, that we weren't horndogs going at it in the middle of every
afternoon, that we watched the kids carefully, that this was a rare
moment. The blur of being told that a social worker would come
to our house unannounced to determine if we were fit parents.
The blur and sting of the shot a nurse gave me to make my milk
dry up when I thought my breasts might explode. The blur of Pia
arriving, letting me flop against her. The blur of waiting. And
waiting. And waiting so long, and worrying so hard, I wanted to
blur until I disappeared completely.

The only thing that could have brought me back into focus
was my copy of *Leaves of Grass,* but that was still at home, hidden
in the dark reaches of my drawer. Random lines floated into my
head. . . .

*What have I to do with lamentation?*
*It throbs me to gulps of the farthest down horror.*
*Somehow I have been stunned. Stand back!*

A doctor finally came back through the swinging doors and
walked purposefully toward us. We all sat up, every cell at attention, petrified.

"Well," he said, crossing his arms in front of him. It seemed
like a million years before he said anything else. "She has three
broken ribs and a punctured lung. Her liver is slightly bruised.
Given what could have happened, you should consider yourselves very lucky. It's a miracle she's still with us."

*Ever love, ever the sobbing liquid of life,*
*Ever the bandage under the chin, ever the tressels of death.*

Shae sagged against me, his body heavy with relief.

"Can we see her?" he asked.

I felt dizzy. I wanted to see Nori, but I didn't want to see her in a hospital bed. I didn't want to see her in pain. I pictured my mother in her hospital bed, bucking and groaning. I could barely breathe, thinking of Nori's lung pierced.

I was tempted to bolt from the hospital and breathe in some open air (I won't say fresh air—in Riverside, the summer air looks like soup). A police officer was stationed by the nearest exit, though, and I didn't want to get in any further trouble. Anyway, how could I even think of leaving Nori behind?

"She's in the ICU," the doctor said. He looked angry with us, impatient, his eyes dark slits, his Bugs Bunny tie mocking, cruel. Did he know what we had been doing when Nori was hit? Did he think we had hurt her, somehow? "We had to put a tube in her lung to drain the air from her chest cavity. We're going to need to watch her carefully. She's not in the clear yet—her liver could start bleeding, her lung could develop an infection—but we expect her to pull out of this. We'll have a better idea in a couple of days."

"Thank God," I said. Strange how those words just pop out. I forced myself to stand up and follow him to the ICU. I thought of the yellow "C" on the side of the Box Springs Mountains. *See?* A voice inside told me. *I See You. ICU. I see you wanting to run. I see you wanting to get out of this. But you're in it, baby. This is real. This is your life now.*

It's astonishing how quickly something can become your life, even when you resist it. How easily you can slide into the rhythm of vitals checks and blood tests, the clack of gurney wheels on the polished floor, the hum of the radiology department, the whoosh of the tube sucking air and blood from your child's lung.

*Agonies are one of my changes of garments.*

Our second night in the hospital, bleary after tests and worry and staring at Nori's sleeping face, a huge blast shook the walls.

I was dozing in a chair next to Nori's bed and woke up to BOOM! BOOM BOOM BOOM! Car alarms blared, rattled by the explosion. Nori stirred briefly from her medicated sleep, her breath condensing inside her oxygen mask; Shae, shockingly, was still out cold on his hard orange chair. I kissed Nori's head and ran into the hallway to see what had happened. Dozens of other concerned relatives rushed out at the same time.

"Was that a bomb?" someone asked.

"Are we under attack?" asked another.

Everyone had been on edge since September 11. Everyone was waiting for the next catastrophe. We all stood ragged in the hallway, waiting for our lives to change all over again.

"You don't know what day it is, do you?" Gladys, a nurse from Trinidad via Texas, asked us. She had the most wonderful voice—a smooth Caribbean lilt with an occasional unexpected twang. "Poor things, y'all been cooped up in a hospital too long."

Two days was definitely too long. It felt as if we had been there for two weeks. Time had stretched like one of Dalí's clocks. I couldn't say what day of the week it was, what hour of the day.

"And you call yourselves Americans," she said. "It's the Fourth of July! Independence Day? Fireworks? Barbecue? Hello?"

She pointed to the window at the end of the hallway. We

could see a spray of white sparks. They turned into corkscrews and skittered away, out of sight.

She turned the knob on her radio so we could all hear the patriotic music the local radio station played each year to accompany the display. An elderly man and his middle-aged daughter put their hands on their hearts when the "Star-Spangled Banner" came through the speakers. A Latino woman cried. On the radio, a baritone sang "And the rockets' red glare, the bombs bursting in air," his voice jangly through the transistor, and I couldn't help but think of the Suleimans, the bombs raining over their homeland. *The fall of grenades through the rent roof* . . . I wondered how Sodaba and Raminullah were handling the fireworks. Did they even know about Independence Day? Did they think they were under siege? I felt a rush of compassion for the couple, quickly replaced by an urge to jump on top of Sodaba and pummel her senseless. I wondered if she was still in police custody. No one I talked to seemed to know.

"Mount Rubidoux's on fire." Shae pointed to the orange flames licking up in the distance.

"It happens every year," the old man sighed. The fireworks were launched from the top of Mount Rubidoux, more a hill than a mountain, crisscrossed by paths for joggers and bikers, just a few blocks from the hospital. Like the Box Springs Mountains, Mount Rubidoux was dry and brown every summer, except for patches of cactus and some hardy weeds and herbs. The city performed controlled burns on the hill before the Fourth and saturated the ground with water, but it still managed to catch fire year after year.

The river in Cleveland caught fire several years before I was born. My dad talked about it often, the day the Cuyahoga, slick with oil, ignited. I always hated those stories. If water, the thing that could save us from fire, had the potential to burst into flame, then the whole world could combust at any moment. The thought used to make my feet fall asleep; the ground would feel like static electricity beneath them, no longer solid.

The fireworks kept exploding—red, white, and blue barreling toward us like fists. They were so loud and bright my temples began to ache. The flames on the hill grew higher. What would happen if the flames barreled all the way down the hill? Would we have to evacuate the hospital? What would happen to Nori's ventilator? I looked around, but no one else seemed nervous, at least not about the fire.

Gladys began handing out little toothpick American flags to everyone, the kind you would use to hold a club sandwich together or stick on top of a cake. I doubted there was room for fifty stars in the corners of the stiff paper banners—it looked like there were only twelve or so on each one, which I found strangely depressing. I thought of Walt Whitman proudly calling himself *an American, one of the roughs, a kosmos*. You can't make a kosmos out of twelve paper stars. I went back to Nori's room before Gladys could offer one to me.

I learned a few things those first couple of days. Primarily, I wasn't a good hospital person. Everything inside that building was too new, too bright and clean. I missed the dust and dinginess of the storage units, of my auction room, my whole broken-in life. The air was so antiseptic I couldn't sit still. I couldn't look at Nori's tubes and blood and bandages without feeling lightheaded. I kept pacing the halls, wandering over to the cafeteria for a cup of coffee or a bagel or some gummy entrée. I went to the nursery to look at the new babies, to the gift shop to peruse, yet again, their assortment of breath mints and stuffed animals.

Shae, on the other hand, was made for the job. He was used to sitting around all day, watching TV on crappy sets. He showed no signs of fatigue or impatience. He was traumatized, sure, but he could have sat there forever if that's what Nori needed.

"Why don't I go home and spend some time with Noodle?" I suggested. Noodle had been staying at Pia's house since the accident. He was too young to visit Nori's room. "Nori's stable now. I think one of us should be with him—he must be all scared and confused. . . ."

"I could go . . ." Shae started to rise from his chair. I put a hand on his shoulder; he sat back down, shrinking away from my palm. Touch had become a dangerous thing between us.

> *To touch my person to some one else's is about as much as I can stand.*

"No, no," I said. "I'll do it. You can stay here with Nori." I made it sound like I was making a sacrifice. I didn't want him to know how eager I was to get out of that place.

I kissed Nori's sleeping head. Her hair smelled musty, sweet and dank with sweat; it needed to be washed. Her eyelids were dark, swollen, almost scrotal. I could barely look at her. *I'm leaving the hospital,* I wanted to tell her. *I'm not leaving you.* I hoped she would understand.

When I stepped outside into the parking lot, I blew out a long hard exhale to purge the antiseptic from my lungs. When I took a deep breath in, I felt lightheaded. I felt light as air.

A woman with a notepad strode up to me, a man with a camera close behind her. "Excuse me," she said. "Are you Flannery Parker?"

I shook my head and staggered to the car.

The courtyard was full of people when I pulled up to the curb. At first I thought they were the same people who had been standing there as I left in the ambulance. Maybe normal life had stopped for everyone in the courtyard, not just us. Then I noticed the signs in their hands: SUPPORT OUR TROOPS IN AFGHANISTAN, PRAY FOR AMERICA, AL QAIDA LIVES HERE! on one side of the courtyard, near the Suleimans' house; GOD BLESS HUMANITY, U.S. OUT OF AFGHANISTAN, PEACE, PEACE, PEACE, PEACE closer to our door. I was shocked so many right-wingers were on campus. Maybe they were from the wider community. Maybe Sheila or the mom from the park had told the guards to let them in. Or maybe 9/11 really had changed the tenor of the university. Fear does unusual things to people.

Pia emerged from the crowd. I was so happy to see her I just about fainted into her arms. She smelled good—like lettuce, apple juice, almond lotion. Pia's scent. "What's happening?" I asked.

"Just your average patriotic bedlam," she said.

A pickup truck drove by slowly, an American flag snapping from the back. Another flag whipped around, shredded, from the antenna. "Go Home!" at least two people shouted through the open windows.

"We *are* home," Pia yelled back, and she was promptly hit by a flying soda can, thankfully an empty one.

"They probably thought I was Sodaba," she said as she pulled me toward her house. She tossed the red can into the recycling bin outside her kitchen door. "Although I think everyone with dark skin is a target right now."

"It's her," I heard someone yell before we disappeared inside. "Baby killer!" another voice roared.

"Oh my God." I collapsed on Pia's couch. "I thought I was coming home to relax."

"No rest for the weary here, my friend." She kissed the top of my hand. The wet imprint of her lips lingered over my veins.

Noodle ran into the room. I had forgotten about his short hair. He looked grown up, his face newly angular.

"Mama!" he cried out, and dove into my lap. He was wearing one of Ravi's shirts; he smelled like a new kind of shampoo.

"My boy," I whispered into his neck, even though he didn't feel like mine anymore.

"The cops should be breaking this up soon," Pia said, peering between two blinds. "They do every day about this time."

"What's going on?"

Pia grabbed a newspaper from her faux marble coffee table. She pointed out a small article, on the third page of the local section: "Afghani national runs over toddler."

I scanned the piece quickly. It was only a few short paragraphs. Most of the article focused on Sodaba and the fact that she didn't have a license. She had apparently tried to apply for one in her burqa, but was denied. Our family wasn't named. The article didn't mention that Shae and I had been having sex, either, although it did say we were "indisposed," so people might be able to guess what we were up to. It listed Nori ("the toddler girl") as being in serious condition. I felt a twang of shame. Why wasn't I at the hospital with her? I burrowed my face into Noodle's hair.

"That was in the paper yesterday," said Pia. "This is what's been happening since."

She put another paper in my lap, open to the Letters to the Editor section. Most of the letters demanded that Sodaba be sent back to Afghanistan, demanded that all "towel heads" be sent back to Afghanistan, demanded, essentially, that anyone with Arab blood be sent back to the Middle East, or at least rounded up and detained.

Other letters appeared, too, deeming me and Shae selfish and negligent parents, saying we were unfit to raise our children, saying the writers would be happy to adopt the toddler girl after she got out of the hospital. "We've been trying for six years to have a baby," wrote one woman. "We know how precious children are. We would never allow this to happen at our house."

"Some TV people have been by, too," Pia told me. "News vans. I asked them to leave, but they'll probably come back looking for you."

"Shit," I said. "What do we do now?"

"We wait for the police to show," said Pia. "After that, we go back to your house and clean you up and get you some rest. If any camera people come by, I'll kick their asses."

A sharp laugh punched out of my throat at the image of Pia kicking some journalistic butt, but it quickly turned into a coughing fit. How dare I laugh when my daughter was hurt?

"I could write an official statement for the media, if you want," she said. " 'The Parker family thanks you for your support and asks for privacy during this difficult time'—something along those lines."

"Thanks, Pia." I couldn't have asked for a better spokesperson.

I leaned back toward the window behind the couch and

spread two of the metal blind slats apart. I noticed a cluster of women dressed all in black outside, some with black veils over their heads; they stood together in silence. If anyone yelled at them, they remained silent and still. If anyone shook their fist at them, they remained silent and still. If anyone asked what they were doing, they remained silent and still. I never could have done it, myself.

"Who are they?" I asked Pia.

"They're Women in Black," she said.

"Like that movie with the guys with the sunglasses?"

"You dork," she said. "You think they're fighting aliens out there?" She told me Women in Black stand in silence to give voice to the voiceless. She said the movement started in Israel and Palestine, but I was too tired to absorb much beyond that.

I thought of Julia living her life at the Zen Center mostly in silence. I wondered if she had come down the mountain, if she was one of the women in black, one of the women under a veil, standing right there on my lawn. Wouldn't that be amazing if Julia was out there? I felt a little *zing* run through me, a little jolt of Yes. I tried to study the women's faces through the slit in the blinds, but I couldn't make out any individual features.

Noodle's head grew heavier on my lap, then lighter, then heavier, as he drifted off, then resisted it, then drifted off again. I wondered if he had slept at all since he'd been here.

I watched the candles flicker in the grass outside the window. The flashing lights from a police car joined them.

"Pia." I looked at her, but I didn't know what else to say. Exhaustion bore down on me like a strong, steady hand.

"Let's get you back home," Pia whispered after the courtyard was quiet. She lifted Noodle and carried him outside. I followed in a daze, close behind. The grass was strewn with scraps of paper, soda cans, stubs of candles, along with the usual acorns. It looked like the aftermath of a concert.

Our house was stuffy and hot, a little ripe with the garbage that should have been taken out a few days before. I followed Pia into the bedroom. She poured Noodle onto one of the twin mattresses, then lay down on the futon beside me.

"Have you seen Sodaba lately?" I whispered, turning to face her. I tried to sound casual, but inside I was churning. I wanted to shake Sodaba, to hug her, to rip the veil off her head and slap her across the face. Or kiss her. Maybe kill her.

*Do I contradict myself? Very well then, I contradict myself.*

I had no idea what would happen if I actually crossed paths with her.

"I haven't seen her for days," Pia whispered back. "I heard the police released her, but I don't know if she's come home."

"Have you seen Raminullah?"

"It's been a long time since I've seen that guy," she said, and I realized that I hadn't seen him for a long time, either; not since the day he found all his stuff in my back yard. Almost a month.

"Are you going to press charges?" Pia smoothed down my hair.

"I don't know." I started to cry. Pia let me sob against her until I fell asleep.

It was such a relief to wake up to the smell of my dingy pillowcases, my weeks-unwashed sheets, instead of antiseptic air. I was tempted to stay in bed all day and watch dust motes travel through the planks of light that fell across the room. Pia and

Noodle had already gotten up. I could hear cartoons blaring out of the TVs. I wondered if Nori was awake yet, watching cartoons from her hospital bed.

"Pia signed me up for camp, Mama," Noodle said when I walked into the living room. He was already dressed, wearing his green dolphin shorts, faded purple tiger T-shirt, and orange jelly sandals (which were probably girl sandals, but he loved them, anyway—in his mind, orange was a boy color). "Today's my first day." He sounded like he was trying to be brave, but when he lifted a spoon full of Fruit Loops to his mouth, his hand wavered a little.

I called Pia's cell phone. "What's this about camp?"

"I meant to tell you last night," she said. "He needs a place to go. I'm at the lab. Michael has to work. You have to go to the hospital. It's at the Child Development Center. You better head over there—it opened half an hour ago. He's registered and paid for. All you need to do is drop him off," she said.

How did I deserve such a good friend?

The Center was only a couple of blocks from our house. Noodle went to preschool there, so he knew the place well, but as soon as I said "Let's go," he started to cry.

"I want to be with you, Mama." He glommed on to me, his milky lips finding a space where my shirt had ridden up in the gap of my overalls.

"I have so much to do, Noodle. . . ."

I practically had to drag him to the Center. It was a hot day. The grass was parched, crunchy beneath our feet. He cried the whole way there.

When he saw a couple of his friends, including Ravi, he took some deep shuddery breaths and braced himself. I watched him disappear through the door into a room where kids were dipping yarn into glue and squiggling it across pieces of paper. I left as soon as possible. I didn't feel ready to be at the receiving end of all the concerned glances, the dirt-digging "How are you *really* doing" questions from the few parents who were milling around.


I should have gone straight to the hospital, but the thought of those hallways made my head ache, so I called Shae and told him I had some things to do around the house. He said there was no reason for me to rush back—Nori was staying awake for longer periods and didn't seem to be in too much pain. I think he was actually relieved to have me away for a while.

I probably should have taken the time to clean up a little, to take the smelly, wet laundry out of the washing machine, to rinse some of the dishes crusting in the sink, take out the trash, hop into a shower, check my eBay listings, but I couldn't do much of anything. I pulled *Leaves of Grass* out of my underwear drawer and ran my cheek over the mustard cloth cover. The weight of it in my hands was a comfort in itself. I carried the book to the living room and slumped onto the couch. I felt closer to Shae than ever, sitting there. At the hospital, I couldn't sit still, but at home I couldn't do anything else. I turned each of the seven TVs on to different channels, a couple of them pure static, all of them blending into fuzzy Technicolor chaos. I stared in their direction, not really watching any of them. The book on my lap felt like the only solid thing in the world. Days seemed to go by as I sat there, but when I looked at the clock, only a couple of hours had passed.

Pia had left the newspaper on the couch; I picked it up and absently flipped to the Public Notices. There was an auction that day, which seemed absurd to me. How could life keep chugging along as if nothing had happened? I thought about Nori and something like seasickness washed over me. My baby. I was desperate to see her. Why wasn't I at the hospital already? When I got in the car, though, my mind lost out to muscle memory and I found myself in the parking lot of Store It Your Self.

"It's Flan!" Mr. Chen-the-elder broke into a smile when I entered the office to register.

"Where have you been, girl?" Yolanda slapped me on the arm. I had only missed an auction or two; I was surprised anyone had even noticed I was gone. Her long nails left dents in my skin. Her mouth smelled like bagels. Like onion and yeast. A few poppy seeds were stuck between her teeth, wedged up near her gums.

"We had some family stuff to deal with," I said. If I said anything further, I knew I'd fall apart. I didn't want to fall apart; I wanted it to be a normal auction day. I hadn't had a normal day in what seemed like forever. I was so tired, I felt like I was hallucinating.

"It wasn't that accident, was it?" asked Mr. Chen-the-younger. Shit. I nodded. My eyes prickled. I blinked them furiously.

"We read about it," he said. "I recognized the name of the street. I was hoping your family wasn't involved."

"The girl. How is she?" Mr. Chen-the-elder asked.

"She's going to be okay," I managed to choke out.

"Your girl is the little girl who got hit?" asked Yolanda. I nodded again. I couldn't stop the tears this time. "Oh no. Oh, baby. Oh, you must be hurting and hurting." Yolanda wrapped her plump arms around me and I started to sob. I felt hands pat my head, my shoulders, my back.

"Such a nice neighborhood, my son tells me," said Mr. Chen-the-elder. "He says maybe we can move there someday."

I was grateful, once again, that the media didn't say anything about Shae and I having sex. I doubt people would be as quick to comfort me if they knew what I had been doing when Nori ran out of the house. I guess the press wanted to demonize Sodaba, not us. If the blond people had been doing something naughty, then the woman in the burqa wouldn't look as bad. The press definitely wanted the woman in the burqa to look bad.

"She's a handful, that baby girl," said Yolanda. "I seen her in action. You have to watch a child like that like a hawk."

I snuffled. "I just turned my back for a second. . . ."

"That Arab woman hit her, right?" Norman grunted and took a drag off his cigarette. "That lady from Afghanistan? That lady thinks she should get a driver's license with that rag over her head?"

I nodded.

"They should send her back to the Taliban, let them cut off her hands."

"Those bastards don't belong on American soil," said Yolanda's husband, Rafael.

Yolanda shot him a look. "Then you don't belong here, either, pinchè," she said. "Then Mr. and Mr. Chen don't belong here. Flan, neither—she don't look Native American to me. Everyone belongs in America. That's what America is for." Mr. Chen-the-elder nodded enthusiastically. I wanted to give her a hug

"That's not what *my* America is for," said Norman. "Let them cut off her head."

My own head was reeling. There was no way I was getting sucked into this conversation.

"It was an accident" was all I could say, but I'm not sure anyone heard me.

"If they get deported," said Mr. Chen-the-younger. "Do you think we could have their house?"

I was relieved when the auction started. I just wanted to forget about everything and look at the lots, shine my dim beam into the lockers, hear the auctioneer do his roadrunner-on-speed spiel, watch the different ways people bid—lifts of hand, of chin, of eyebrows. During the first lot, though—not a Flan lot; this one was full of huge machinery—Yolanda pulled me aside. "You shouldn't be here," she told me. "What are you doing here? You should be with your girl."

"I need to make some money," I told her, my mouth dry. "We have to pay for the hospital bills."

They didn't know I had stopped my yard sales. It was a decent excuse.

I ended up not bidding on anything. Lethargy swept over me. I couldn't seem to lift any part of my body to respond to the auctioneer. Before everyone left, my auction friends gave me the best items in the units they had just won—a zirconia necklace, a set of collectible spoons, a laptop, a small locked safe. "For the girl," they told me. "For the bills."

"You want us to start a fund?" Rafael asked. "We could have a car wash. We did that for my nephew's funeral. . . ."

Yolanda smacked him. "Don't you say nothing about a funeral. Jesus Christ." She turned to me. "I apologize for my husband."

"It's fine," I told her. "We'll be fine." I was grateful for the outpouring of generosity from my little community, but I wished I could just crawl into one of the dark storage lockers and sleep.

I gave the safe back to Mr. Chen-the-elder. "I really can't keep this," I said.

"Let's at least see what's inside," said Mr. Chen-the-younger. "Maybe we can share the loot."

He put his ear to the metal door and fiddled around with the built-in combination lock. It wasn't long before he figured out how to open the thing.

The door opened with a creak. We held our breath. Would it be cash? Bonds? Jewels? Mickey Mantle baseball cards? My nose wasn't registering anything. Maybe because it turned out to be a stash of gay porn magazines. I guess my nose hadn't been calibrated for those.

"Oooh," said Yolanda. "Someone was in the closet."

"What was in the rest of the lot?" I asked, glad to have someone else's drama to think about for a minute or two.

The Chens looked through their haul. "Toys, kid clothes, changing table, playpen, thirty-six-inch TV . . ."

"You never know what a family man is hiding," Yolanda chortled and nudged her husband in the ribs. "You keeping any secrets from me, Rafael?"

Rafael puffed himself up and said, "Yeah, I got a secret. My wife's a crazy *puta*." I could tell he was mostly joking, he wasn't really trying to be mean, but still it was a shock to hear him say it.

"And you can't afford me, baby." She jutted her hip in his direction.

I had never heard the Garcias talk like this before. They pretended to punch each other, and ended up practically having sex right there on the asphalt. Was everyone going insane?

"I guess these won't help your girl," said Mr. Chen-the-younger, ignoring the Garcias' display. He put the safe, still full of magazines, in the back of his truck.

Norman watched it all, shaking his head in disgrace. Before I left, though, he grabbed my arm and said, "You take care of her, you hear me?" His eyes, full of compassion and pain, disconcerted me. If I kissed him, I thought with a start, he would taste bitter, like smoke. But once I got past that, once my saliva washed away some of his saliva and found what was underneath, his kisses would taste like licorice and pipe tobacco, something dark and sharp and sweet.

I wondered what was wrong with me, why my body felt pulled to other bodies even when my daughter was in the hospital, her own body in pain.

*You villain touch! what are you doing? My breath is tight in its throat;*

*Unclench your floodgates, you are too much for me.*

Noodle seemed no worse for the wear when I picked him up at camp. He was holding two crossed Popsicle sticks latched together by diamonds of orange and purple yarn.

"Is that a kite?" I asked, clobbered with exhaustion, as we started to walk home. I could barely see straight.

"It's a God's eye," he said, looking at it with reverence, maybe a little fear. "Do you think God can see through it?"

We hadn't really talked about God before. I had never known what to tell him. *Why should I wish to see God better than this day?*

"I don't know, Noodle," I said. His hand felt good in mine, just the right size. "I don't know if God can see through yarn."

"But I thought God was everywhere."

"Maybe so."

"Ravi had to go home early, Mama," he told me.

"I hope he's not sick," I said, and Noodle's face creased with concern.

"Maybe if I look through the God's eye, I can see him," Noodle said. "Maybe that's what a God's eye means—it makes me see everything like God sees everything."

"You can try," I said.

He held the bright scratchy cross to his face.

"What do you see?"

"Colors. And little stringy things. And some sun. And I can see you through the holes." He looked disappointed.

"That's a lot," I tried to reassure him.

"Mama," he said. "What color eyes do you think God has?"

"I don't know if God has eyes."

"How can God see us, then?" he asked.

"Maybe all our eyes are God's eyes." I felt like one of the cheesy resident Grounded gurus saying this, but Noodle seemed to like this idea.

"Maybe God's eyes are every color in the world," he said, looking to me for confirmation. As if I had a real answer.

"Maybe so."


Noodle was adamant about stopping by the community garden, halfway between the Center and our house. I was glad to delay the trip home. I didn't want to see all the people camped out in the courtyard, singing "God Bless America" or standing in silence or screaming or doing whatever it was they found it necessary to do on my behalf.

Our section of the garden was a mess. Most everything was dead. Only a solitary giant zucchini was flourishing.

"Remember how Nori used to lie down next to that uzini, Mama?" Noodle asked. Uzini was Nori's word for zucchini.

"Mmm hmm." My stomach folded into itself. I couldn't think about Nori without my body shivering or contracting in some way.

"Remember how it was as long as her, Mama?"

"Mmm hmm." His questions were starting to wear on my nerves, but I didn't want to tell him to stop.

"Do you think it's still as long as her, or did Nori get bigger?"

"I think she's about the same," I told him. I didn't tell him how much smaller she looked in that hospital bed.

"Can we bring it home, Mama?"

"The zucchini?"

He nodded gravely.

"To eat?" I asked. He looked at me as if I had suggested eating a pet.

"To remind us of Nori." He lifted the God's eye to his face.


We carried the zucchini across the field, smuggled it past the chanters and the meditators and the screamers. Ravi was in front of Pia's house, sitting on the steps, absently playing with a rubber ball.

"Ravi!" Noodle ran over to him.

Michael came outside. He stepped over the boys and walked up to me.

"Pia's mom died this morning," he said. "We're about to take her to the airport."

Pia came out the kitchen door, lugging a giant floral suitcase from one of my auction lots. I set the zucchini on the grass before I raced over and hugged her for what felt like a million years.

"Don't you wait, Flan," she told me, her voice congested with tears. "Don't you wait to go see that girl."

"Babykiller!" one of the protestors yelled at Pia. The number of protestors had dwindled considerably, but both sides continued to stake out the courtyard in shifts, one or two people at a time. They probably wanted to take advantage of the sporadic

visits from reporters. I had mercifully been able to avoid the reporters myself, thanks to Pia.

"Asshole!" I shouted back. I wanted to go punch her in the
mouth.

I took the cubic zirconia necklace from the auction out of my
pocket and slipped it over Pia's head before Michael led her and
Ravi to their car. She didn't seem to notice the jewelry, glinting in
the sun. I put my arm around Noodle. He lifted the God's eye to
his face again and we watched them drive away in their old Ford
Fairlane, their dark heads rounding the corner, driving toward
more and more sadness.

When they were out of sight, I marched over to the protestor
who had yelled at Pia, a thin woman with dyed red hair and a
narrow, pinched face. "No babies were killed in the making of
this movie, so shut your pie hole," I hissed at her.

"When you aid a terrorist, you become a terrorist." How anyone could think Pia was a terrorist was beyond me. It would be
hysterical if it wasn't so hideous. Why would a woman in a burqa
change into Bermuda shorts showing her sturdy knees?

I pulled the KEEP AMERICA SAFE sign from the woman's
hands and threw it to the ground.

"Mama!" Noodle had picked up the zucchini. It was cradled
in his arms, the God's eye resting on top of it. "God can see you."

"Out of the mouths of babes." The woman picked up her sign.

"If you want to keep yourself safe, I suggest you go home
now," I told her.

"My son is serving in Afghanistan," she said, her voice starting to break. "He's the one keeping all of us safe." I noticed the
button pinned to her purse—a gangly young man in full army
dress, trying hard to look stoic for the camera.

I had an urge to wrap my arms around her, but I just nodded,
grabbed Noodle's hand, and walked back to the house.

.   .   .

Noodle said he was starving, so I tried to pull together a decent square meal. I found a box of macaroni and cheese in the back of a cupboard. The smell of boiling water made me feel like a nearly normal mom, my normal child watching normal cartoons in the next room. After the noodles were done, though, I realized I didn't have any butter or milk; I poured the fluorescent orange cheese powder directly on the pasta and stirred it around. It turned clumpy and diseased-looking. I added a few tablespoons of olive oil. It didn't help much. If Noodle didn't like the bowl I put in front of him, he didn't say. Then again, he didn't say he liked it, either. He didn't say much of anything. We just sat together in silence, crushing blobs of powdered cheese against the roofs of our mouths with our tongues.

I had planned to go back to the hospital that night, but then Noodle fell asleep curled around the zucchini, and I didn't want to leave him. I called Shae to say I would be there tomorrow.

"I thought you were going to come today," he said, a hint of reproof in his voice.

"I tried . . . ," I started, but it sounded lame even to me.

"They took out Nori's chest tube," he said. "She's sleeping, but I can hold the phone up to her ear for you." I was going to say he didn't have to do that, but I didn't want to do even more to earn his disdain.

I wanted to tell Nori an endless number of things, but I didn't want to disturb her sleep. I beamed silent thoughts to her, instead, tears sheeting down my face—*I love you, Nori. I'm sorry I'm not there with you right now, but you'll be home soon. You'll be good as new before we know it. You're so strong, my sweet girl.* I sat on the couch listening to her breathe until Shae got back on the phone.

"You need to be here tomorrow," he said. I could hear the tension in his voice.

"I will," I told him, though the thought of it made me want to pass out.

"It's important," he said, and I wondered if there was something he wasn't telling me. Could a doctor have said she only had one more day to live? Did they take the tube out because there had been complications?

"I could come right now," I said, frantic. "I could see if Michael can stay with Noodle...."

"Just be here tomorrow morning," he said.

"I hope you're able to get some sleep," I told him. He seemed very far away. I almost couldn't remember what it felt like to sleep next to him.

I could hear him sigh. "Good night, Flan."

After I hung up the phone, I walked into the auction room. Normally I was able to make sense of the chaos there, but the room just looked like a jumble, a disaster. The furry blanket still lay on the floor from my encounter with Shae. The sight of it turned my stomach. When I kicked it toward the wall, it felt heavy as a carcass against my foot.

I considered wading across the piles and turning on the computer to check my eBay listings, but that seemed too overwhelming. I didn't want to know about all the packages I needed to assemble and ship off. As long as the monitor was blank, I wasn't beholden to anyone.

On my way out of the room, I unpinned the passport from the door and flipped through its pages. I envied Samantha Walker with all my heart. As a Walker, I imagined, she was free to move wherever she pleased. As a Parker, I was stuck in a single, stalled, gear. I couldn't do anything right, not even visit my own daughter in the hospital.

I held the passport to my face and breathed in its musty possibility. How hard would it be to drive to Ontario Airport and buy a ticket with this passport? Would the post-9/11 security people let me through? Could I get on a plane and fly to Bermuda, or Zimbabwe, or the Philippines? Pia would want me there at her mother's funeral, wouldn't she, especially since Michael and Ravi weren't able to go? Wouldn't she want someone from her Riverside life there? I was seized with the need to see her in her Filipino blouse, to see the huge insects she told me about, the ones she and her brother used to trap in pickle jars, the ones that first made her want to be an entomologist. I wondered how long the flight would take, what the air would feel like when I got off the plane—I was sure it would be humid, fragrant, different from our dry summer heat.

"Mama?"

I guess Noodle hadn't fallen asleep, after all. I pinned the passport back to the door and went to join him.

In the morning, the bedroom smelled peaty; the zucchini was already softer and darker than it had been in the garden. I worried that it would split and ooze seeds all over our faded Underdog and Aquaman sheets. My substitute daughter rotting in our bed. My real daughter recovering, I prayed, in a different bed four miles away. I took Noodle to camp, then went home and sat in front of the TVs, paralyzed, for an hour. It took me almost another full hour to convince myself to get in the car.

· · · ·

The hospital hallways were fuzzy smears of light as I stumbled down them, holding my breath. The first solid thing I remember is Gladys, standing in front of the nurses' station like a boulder in the middle of a river.

"So the queen mother has decided to make an appearance," she said, crossing her hands on top of her breasts. She was wearing Tasmanian Devil scrubs. The graphics gave me vertigo. *The whirling and whirling is elemental within me.* I blinked, too discombobulated to say much. "You gonna stay this time?"

"I haven't been gone that long," I choked out. "Just a little over a day."

"A lot can happen in a day," she said sternly. "A lot can happen in even a minute."

"I love my daughter," I choked out.

"I'm sure you do, baby." Her face softened.

"I have trouble with hospitals," I said.

"Lots of people do," she said.

"I didn't mean to stay away. . . ."

"She's been in good hands," she said. "That husband of yours, he's a good man. He even learned how to clean your girl's stoma."

"Stoma?" I was sure I was going to pass out.

"The hole in her chest," she said. "For the tube. It's out now."

I had to lean against the wall; neon streaks burst across my vision.

"Now he helps her with her breathing exercises. He changes her diaper. He sings to her when they do the needle sticks."

I was stunned. Shae did all that? My couch potato husband?

She must have seen the disbelief on my face. "Some people rise to the occasion," she said. "And some people fall." She gave me a look that made my stomach plummet before she turned and walked purposefully back to the nurse's station, her cartoon scrubs swishing around her large body.

Nori was asleep when I stepped into the room. Shae was writing on the back of a flyer and didn't see me at first. I tiptoed toward the bed. The room was quiet, except for the occasional beeping of a monitor. Nori didn't have too many tubes. Just an IV. She wasn't full of holes. She was Nori. Still Nori. Nori with the corn silk hair. Nori with the lovely dip between her nose and her lips. Nori with the long eyelashes. Nori with the little birthmark under her left eye. My Nori. My baby girl. How could I have stayed away from her for so long?

*The little one sleeps in its cradle,*
*I lift the gauze and look a long time*

I leaned down and breathed her in, caught a whiff of her natural bubble gum smell, hidden beneath the hospital fumes. I touched her hair, lightly, scared to wake or hurt her; her lids looked less swollen than they had, but they still looked a bit bruised and greasy. She slowly opened them.

"Mama." Her voice was scratchy. I thought she would be upset, I thought she would ask me where I had been, but she was thrilled to see me. I wrapped my arms carefully around her body. I didn't want to crush her. But she squeezed and squeezed me—*Long I was hugged close . . . long and long*—and I cried so hard I thought I would need a breathing tube myself.

When I came up for air, I realized Shae was standing next to me.

"She's eating now. Aren't you, Nori girl?" He smoothed her hair back. She smiled sleepily up at both of us and then closed her eyes again. "Well, not eating exactly. Eating would be too hard on her ribs. She's drinking Ensure now."

I couldn't look at Shae full on. Out of the corner of my eye, I noticed he was wearing hospital scrubs. He smelled different, like industrial soap. I felt horrible that I hadn't brought him a change of clothes. "Do you want to go home and take a shower and change?" I asked. "I can stay here."

"You can stay here." I could feel him shake his head in disbelief. "Flan, you couldn't stay here if you were in traction."

"I can," I said, but panic crackled up my spine.

"I'll believe that when I see it." I had never heard such sarcasm in his voice before. Over the phone, he hadn't sounded mad at me. He had been hiding it well.

"You should go home and change," I told him.

"I can change here," he said. "I can shower here. I'm getting a lot of work done." He gestured to the stack of papers on the adjustable tray near the window.

"Noodle misses you," I said, and I could feel him pause.

"Noodle can come visit," he said.

"He's too young," I said. I thought of myself in my mother's hospital room, being pinned still by my dad's arm, my mother grunting, her face twisted.

"He can't come in the room, but I found out there's a family visiting room. I can wheel Nori out there. I know she wants to see her brother. She's been asking about the two of you." He said it as if I had been gone a month.

"What do you tell her?"

"That you're busy," he said curtly. "That you love her. That you're busy baking a big fat strawberry cake for when she gets home."

"So now I have to bake a cake?!"

"Shit, Flan. Don't sound so put upon. It's the least you could do," he said.

We turned and faced each other. He didn't look as angry as I thought he would. He mostly looked sad. Sad and tired and confused.

"I'm sorry I didn't come sooner," I whispered, and started to cry again.

He wrapped me in his arms and started to cry, too. It made me cry even harder. We cried onto each other's shoulders. We cried into each other's hair. We cried onto each other's faces. We cried into each other's mouths. Wet, salty, sobs that, from the outside, probably looked like deep, passionate kisses.

When we let go of one another, I could tell someone else was in the room. A doctor, I figured. I blinked a few times, and the person came into better focus. He wasn't a doctor. He was an old man, around my height, balding, wearing a short-sleeved, brown-checked dress shirt, tan shorts, black shoes. Baggy elbows. Spotty hands. I thought he had wandered into the wrong room.

"Can we help you?" I asked, still snuffling.

He stared at me for a while before he said "Come on, Flan, don't tell me you don't recognize me." As soon as I heard his voice, I knew.

"Dad?" The word sounded rusty in my mouth. He had become an old man. How had that happened? How could a person get this old in just ten years?

Shae kissed my forehead and said, "Maybe I'll go home and take a shower, after all. You should have some time alone." He kissed Nori's sleeping face and shook my dad's hand before he left the room. Their eyes locked in a moment of understanding that made me wince. I wanted to race after Shae and tell him to come back, but I couldn't seem to move.

A person supposedly sloughs off all their cells every seven years. If that's true, how can we remember what came before each new seven-year set? I barely remembered my life before I came to Riverside—my first seven years with my mom in the world, my next seven years with my dad, my third seven years, partly in Cleveland, partly in Riverside. These past seven years with Shae, the kids. Since I last saw my dad, he and I had become entirely new people.

"How did you get here?" I whispered. "How did you know to come?"

"Your husband phoned me," he said, with the same mouth that once called me "You little bitch" and said "You can't talk to me that way" and "What the hell is wrong with you?" The mouth that sometimes sang "Climb Every Mountain" to me at night.

"I didn't know you had a husband until he phoned," he said. He was shaking as much as I was.

"I have a husband," I said. "I have a husband and two kids."

"I know, Flan," he said. He looked so splotchy and frail. "I wish someone had told me before now."

I wasn't sure how to answer him. Silence settled into the room again. We sat on orange molded chairs, Nori's adjustable tray between us. So much time between us.

I took a deep breath and asked, "How have you been, Dad?"

"Oh, you know," he said.

How could I possibly know? When he yawned, I could see the fillings in his molars. I vaguely recalled having been scared of those fillings.

"Still working?" I asked him.

"Nah, I retired a couple of years ago." He picked at his shirt. "You know those little cars and boats I was always making in my shop?"

I had no memory of them at all, but I said "Of course."

"I'm making a business out of them. I sell them at street fairs and the like. I even have a website."

"That's great," I said.

"I looked for you online," he said. " I couldn't find you any-where."

"I'm no one," I told him. "Plus I have a different last name now." It gave me a little pang to learn he had been looking for me. In all my Web searching, I had never once typed in his name.

"Anyway, I brought some for the kids," he said. "I would have sent them earlier if someone told me where you were, and that you had kids." He reached down and pulled a car from his duffel bag. I remembered the duffel bag, navy canvas with burgundy piping. It was the one he used when he went off for weekends with his hunting buddies and left me in the care of one neighbor or another. It was a little shabby, but remarkably intact.

The car he held was beautiful, made of two different kinds of wood, buffed to a glossy sheen. It was shaped like an old roadster, curvy and smooth and sporty. The number 9, my favorite num-ber, was inlaid on the hood.

"You used to love to come into my shop, remember, Flanny?" he said. "You used to love to play with all my hand tools." I could faintly conjure up the smell of sawdust, a Mexican restaurant cal-endar on the wall, but I wasn't sure if those were real memories or just figments of my imagination. Then more images emerged from the murk of my brain. My dad's furred arm pushing a sander across a piece of wood. His hand guiding my small hand as I tried to use the drill. Him putting a bandage around my finger after I almost sliced myself to the bone. How could I have forgotten all that?

"It's a great shop," I told him. I pictured him there alone, and I was overwhelmed with grief.

"I'm sorry, Dad. I'm sorry I've been so out of touch."

He put the car in my palm, the heat of his hand infusing the wood. We sat together in silence and watched Nori breathe until a nurse came in and told us Shae and Noodle were in the family waiting room. She gently woke Nori and helped her into a wheelchair. I pushed her down the hall, my dad walking a few steps behind us. Nori's grogginess turned into excitement at the mention of Noodle. I was worried she would exhaust herself by swinging her legs around, but I was thrilled to see her so happy.

Shae jumped up immediately when we entered the waiting room. "My girl," he said, and I felt a flush of pleasure until I realized he was talking about Nori. I saw that he had packed a bag for himself; it was sitting on the chair next to him. It made me wonder if we'd ever live in the same place again. The room was filled with sagging couches, old issues of *Highlights for Children* and *Yacht Living* splayed across the scuffed tables. A TV in the corner blared an old cop show from the eighties. Noodle looked nervous; a Goofus and Gallant page lay open on his lap, unread. I think he was worried, as I had been, that Nori wouldn't look like Nori, that she would be someone else. I saw his relief when he realized that Nori was still his sister.

"Noodie!" Nori yelled. She tried to jump out of the wheelchair, but couldn't. Her ribs were taped, her chest stapled. I thought about all the times I wished she could stay still, stay in one place. I would have given anything to chase after her again.

"Where are your broken ribs?" Noodle asked.

"I eated them." Nori grinned.

"Gross!" Noodle wiggled around, being a big goofball for his sister. He started to do a crazy, manic dance around the room, to Nori's delight.

I hadn't warned him that laughing hurt Nori. A lot. Her laughing quickly turned to shrieking, and Shae had to wheel her back to her room.

"What happened?" asked Noodle, frantic, as they left.

"Her ribs still hurt, sweetie," I told him. "If she laughs too hard, they hurt more."

"I hurt Nori?" he asked, pale.

"She'll be fine," I told him. It was the first time I said it out loud that I actually started to believe it myself.

I noticed my dad out of the corner of my eye. I had been so glad to have my family all in one place again, I had forgotten that he was in the room with us. That he was part of our family, too.

"Noodle," I took a deep breath. "This is your grandfather Ray."

Noodle stiffened. He let his eyes briefly dart to my dad before they settled back on me.

"Ray, like a manta ray, or Ray, like a ray gun?" he grilled.

"Ray, like Raymond," my dad said. He looked nervous, too, as if he were worried about disappointing Noodle.

"And I'm not Noodle, like spaghetti," Noodle said, still looking at me. "I'm Noodle, like Newton."

"Pleased to meet you, Newton," my father said. He extended his hand.

Noodle finally looked at him. He tentatively took my father's hand, gave it a quick shake. "Nori got hit by a car."

"I know," my dad said somberly. They looked at each other, and I recognized my dad in the curve of Noodle's jaw, in the pale blue of his eyes, the slightly droopy eyelids. I had never seen my dad in my son before. I almost couldn't bear to think of my dad as a little boy. It made me feel even more remorseful about being out of touch.

What had he done that was so bad? He had found my journal, where I used to record my romantic exploits. Back then, I guess I wanted to kiss everyone, too. My dad had written "slut" all over the pages with lipstick—mine, or my mother's ancient tubes, I wasn't sure. I couldn't bear to be in the same room with him after that, and the feeling appeared to be mutual. I was deeply ashamed. I was sure he hated me. He so wanted me to be a good girl, a perfect girl, a carbon copy of my mother who had saved herself for him. Part of me wanted to be that, too, but the more insistent part of me wanted to know the smell of boys, the taste of them, the feel of their fingers slipping under my clothes. When I had a chance to leave town with the last boy chronicled in the journal, I jumped and never let myself look back.

Over time, the prospect of contacting my dad got harder and harder. I was tempted to call him after Shae and I got married at the county clerk's office, and later when I had each of my kids, but as soon as I started to dial his number, I lost my nerve. I didn't want anything to sully my happiness. I didn't want the reek of the past on my babies' new skin. How could I have been so self-centered and neglectful? My dad probably just got freaked out about his teenage daughter's sexuality and didn't know what to do. That was understandable. The thought of my kids having sex freaked me out, too. It wasn't something I'd want to read about in graphic detail. I wondered if he knew that Shae and I were having sex when Nori was hurt. I almost expected him to say "I told you—something bad was sure to come from all that screwing around," but he looked too feeble to say anything harsh. Besides, my years of silence were much harsher than any words he could spit at me.


My dad tried to comfort Noodle, something I never could have visualized.

"Her ribs hurt when she laughs," he said, bending down to pat Noodle's shoulder. "That's all. She'll be right as rain before you know it."

Noodle flinched against his touch at first, but then seemed to get used to it. We stood together in silence for a few breaths after my dad stopped with the patting. I remembered his hand on my forehead when I had a fever, his hand on my back when I threw up.

"Well, folks, I better be going." My dad slapped his palms against the sides of his legs. The sound echoed through the room like a gunshot.

"You just got here," I said, flooded with sorrow and relief. What would we talk about if he stayed? Where would he sleep? The house was too much of a mess for an overnight guest. But how could he leave this soon?

"I have to get to the airport. Big craft fair tomorrow in Hinckley." He fished a couple of wooden cars and boats from his duffel and handed them to Noodle. "I made these for you and your sister," he said.

"Thanks, Raymond." Noodle carefully lowered a car to the ground and started to push it over the flat carpet. Little sparks of static electricity jumped up beneath the wheels. My dad bent down and rumpled Noodle's hair.

"It's good to see you, Flanny," he said, righting himself with a grunt.

"You, too," I told him.

"Maybe you could come visit me sometime, after Nori gets better," my dad said.

"I would like that," I said. Images from the Cleveland house flashed through my mind. It had been a long time since I had let myself picture the Dutch girl pot holders, the fuzzy green toilet seat cover, the blue- and yellow-striped washcloths. Things that would look like trash in an auction box but filled me with affection when I thought of their steady presence in my childhood.

We hugged, lightly, our bodies barely touching. My dad felt brittle. His cheek, stubbly and rough, pressed against mine, and I could smell the mustiness of age on his breath. This was my father. This old man was my father. By the time we let go, I had dissolved into tears. I could barely see him as he left the room. My blurry father, going home.

I sat down on one of the dilapidated couches, winded.

"Are you okay, Mama?" Noodle asked.

My eyes and nose were both running unchecked, but I nodded. He sat down next to me until I caught my breath.

"I should go say good-bye to your dad and Nori," I sniffled. "Will you be okay for a minute in here by yourself?"

"I have Raymond's toys," he said. He knelt down on the floor and started to play with one of the boats in earnest.

Nori was sleeping and Shae was stretched out on the empty bed next to hers, writing, when I came into the room. He immediately turned the papers over as soon as he noticed me.

"Is she okay?" I asked. She looked pale.

"They gave her some pain meds. She'll sleep it off," he said.

"That was intense." I leaned against the wall and set Shae's bag on the floor.

"How are you doing?" Shae asked.

I shrugged, letting out a long held breath. "Why did you call him?"

Shae pushed a button to make the bed sit up higher. "It just seemed like the right thing to do," he said over the mechanical hum. "What if something happened to Nori and your dad never got to meet her? You'd never be able to live with yourself."

I ran my hand down the edge of the privacy curtain and shivered.

"And what if he died before you tried to reach out to him? You'd never be able to live with yourself then, either, Flan."

I went to grab a tissue from the stand between the two beds. Shae brushed my hip with his fingers.

"I want you to be able to live with yourself, because I want to be able to live with you." His own eyes had started to fill. He opened his arms and I climbed up into the bed with him; he pushed the button to make the top of the mattress whir back down again. We lay with our arms wrapped around each other, my face getting his shirt wet.

From the bed, I could see Mount Rubidoux out the window. The hill was charred from the fireworks; a black swath marred the side of it like a bruise. It didn't look like anything could grow there again. But I had heard that fire is part of the natural cycle of a mountain. The areas that look the most ruined and desolate will one day be full of life, the soil nourished by what had burned there. Certain pinecones actually need fire to burst them open so they can release their seeds into the world.

Maybe this accident was the fire that would break us open so we could grow close again.

Shae and I decided I would bring Noodle every afternoon until Nori came home. Shae was adamant about staying in the hospital; I promised I would come by every day, at least once. Having Noodle with me would make it easier. We asked a nurse to keep an eye on Nori so Shae could kiss Noodle good-bye before we went home.

Through the narrow window in the waiting room door, I could see Noodle was still sitting on the ground, probably trying not to worry about why I was taking such a long time. As soon as he noticed us, he started to push my dad's boat around again, as if he wanted us to think he had been doing it the whole time.

Shae scooped Noodle into his arms. "I'll see you tomorrow, okay, little man?"

"I won't make her laugh, I promise," Noodle said, solemn as any oath.

"You can make her giggle." Shae stared at Noodle as if he wanted to soak in every centimeter of him. "Just don't make her guffaw. Or chortle."

"Snickering is probably okay," I said, wrapping my arms around Shae.

"And Butterfingering." Noodle piped up, looking proud of himself.

"But not Three Musketeering." Shae shook his finger at Noodle mock-sternly.

How long since we had had a silly conversation? How long since we had all had fun together? It was like a rush of oxygen, this short sweet exchange. So was the kiss Shae planted on my lips. So was having seen my dad—as shocking as it had been, his visit had aerated me somehow, made my brain a shade lighter. I remembered his favorite candy—the Necco Sky Bar, four candy bars in one. I hadn't thought about Sky Bars in years. Sometimes he would break off the vanilla section and give it to me. He favored the peanut butter, himself.

"Don't make Nori Baby Ruth," Noodle told Shae before we left. He laughed in the car the whole way home, sailing my dad's boat over the backseat.

Now that I had seen my father, I could picture his life in Cleveland, his aloneness, with heartbreaking clarity. I had the luxury of being in California, a place not swarming with memories of the past, but he was living in the house I had left, the house my mom had gotten sick in. He was confronted with memories every single day; they must have clotted the air. I wondered how his craft fair went in Hinckley. I had a memory of us driving to Hinckley, about half an hour south of Cleveland, when I was eight for their annual Buzzard Day. There was a pancake breakfast at an elementary school; afterward, everyone hiked to a park and stared at the air, ceremoniously waiting for turkey vultures to appear. I couldn't understand why everyone was excited about such ugly birds. Scavengers. I was scared they'd be able to smell my mother's death on me.

I went to my computer in the auction room that night and searched for my dad's name. His website, Ray's Woodworking Wonders, was unexpectedly professional, with well-lit photos of his boats and cars and a few hand-carved bowls. I had somehow expected a chintzy site, something with clip art and canned music. I wondered if he had designed it himself. I searched for a photo of him—I wanted to see how he looked outside of the hospital—but all I could find was a black-and-white shot of his hands holding a chisel. His hands looked much older, but I recognized the square fingernails, the mole near the base of his thumb. His bio simply read "Ray Michaelson, Woodworker." In the Guestbook area, one customer had written "We love Ray's race cars." Another gushed "Ray's the best!!!" I wasn't sure if it made me feel better or worse to know he had been getting love from strangers. Maybe they were friends. I hoped so. I typed a short note on the "Write to Ray" page, then turned off the computer. It was a start.

I wondered what else might come back to haunt me someday. I lay down between the heaps of women's clothes and handbags, closed my eyes and waited to see if anything bubbled up. Nori was a given. Sodaba materialized, too. As much as I wanted to, I couldn't push her out of my head. Shae wanted me to be able to live with myself, and to be able to do that, I realized, I needed to talk to Sodaba. The sooner the better.

After Noodle was sound asleep, I snuck outside. The ground was littered, again, with the detritus from the demonstrators. For people worried about keeping America "clean" and "pure," they left a shocking amount of trash behind. I could hear my pulse in my ears. The moon bled through the smog, diffuse, orange, like the tip of a large cigarette. It made everything on the ground look black and white.

Acorns flashed like silver bullets from the crispy grass. I tried not to slip on them as I tiptoed toward the Suleimans'. All the lights were off at their house. I had forgotten to check the clock—it could be nine P.M. or it could be midnight. I had lost all of my bearings as far as time was concerned. The glassy-winged sharpshooters in the mimosa tree peed or spit or whatever it is they do onto me, little pinpricks of liquid on my arms. I crept under a window and slowly raised myself up to try to get a peek inside. Before I knew what was happening, I found myself on my stomach on the ground, my hands pinned behind my back, dry grass pushing into my mouth. I felt a ringing in my head, like a hammer against a metal pole. A cloud of heavy, expensive cologne engulfed me.

"What do you want?" a man's voice boomed. "Why are you sneaking around here?"

"Raminullah?" I asked, my voice muffled. I imagined his chapped lips careening toward mine after he let go of my wrists, his small teeth clinking against my larger ones. I was terrified and strangely turned on all at once.

The man got off me. When I turned my head, I could see he was not Raminullah. This man was younger, clean shaven, but his eyes were dark and wet, ringed with long lashes, like Raminullah's. Maybe he was a relative.

"How do you know Raminullah?" he asked, suspicious.

"He's my neighbor." I sat up, spit out a few blades. He glared at me, disgusted. A deep exhaustion settled into my bones. "Sodaba hit my girl with her car."

"And you want to make her pay." He crossed his arms.

"We don't have the bills yet." I figured he was talking about medical expenses. I could taste blood in my mouth. I must have bit my tongue.

"Not bills," he said. "You're coming to get your revenge." It wasn't a question.

"No," I said. "Nothing like that."

"Then why are you here?" His shirt was a rough, loose, peach linen, almost a tunic. A shirt Walt Whitman would be at home in. His dark jeans looked new. His sandals were heavy, well made.

"I just wanted to see if Sodaba was home," I said.

"Why not knock on the door?" He jutted his chin up as he spoke. My bidding movement.

"I didn't want to wake her up if she was sleeping. . . ."

"Come back tomorrow." His voice softened. "In the morning. After ten o'clock." He disappeared into the house. I sat on the ground a while longer. The glassy-winged sharpshooters rained over me, a dainty, prickly shower, until I found the energy to stand and walk back home.

When I got into the bedroom, Noodle jumped out of bed and clutched me like a barnacle. He was shaking. He wasn't wearing any pants. The bottom half of his body glowed pale in the dark room.

"Where did you go?" he asked, hysterical.

"I just went for a little walk," I said. Dry grass was still stuck in my hair. I hoped I didn't smell too much like the cologne of the man who had been on top of me.

"You left me alone?!" I had never heard him so mad before. He had been fine when I left him alone in the waiting room, but that was different. He had known where I was.

"I thought you were sound asleep. I didn't go very far. . . ."

"You're not supposed to leave your kids, Mama."

That stabbed me in the gut. I bent over to catch my breath.

A cloud of urine rose from the sheets. Noodle had wet the bed, something he hadn't done in years. I looked down and saw he had put a towel over the puddle on the Aquaman sheet. The sight of the towel just about broke my heart. I should have been there when he woke up wet, when he needed me. I had failed both of my children.

"I'll clean this up," I said. I stripped the bed. I started a bath. I washed Noodle in silence. His body felt small under the washcloth, but his anger fanned out, huge. His muscles tensed against my touch when I dried him off. He refused any more help from me, put on his underwear and pajamas by himself, turned away from me on the futon. Even after he fell asleep, his body stayed curled into itself, mad and hard.

He was still upset the next morning. When I dropped him off at camp, he walked away from me, dwarfed by his big backpack, without saying good-bye.

I drove to the hospital and watched *Sesame Street* with Nori.

"Big Bude," Nori said, grinning as I spooned some applesauce into her mouth. She had just started eating solid food again.

"Yep, Big Bird," I said, slipping the spoon back out, watching globs of applesauce dribble down her chin.

I almost told Shae about my impending appointment with Sodaba, but he was still writing up a storm and I didn't want to disturb him. Plus, I didn't know how to put it into words.

"It's great that you're getting so much work done," I said.

"Mmm hmm," he said, his pen still moving.

"You'll be done with your dissertation before you know it," I said. He blushed and kept writing.

I got up to leave after Nori finished her bowl of applesauce.

"Short visit." Shae lifted his head. There was a hint of disapproval in his voice, but I'm sure he was relieved that I showed up at all.

·   ·   ·

When I reached the courtyard, thrumming with nerves, the man who had been on top of me was standing guard at the Suleimans' front door. I felt embarrassed seeing him, and a little excited, too, as if we had had a sordid one-night stand.

"You are here for Sodaba?" he asked. He acted as if he had never seen me before in his life. I wondered if he planned to frisk me. His fingers were long, his nails clean ovals. I anticipated them patting down along my sides, up between my legs, but he just gave a special knock on the door, a circular series of taps. The blinds opened a crack; then the door opened. A woman I had never met gestured for me to come in. She was wearing a head scarf, not a burqa, over her jeans and long-sleeved T-shirt. She was very young, probably a student at the university.

I expected the Suleimans' house to be full of tapestries and silk cushions and ornately carved lamps as I had imagined for their storage unit, but I was wrong again. The house was very spare. A tweedy, sagging couch was pressed against one wall. A card table with two folding chairs sat off to the side. The rug on the floor was a worn rectangle with a geometric print in browns and tans and beiges. The walls were bare, except for a calendar featuring a couple of kittens on a wooden swing. The air smelled like caramelized onions, not incense.

"You are here to talk with Sodaba?" the woman asked. I nodded, my heart balancing like an egg inside my throat. "I'm Naima," she shook my hand. "I'm here as Sodaba's interpreter. I'm sorry about your girl. Sodaba is beside herself."

She wandered off toward the bedrooms. Their house had the exact same layout as ours, but it looked like what we used as my auction room was their bedroom. I could hear some muffled talk. Then Sodaba followed the woman out into the living room. Her burqa looked rumpled, as if she had just been sleeping. I wanted to know if she slept in her burqa, if she was allowed to take it off to bathe or if she had to sponge herself off beneath the cloth. Had she been allowed to wear it when she was detained? I ached to pounce on her, scream at her, but I just nodded hello; she nodded back at me, then said something I couldn't understand.

"Have a seat," said Naima. "She would like you to sit on the couch."

I felt self-conscious sitting down on the long couch all by myself while the two women sat on the metal folding chairs. The springs creaked beneath me.

"You are here to ask some questions?" Naima said.

"I just want to know a few things." My voice trembled with adrenaline.

Naima translated my words to Sodaba, who didn't say anything in return.

"Such as?" Naima asked.

"Such as . . ." What the hell was I going to ask her? Why do you wear a burqa when it's one hundred degrees in the shade? Why are you in America? Why did you hit my daughter? Do you know that you've turned my life upside down? My mind went blank. I finally said, "Why was she driving without a license?"

Naima repeated my question to Sodaba. Sodaba said a few words in response.

"She has a license in Afghanistan," Naima translated. "She tried to get a license here, but they wouldn't let her take her picture in her burqa."

"But she knows how to drive American cars?" It felt funny asking about Sodaba in the third person while she was right there, but I found it much easier to speak to Naima, to look at her uncovered face.

"American cars are no different from Afghani cars. In Afghanistan, they had a Chrysler LeBaron." Naima answered me without consulting Sodaba this time. They obviously knew each other well; they knew each other's stories. At least she knew Sodaba's.

"And she was allowed to drive it?"

"Before the Taliban, yes. After, no. After, a woman could have been punished by death for driving. She hadn't driven for many years, but she needed to get to the doctor. Her husband has been detained, you know, so she had to drive herself."

"I didn't know," I said. "About the detention."

"He went to register at the immigration office—you know how they are making men from Arab countries register?"

"I heard something about it," I said. I'd read an article before the accident; there had been a protest at the local INS office, and a couple of peace activists had been arrested. Maybe the same people who stood on my lawn, standing and chanting for what they thought was right. I wondered if the Arab men appreciated having the protestors there. Maybe they didn't even notice; maybe they were just as numb as I was, the rest of the world foggy around them.

"Zalmai—you met him outside," she said. "They kept him for two days. And Raminullah still hasn't been released."

"Why not?" I wondered if the woman at the park was involved somehow.

"He's a microbiologist, so of course they think he was making biological weapons. But he's not a terrorist. He is just a man from Afghanistan, a scientist studying plant pathogens. And now they've detained him, and we don't know where he is. They're not giving us any information. We fear they've sent him to Guantánamo Bay."

I shivered. I had seen images of men in orange jumpsuits, heard rumors of torture, indefinite detention.

"What about Sodaba?" I asked, my arms beaded with goose bumps.

"We've been talking to a lawyer. He imagines they'll send her back to Afghanistan after the investigation."

I took a deep breath. "You said Sodaba had to go to the doctor. Was she sick?"

"She was bleeding. She is pregnant."

That hadn't been mentioned in any article. I felt my own belly twist inside. So both of us had been scared of losing our babies that day. I thought of all the items in her storage unit, now in my storage unit. Maybe she'd be able to use them after all. "Is she okay?"

"For now. She's had three miscarriages already. One stillbirth."

I turned and looked at Sodaba; I hadn't looked her way in a while—she had been a shadow in my peripheral vision for most of the conversation. I couldn't see her eyes under the mesh window. I couldn't see how big her belly was under the burqa; she was sort of like a fetus herself, hidden inside a large womb, under an opaque skin. I thought of my own baby, hidden inside a building across town. I thought of Shae, sitting patiently with her while Sodaba might never see her husband again. Raminullah might never even know if his baby was born safely. I felt lightheaded.

The front door cracked open. "Sodaba hurts one American girl," Zalmai said from the doorway, "and people call for her death. Meanwhile, your army bombs whole villages, hundreds of children dead this week alone, and no one blinks an eye." He looked at me as if I had ordered the bombings myself.

This was too much to take in. "I'm sorry," I said. "I shouldn't be here. I have to go." I stood up from the creaky couch, my mind filled with hundreds of massacred children, some of them with Nori's face. I reeled through Zalmai's cologne on my way outside.

I could tell Noodle had almost forgiven me when he let me hug him after camp and his body softened against mine. It was wonderful to see him and Nori together in the hospital, playing Connect Four, but I was unnerved. My meeting with Sodaba kept me from fully engaging with anyone, especially Shae. I wanted to pull him closer to me than ever, tell him how deeply I appreciated him, but I found myself holding back. I wondered if he could smell traces of Zalmai on me.

"Did you know Raminullah might have been sent to Guantánamo Bay?" I asked as checker pieces clattered out of the blue Connect Four frame.

Shae said "Good riddance" with such conviction, I didn't pursue the subject any further.

That evening, Noodle was invited to watch a movie at Ravi's house. I was sipping a glass of wine in the kitchen when a dark shape moved outside my window. At first I thought it was the shadow of an airplane; sometimes military jets flew low over the campus on their way to and from the March Air Force Base. Then it passed by again, and I realized, with a start, that it was Sodaba. If I swung the door open quickly enough, I thought, I could knock her over. It would seem like an accident. It would be swift, easy. That smack of wood against flesh would make a satisfying sound. I was filled with a momentary sense of well-being, but then I almost choked on my zinfandel. Stupid conscience.

I opened the door, carefully.

"Yes?" I made my voice sound impatient. "Can I help you?"

Sodaba inched toward me, her veiled face turned downward. She pulled a folded piece of paper from one of her sleeves and held it out for me. The paper was warm between my fingers when I took it from her hand. I unfolded it. It was a lined sheet, the kind with three holes on the side.

"Dear Mrs. Parker," it said, in blue ballpoint. "Sodaba needs your help."

What the fuck?

I kept reading.

"As you know, she is going to be sent back to Afghanistan, deported, if we don't do anything. She doesn't want to go. Everyone from the Islamic Center is under surveillance—she can't come to any of us for assistance. Her own house is under surveillance, too—you may have noticed that dark blue car parked on your street. We think it is FBI. If she is at your house, it means the car is gone. The man takes a break around 10am, for half an hour or so. If you could take her during that window of time and bring her somewhere safe, we would be forever grateful. I know this is a lot to ask of you, considering what happened, but that was an accident, Mrs. Parker, and this is her life, and we don't know where else to turn. The lawyer wants to help us, but he is bound by law. Please destroy this paper after you have read it. Sincerely, Naima." A phone number was written underneath her name, the word "cell" next to it in parentheses.

Couldn't Naima have asked one of the Women in Black to help Sodaba? One of the people with the Peace signs? A sympathetic student? Why would she ask me, of all people, to do such a thing? I felt a little flattered that Naima would trust me with such a task. Unworthy, too. She obviously couldn't see the vengeance in my heart.

"I don't know what to tell you," I said to Sodaba. I had no idea if she understood me.

I could feel her hesitation. She stalled by the step that led up to the kitchen. I wanted to rip off her veil. I wanted to see who this person was, standing outside my door. She almost didn't seem like a person. She was more an idea of a person. An approximation of a person. A mound of fabric with some breath underneath. A dark ghost who had hurt my girl.

"I don't know," I said again. "I'll call her, I guess."

I lifted my hand to my ear to mime making a phone call. This seemed to satisfy Sodaba. She nodded her head, and turned around to leave. I watched her glide to her house. I watched a blue car pull up to the front curb as she walked through her front door. The man inside didn't get out. I read the letter a few more times, looked at the car a few more times, and wondered what in the world I had gotten myself into. I wondered why Sodaba needed my help, why she didn't want to go back to Afghanistan, where she wouldn't stand out as much, where she would blend in with the rest of the covered women, where she wouldn't have to run away from everyone who voiced her name. And if she didn't want to go back to Afghanistan, why did she continue to wear the burqa? It wasn't like the Taliban was breathing down her neck in America. None of it made sense.

*I can say no,* I told myself. *I don't have to do a thing.* But somehow I wasn't convinced. I thought of what Shae said about my not being able to live with myself. Could I live with myself if I did this for Sodaba? Could I live with myself if I didn't? I thought of the bombings in Afghanistan. Could I let her and her unborn baby go back to that kind of life?

That's when I turned to Walt Whitman.

I grabbed *Leaves of Grass* from my underwear drawer, and let the pages spread at random. The book always opens to "Song of Myself," the pages that have been fingered and thumbed and poured over, violently underlined by my mom.

This time, the book opened to the section about the runaway slave:

*The runaway slave came to my house and stopped outside,*
*I heard his motions crackling the twigs of the woodpile,*
*Through the swung half-door of the kitchen I saw him*
*    limpsy and weak,*
*And went where he sat on a log, and led him in and assured*
*    him,*
*And brought water and filled a tub for his sweated body and*
*    bruised feet,*
*And gave him a room that entered from my own, and gave*
*    him some coarse clean clothes,*
*And remember perfectly well his revolving eyes and his*
*    awkwardness,*
*And remember putting plasters on the galls of his neck and*
*    ankles;*
*He staid with me a week before he was recuperated and*
*    passed north,*
*I had him sit next to me at table . . . my firelock leaned in the*
*    corner.*

How could I read this and not help Sodaba afterward? How could I not dial up Naima and say yes? I didn't want to put plasters on Sodaba's neck or soak her feet or do anything else of that nature, plus she probably wouldn't accept any clothes I had to offer her, but I could certainly lean my firelock in the corner, at least for a while. I hoped Shae would understand one day.

I ripped Naima's letter into shreds and put a few of the pieces in my mouth. I chewed them into a wad between my back teeth, but when I tried to swallow, it wouldn't go down. I spit the pasty mess into the sink, pinned the scrap with Naima's cell phone number onto the bulletin board, and hid the rest of the pieces under some coffee grounds and old macaroni in the trash. I took a big slug of wine, then called Naima and hammered out the plans.

The next morning was quiet except for a few blue jays and crows. I had already dropped Noodle off at camp and had just gotten off the phone with Shae and Nori. He said they had both slept through the night; she told me she dreamed about Noodle at the park. Her voice sounded strong.

When Shae asked how I was doing, I wasn't sure what to say. "Still a little shaky," I told him.

"I hope you're not mad at me for calling Ray," he said.

"It was the right thing to do." I hoped helping Sodaba was the right thing to do, too. Even if it meant keeping secrets from Shae.

"I love you, Flan," he said. I couldn't remember the last time he had told me that.

"I love you, too," I said, tears streaming down my face. "I'll see you later today."

It was going to be a scorcher—the air was tinged with a high, thin heat, the kind that threatened to press down on everything by the middle of the day. I pulled Beulah onto the lawn in the back of my house and parked her under the cypress trees, as I often did when I unloaded my auction spoils. I felt a twinge when I unbuckled Nori's car seat and carried it into the house. She should be the one in the car that day, not Sodaba. I almost phoned Naima to cancel the whole thing, but then I thought of Walt Whitman, and my dad, and what awaited Sodaba in Afghanistan, and knew I couldn't back out. When she appeared at ten-thirty, I opened Beulah's door. Sodaba ducked in and lay across the backseat, as Naima had instructed her to do. My heart raced; I couldn't believe I was actually doing this.

I quickly piled old shirts and skirts and sweaters on top of her, making sure I had left space around her veiled head for her to breathe. I probably didn't even need to add the extra piles of stuff—she looked like a pile of black material all by herself; few people would have guessed there was a person in there—but I wanted to be on the safe side. As I drove to Store-U, I kept glancing at the heap in the rearview mirror to see if Sodaba was still breathing. It must have been hot under all those layers; I was worried she would suffocate.

When the kids were babies and had to sit in rear-facing car seats behind me, it made me crazy. I hated not being able to see their faces or watch their ribs rise and fall. I was sure they were going to die of SIDS when I wasn't looking. I would often reach my hand back blindly until I touched their torsos, felt the slight movement of their inhale, their exhale, through their terry-cloth onesies. I was tempted to reach back and touch the fabric pile, see if I could find Sodaba's pulse through the layers, but I didn't want to alarm her. There were probably Muslim taboos regarding touch.

The Store-U manager saw me punch in my code and drive through the gates. Unfortunately he was someone I knew from my auctions; he used to manage Quickie Self Storage over on Monroe. He followed me over to my unit on foot.

"Hey, Flan," he said as I got out of the car. He was a burly, hairy guy—big hairy arms, a big hairy face, chest hairs curling up over the collar of his blue work shirt, curly hair spilling down on the other side. "How ya doing? I haven't seen you in ages."

"I'm okay, Mitch." I looked quickly at his name patch to refresh my memory. I tried to send telepathic messages to Sodaba to not get up in the backseat. I could see the pile begin to shift and stir. "How about you?"

"Can't complain. Still going to auctions?"

"Every once in a while," I told him. I didn't want to give him my whole life story.

"How are the kids?"

"Doing fine," I said. If I started telling him about Nori, I would collapse. The clothes in the backseat shivered. Sodaba must have sneezed. "You know, I don't mean to be rude, but I'm kind of in a hurry. . . ."

"Here, let me help you." He opened Beulah's back door, reached toward the clothes.

"No!" I yelled, too loudly. His back stiffened.

"Jesus, Flan," he said, obviously stung. "You got a dead body back there or something?"

I tried to laugh. "It's just some personal stuff. You know how it goes."

"Hey, no problem," he said. "We got a lot of secrets stored here."

"It's not anything secret . . . ," I started, but didn't know what else to say. All of it was secret.

"I got work to do in the office, anyway," he said, businesslike now. "Good to see you, Flan." He nodded curtly, didn't reach to shake my hand before he walked back toward the small prefab office building.

I slumped against Beulah and took some deep breaths to try

to regain my composure. When I was sure Mitch was squared away in his office and no one else was coming, I opened the padlock and rolled up the door. I hoped Sodaba would be okay with seeing all of her stuff. I hadn't considered the potential impact of her hanging out with her dead baby's things. I began to peel layers of clothing off of Sodaba—T-shirts advertising Mexican bars and basketball teams and obscure summer camps; sweaters knit by hand in Ireland, sweaters knit by machine in Bangladesh; denim mini skirts and long prairie skirts and sensible office skirts—and toss them into a pile on the concrete floor of the unit. Bit by bit, her black burqa emerged. Her bare hands emerged. I touched one of them briefly, on the back, not the palm; that felt safer, although I wasn't sure any touch was safe. She lifted her head slightly.

"Are you okay?" I whispered, but she didn't say anything. "You can come out now," I said. She looked around; I wondered how much she could actually see through the mesh window in the veil. Her peripheral vision must have been severely compromised. "Come on," I said. She grabbed on to my wrist and pulled herself up to sitting. Her fingers felt bony, her nails sharp. She shifted across the seat, ducked into the storage unit, hid in the farthest, darkest corner. She reminded me of an animal at the zoo. I felt horrible thinking that way, but it was kind of true. This was her new cage, and I was her keeper.

## part four

Behavior lawless as snowflakes

I called Naima so she could translate while Sodaba and I passed my cell phone back and forth. I told her to tell Sodaba I would leave the rolling door unlocked and open a crack. I would keep the standard door cut into the rolling door unlocked, too. I told her the office closed at six; Sodaba could get out and use the bathroom in the complex after that. If that was locked, she could use the patch of grass in the back of the yard where people stored their RVs and boats and old cars. It wasn't ideal, but it was something. I suggested that if she had to go before six, she could use a large bowl like a chamber pot and dump it out later. I had seen a big green mixing bowl among her things. There were no guards, I assured her. No guard dogs. I was pretty sure that was true.

Sodaba pressed the phone to the side of her head without lifting her veil. She occasionally murmured a few syllables to Naima. What she said, I don't know. Naima didn't translate any of it back to me after Sodaba handed me the phone.

I said good-bye to both Naima and Sodaba, and took off, feeling like a good Samaritan and a villain all at once. What in the hell was I doing? Was I betraying Nori by bringing Sodaba to this place? Was I being a model of forgiveness? Was I even helping Sodaba at all? When I was about halfway home, I realized I hadn't given Sodaba any food for her overnight stay. I drove to the Gus Jr. drive-through. I knew Muslim people had some dietary restrictions, but I wasn't sure what they were. I had a vague recollection that beef was forbidden. Chicken seemed safe enough. I picked up a fried chicken sandwich and ginger ale for each of us, and drove back to Store-U.

I was worried Mitch would ask me why I had returned so quickly—I prepared a story about how I had left my wallet inside the unit by mistake—but he barely looked up from his desk as I drove through the gate.

Sodaba was sitting on one of the blue recliners in the dark. She startled when I opened the door. I could see her body flinch inside the fabric.

"I brought food," I whispered.

Sodaba didn't get up. I put her sandwich on the other recliner, her drink on the floor. I considered staying to eat with her, but the air felt too charged. I did an awkward little bow before I left. When I ate my sandwich in the car, I wondered if we were tasting the same thing at the same time.

My secret rattled inside of me as I picked Noodle up at camp and we drove to the hospital. It itched and burned and bloomed inside my body. I knew I couldn't get Shae to understand why I had been spending time aiding the woman who hurt our girl. I could barely understand it myself.

"Nori had a bit of a setback after you called this morning," Shae told me. "She spiked a fever. The doctor thought that her liver might be infected—we had to race down and get an ultrasound. But everything looks okay. The Tylenol helped. And she's on antibiotics, just in case." There was a slightly accusatory tone in his voice. I knew I deserved it. I should have been there with them.

"She looks a little yellow," I said as Noodle read a picture book to Nori, careful to skip over the funny parts so she wouldn't laugh too hard.

"I tried to call you," he said, "but there was no answer at

home, and I couldn't get through to your cell." He must have tried while I was on the phone with Naima.

"I had some errands to run," I said. I was flooded with a strong urge to kill Sodaba. I wanted to go back to the storage unit and bang her over the head with a pan or take off her burqa and use it as a noose. I couldn't believe I had agreed to help her. The woman who had put my daughter in the hospital, who had punctured my daughter's lung, maybe infected her liver. What in the hell was I doing helping her?

*I and nobody else am the greatest traitor.*

When I visited the hospital again the next morning, Shae told me Nori had had an allergic reaction to the antibiotics. Her whole torso was covered with hives. I watched a nurse give her a shot of Benadryl and wanted to plunge the syringe into Sodaba instead. She should be the one screaming in pain, not Nori.

When I got to the storage unit, though, I was disturbed to find someone had pulled down the rolling door and clicked the padlock shut. I unlocked the regular door cut into the corrugated metal and stepped inside. The door swung closed behind me, leaving only a sliver of light. It was stifling in there, surely over one hundred degrees, and dark—it must have been pitch black with the door all the way closed. It took a while for my eyes to adjust, to make out the shape of the recliners, the edge of a crib railing. The room smelled horrible. Sodaba had probably used the bowl, or maybe the floor, as a toilet. Body odor filled the air, too—a sharp, nervous stink. I couldn't imagine what it must have been like for her to spend hours inside that dark, smelly locked box.

I finally caught sight of her. She was crouched down, her burqa flipped off her face, some hair plastered against the side of her neck. Her face was turned away, her cheek glistening with sweat. There was a bruise on that cheek. A big dark one. I thought it was a shadow at first, but then it shifted with her. I wondered if Raminullah had hit her, but then I remembered how long he had been detained. Maybe someone had attacked her on the street. Maybe she had fallen in the dark storage unit while trying to find a place to pee.

She may have been going to the bathroom at the very moment I walked in. She was crouching down like a person going to the bathroom in the woods. Or maybe she was praying. All my murderous thoughts drained through my feet. Seeing her skin, seeing that bruise, made me feel humble, somehow, shy.

"Sodaba," I said.

She stood up. I could barely see her burqa in the dim light, but I could feel her there. I could smell her, too.

"I'm sorry the room got locked," I told her. "I didn't do that. I promise."

I had no idea if she understood me.

"That must have been scary," I said. She barely moved.

I noticed the chicken sandwich, still wrapped in greasy paper, sitting on the recliner. "You didn't eat?" I pointed to it and mimed eating. The cup appeared to be empty, on its side.

"No halal," she said.

"Excuse me?" I asked.

"No halal," she repeated in her deep voice. I thought she might be saying "No way in hell."

"Are you vegetarian?" I dropped my voice, hoping she would drop hers, as well. I didn't want anyone to know we were in the unit.

She didn't respond.

"Halal," she said again, trying to get me to understand. "Halal."

"I'm going to call Naima," I told her. I dialed her number on my cell phone.

"Yes?" Naima answered.

"What does halal mean?" I asked.

"Sodaba must be hungry." Naima sounded tired. "We should have made arrangements for food." She told me that halal referred to the rules I had wondered about—food prepared a certain way, in accordance with Islamic law. She told me I was to avoid giving Sodaba pork, alcohol, meat from animals or birds without external ears, meat from animals who had been slaughtered in the name of anyone other than Allah.

I tried to imagine which animals didn't have external ears. Frogs?

"Do chickens have external ears?" I asked Naima. "I bought her a chicken sandwich. . . ."

"Eating out is tricky," Naima told me. "If halal food is fried in the same oil as nonhalal food, it is no longer halal."

"What should I feed her then?"

"There is a halal market on University," she said. "The Salaam Market, near the Taco Bell. I'll reimburse you for whatever you buy."

"I can't keep her here," I told Naima. "She got locked in by mistake last night. It's like an oven."

"Do you know where you're going to take her?" she asked.

Julia's house flashed into my mind. Julia shouldn't be there—

she'd be at the Zen Center. Hopefully she hadn't sold the house or rented it out. "I have some ideas," I said.

"Just keep me posted," she said. "But don't use your name. I don't want you to get in trouble."

"If they've tapped your phone, they already know who I am," I said. I was surprised by how alive that made me feel.

𝒞𝒪𝒪 We drove to the Salaam Market, Sodaba curled in the backseat, a pale yellow sheet draped over her.

"I don't think you should come out," I told her as I pulled into the parking lot. "The FBI probably has this store under surveillance, too." I hoped she would understand. She seemed to; she stayed hidden, even when I turned off the ignition. "Stay here," I said. Somehow it didn't scare me that I might be under surveillance myself. It made me feel like Samantha Walker, like a spy, someone worth paying attention to.

Once I stepped into the small store, I wished I had brought Sodaba with me. I had no idea what she liked or wanted. The air smelled of dusky spices, maybe a little stale. A small produce cooler sat against one wall, filled with vegetables I didn't recognize—something that looked like a cucumber, but was ridged and yellow and curved almost into a circle. Something that could have been a very large radish. A tangle of bumpy green pods—beans, maybe. The tomatoes, I recognized. The parsley, the onions. Everything else in the cooler was a mystery. Is this what life was like for Samantha Walker—learning new foods, navigating new ways of being in the world? I pictured makeup spontaneously rising from my pores, spreading evenly across my face, my hair growing long and lush. My legs took on a new energy as I strode toward the deli counter tucked into one corner of the room.

Metal containers under the plane of glass held at least six different types of olives bobbing in brine—from dark, wrinkly, raisin-looking ones to some as green and huge as eggs. Other containers held chalky-looking bricks of cheese, some slick with oil, others doused with paprika, a couple floating in liquid. Other bins featured strange pickled vegetables—bright pink, acid yellow, puke green, colors so vivid they didn't look edible. The air smelled different in this corner of the store—sharp and vinegary, a sick room odor. I held my breath.

The walls were plastered with newspaper pages I presumed were in Arabic. An American flag was draped over the door. There was no music, no background noise, just the low humming of the coolers. I glanced out the window; I knew I shouldn't leave Sodaba in the car much longer. It would be hot in there even without any extra layers of fabric, even with the windows cracked open. A heaviness settled over me as I wandered around the low, crowded shelves, grabbing things at random—a bottle of rose water, a can of fava beans flavored with cumin and lemon, a floppy package of flat lavosh bread, almost as big as a pillowcase. Samantha had left the building, it seemed. I was back to being Flan again.

A stooped man emerged from a back room and peered at me from behind the counter. "Can I help you?" he asked.

"I'd like these, please." I plunked my items down. "These are all halal?"

"You eat halal?" He seemed amused.

"Of course." I tried to look convincing. Why wouldn't a blond woman with naked shoulders eat halal?

The man grabbed two cookies—breastlike mounds heaped

with powdered sugar—wrapped them in waxed paper and slipped them into the small paper bag with the rest of my groceries. He said something about Allah as he handed it to me.

I mumbled what I hoped was the same thing back at him, did a little bow, and hurried out to the car.

"Are you all right?" I asked Sodaba as I got inside. She had taken the sheet partly off her head, probably to try to get some air. I realized I should have bought some beverages, something cold for her to drink. She must have been incredibly thirsty. I hoped rose water was drinkable. I passed the bag of groceries to the backseat. I could hear her rustle through it as we pulled out of the parking lot.

Later, when we crossed the border into San Bernardino County, I felt a tap on my shoulder. I turned my head; Sodaba's hand dangled over my seat like a disembodied puppet. She was trying to give me one of the cookies.

"Mamool," she said. I wasn't sure what that meant, but I took the cookie anyway. I was starving. It was grainy and fragrant, tinged with almond, maybe a little bit of rose water. When I took a bite, a large piece crumbled and fell into the pocket on the bib of my overalls. The powdered sugar that stayed on the cookie dissolved and coated my tongue.

"It's good," I said, but it was dry, too; I wished I had something to wash it down.

"Mamool," she said again. It sounded so much like Mama, I felt tears sting my eyes. I was tempted to turn the car around and point it toward the hospital, but I needed to get rid of Sodaba first. No way was I bringing Sodaba anywhere near my girl. I wondered if her pregnancy would be successful, if she would ever hear someone call her mama, if that's what babies called their mothers in Afghanistan. I choked on some powdered sugar and started to cough so hard I almost had to pull over.

ᘓᕰᕲOnceᅠweᅠturnedᅠonᅠtoᅠtheᅠroadᅠleadingᅠupᅠtoᅠtheᅠmountain and I was sure no one was following us, I told Sodaba she could sit up. I wasn't sure she would understand me, but a black shape, lightly dusted with sugar, rose in the backseat in the rearview mirror. It was a disconcerting sight, like a shadow taking form, a ghost materializing where Nori's car seat was ordinarily buckled. I hated to think of Nori's car seat sitting empty in the auction room, as if it were just another thing to sell. I would hook it back into the car as soon as I got home.

"You can come in the front, if you'd like," I said. "I'll pull over and you can get in front." If she understood, she didn't acknowledge it. I was actually kind of glad. Her burqa was seeped in sweat. It would have been even more pungent next to me.

The ride up the mountain was long and nerve-racking. Sodaba was like the Grim Reaper, breathing down my neck in those dark robes; I worried her presence would somehow send us veering over the edge of the cliff. I was grateful when we reached the village and were able to get away from the precarious drops.

It took a while to find the nonroad road. This time, I could see the blue house off in the distance, behind the trees. A lot of leaves must have fallen; it hadn't been visible from the road before. The branches smacked against Beulah's windshield again as we drove down the rutted path. I was thankful to reach the clearing.

"Wait here," I told Sodaba before I got out of the car. I didn't want her to have to break into the place with me. She was in enough trouble. If anyone was going to get arrested for this, it should be me. It was a pleasure to be outside—the air was much cooler up the hill than it was in our smog-choked, summer-baked valley.

The door, as I suspected, was locked. I walked around the perimeter of the cottage, dead pine needles crunching under my feet, peering through the windows to make sure no one was there. To my relief, the house appeared to be unoccupied. The window over the kitchen sink was loose. I hoisted it up and squeezed myself through the narrow opening. I became half stuck in the dry basin of the sink before I wriggled to the ground. I touched a couple of the glass baubles dangling from the ceiling. A little thrill zinged through me as they swung and clinked together, stirring the air.

I opened the fridge; it was empty save for a squat jar of quince jam. I unscrewed the lid, plunged a finger into the cold goo, licked the slickness off. It tasted unfamiliar but comforting. I had the sensation that I was Julia, that Julia was me in a couple of decades when I was living a child-free, maybe husband-free life. It seemed almost inevitable. I tried not to cry as I wandered through the rest of the house, touching every object, thinking *mine, mine, mine.*

I was so wrapped up in my fantasy, I almost forgot Sodaba was waiting in the car.

The house felt different, smaller, once Sodaba was in it. Neither of us seemed to know what to do. Sodaba went to use the bathroom, and I busied myself with the bag of groceries. The contents all smelled like the Salaam Market. I tried to figure out what sort of meal I could pull together; the cookies probably weren't enough to break Sodaba's fast.

I opened the can of beans and dumped them into a cast-iron

pan. They were coated in a waxy glop that held the ridged shape of the can. I pushed the mass down with a spoon. The stove was temperamental; I needed to light it with a long match from the box on the counter, and even then the flame kept going out.

I was so preoccupied with the burner, I barely noticed the kitchen door opening.

"Hello?" Julia, much to my shock, stepped cautiously into the kitchen. She looked more surprised than scared.

"Hey!" I said, stirring the beans. Heated up, the glop dissolved into a rich sauce; it started to smell delicious—savory and tangy and nourishing. "You're not supposed to be here."

"This is my house," she said slowly. I couldn't tell if she was pissed off or bemused.

She wasn't wearing overalls. She was wearing sandals, jeans, a fitted red T-shirt; her sunburst tattoo peeked out from the scoop neck like it was rising from, or setting down into, her chest. No paint splatters. No monk's robe. She didn't look like me at all. Her hair had started to grow back; it stood up from the top of her head like a thistle. It was vaguely thistle-colored, too, a sort of lilac-tinged white.

"I suppose I should ask you what you're doing here," she said, her voice dry, her hands on her hips.

"I didn't think you'd be here." My heart knocked like a small fist.

"So you thought you'd just break in?" She flung her arms out.

"I didn't know where else to go." I tipped my head over the pot. I could hardly look at her. Maybe she had just come home from a date. Could nuns go on dates? In the middle of the day? I felt a pang of jealousy.

"What happened?" she asked. "Where are your kids?"

"Nori got hit by a car." As soon as I said the words, my face crumpled. I dropped the spoon into the pot and turned to face her.

"Your daughter?" She looked stunned.

My nose dripped, but I didn't do anything to stop it.

Julia approached me hesitantly. First she touched my shoulder. Then she touched my hair, then my eyebrow, then my cheek. She smelled like caraway seeds. "Is she . . ."

"She's going to be okay," I cried even harder. Julia wrapped me in her arms. We stood there, melded into each other, until Julia jumped back.

"Holy shit!" she yelled. "What the hell?"

Sodaba had appeared in the doorway.

"This is Sodaba," I said, wiping my eyes with my forearm. "She's my neighbor. She's from Afghanistan. She's the one who hit my girl."

"Hold on a second." Julia rubbed her head. "I think I'm going to have to sit down." She folded herself into a kitchen chair.

I tried to explain the situation to Julia as Sodaba crossed the kitchen and walked to the sink. She said some sort of prayer, and then turned on the tap. She washed each hand three times. Then she lifted the hood of her burqa; I couldn't see what she was doing from the back, but it sounded like she was rinsing out her mouth, spitting the water into the basin with great gusto. Then it sounded like she was sniffing water up her nose and blowing it back out. She moved on to some sort of vigorous cleaning of her face and head, her ears, her neck. Then she reached down and wiped off her bare feet three times. She walked back out of the kitchen; her burqa was still dense with perspiration, but she was coated with a glaze of fresh water.

We watched as Sodaba began to do her series of prayers on the living room rug. It looked almost like calisthenics—the different arm postures, the sitting, the bowing, the lying down, the getting up, the changing of direction, the getting down again, all accompanied by guttural recitations. I wondered what she was praying for. Could she sense the location of Mecca wherever she happened to be, or did she pray in all directions just in case she didn't know which way to face?

Julia stood. She briefly touched the top of my head before she walked into the living room, pulled a small hard-looking round cushion out from under an end table and assumed the classic meditation posture, only a few feet away from Sodaba. Julia began to chant in a quiet murmur. Sodaba hesitated for a moment; she tipped her head up from her own prayers at the sound before she resumed her routine.

I watched the two women, their voices blending into a drone; both were so certain of what they were doing. I sat on the kitchen chair, fidgety, not sure what to do with my hands, my legs. Eventually I remembered the beans. I couldn't pray, I couldn't meditate, but at least I could keep the beans from burning.

As I scraped the spoon against the bottom of the pan, I tried to invoke Whitman, my own higher power, but the only line that popped into my head was *I think I will do nothing for a long time but listen.*

Sodaba and Julia wandered into the kitchen several minutes later. I handed each of them a plate with a pseudoburrito of lemon-perfumed fava beans wrapped in the thin, pliable lavosh bread. They each took a plate in silence. Sodaba followed Julia into the living room. They seemed to have reached some sort of accord in their shared prayer. I brought my plate into the living room, too, and we sat on the floor in companionable silence, Sodaba turned slightly away as the lavosh disappeared under her veil. The beans were warm and cumin-y, a little oily for my taste, but satisfying.

After we rinsed off our plates, Julia pantomimed pulling her clothes over her head and putting them in the washing machine to convince Sodaba to take off her burqa so she could wash it. Sodaba locked herself in the bathroom. The door eventually opened a crack and Sodaba's bare hand emerged, holding the heavy fabric. I had to refrain from pushing open the door so I could see her naked in there, see what she looked like under all that black, but after Julia took the burqa, Sodaba closed the door again and turned the lock. Soon I heard the bath running. I imagined Sodaba invisible under the burqa, invisible in the bath other than her hands and feet and the side of her cheek, her body clear as the rushing water.

෨෮෩ "So I took your advice," Julia told me as we stood in the kitchen, the washing machine gurgling and shaking, Sodaba's burqa tangled up inside. I wondered if it would turn the water black. "I showed up at the Zen Center, ready to sign up for life, but then a question popped into my head: Does this make me say Yes inside? And it didn't. The answer was no. It stupefied me, but there it was. So I apologized to the abbot, turned around, came back home, and knocked out the best piece I've ever painted in my life."

"Wow," I said. I felt humbled. I wasn't sure anyone other than Noodle had ever followed my advice before.

"It was kind of silly for me to let some boxes determine my future, anyway," she chuckled. "I was trying to be Yoko Ono, but I think I turned out more like Monty Hall."

"Do you think you'll ever get the No box back?" I wondered if the word "No" was written in gold, too, or if it warranted some other color. A cooler metal, maybe silver.

"I have no idea," she said. "I left it in a locker in Rialto and stopped paying after the first month. If it wants to find me, it will. But it doesn't really matter; I've made up my mind."

"I'd love to see the painting," I said, moved that I played any role in her decision.

"It's behind Door Number One." She swung both arms with a game-show flourish toward a door I assumed led to a closet.

The studio inside was surprisingly large—it was probably originally a bedroom—and full of light. A giant canvas leaned against the wall. Most of it was a riotous swirl of color, like the inside of the cardboard box and the outside of Julia's car. At the center of the canvas, though, she had painted a pair of overalls, just like the ones I was wearing. Every fold and shadow was perfect. They were shaped like a body was inside of them, rounding them out, but the body was invisible; it was just the overalls, standing, legs about shoulder-width apart, the fabric rippling as if in the breeze. Light shot out of all the holes, like divine shafts of sun. When I bent closer, I noticed that the radiant filaments were really strands of hair adhered to the canvas, some white-blond, some painted gold.

"Is this the hair I cut?" I asked. I wanted to touch the canvas, but didn't dare.

"It is," she said.

"I thought you were going to leave it for the birds," I said.

"I changed my mind."

I was overcome seeing Noodle's hair there, so similar to

Nori's before the accident. Her tresses had gotten so smushed and tangled against the hospital pillow; I couldn't wait to give her a proper shampoo. Julia's hair surrounded Noodle's, all the blueness gilded away.

"Is that supposed to be me?" I asked.

"Maybe." She gave me a sly smile.

Each follicle in my arms perked up.

"Does it have a title?"

"It's kind of long," she said. She pointed to a title painted in gold along the edge of the painting. *I depart as air—I shake my white locks at the runaway sun.*

I gasped. "No way."

"I know it's not the easiest title in the world. . . ."

"It's Walt Whitman."

"Of course," she said.

"But how did you know?" I couldn't find any more words.

"Everyone knows Whitman," she said, and a hot spurt of jealousy, maybe joy, traveled through me. "I love him. He's very Zen."

She pulled a tiny book from a shelf. It was copper-colored, with Whitman's face on the cover. My favorite photo of him, the one where he's young and his eyes come across as a languid blue even in the black-and-white photo, his lips tender between his mustache and beard. A book composed entirely of "Song of Myself."

"I turn to it often," she said, handing the book to me. It felt wonderfully cool in my palm. I flipped through it; the pages were copiously underlined. Not every line, but many of them. In pencil, hard-pressed.

I was bowled over. Literally. I landed with a thump on the paint-spattered wood floor. When I looked up at Julia's face, it was so filled with concern I wanted to weep.

"Mom?" I whispered.

"Excuse me?" she asked.

I blinked several times and said "Sorry. My mom really loved that poem." What I wanted to say was: *I think my mother is speaking through you.* What I wanted to ask was: *Are you my mother? Are you Nora now?* It seemed well within the realm of possibility that this odd, familiar, woman could somehow be my mom. It would make as much sense as everything else from the last week had. My father had materialized; why not my mother, too?

"I miss her so much." I started crying all over again. I hadn't realized I had been looking for my mother all this time, in storage lockers, in boxes of clothes, in underlined pages of books. When Julia wrapped her arms around me again, it didn't feel romantic or sexy. It just felt warm, like mashed potatoes, like a good winter coat, like home.

Sodaba was still in the bathroom when I left. I couldn't wait until her burqa was dry. I was already running late—Noodle was going to be getting out of camp soon and I had a long drive ahead.

"She'll be in good hands," Julia assured me. "I have people I can contact. We'll find someplace for her to go."

Where would Sodaba end up? Would she and Raminullah ever see one another again? I wanted to say good-bye to her, but she probably wouldn't hear me over the faucet, and if she did, she might not understand me, anyway. I sent her a silent wish of good luck instead. I was going to miss her in some peculiar way. Sodaba had been my secret. My shadow. My unopened box.

Julia tried to give me her copy of *Song of Myself,* but I wouldn't let her. I gave her Naima's phone number and my own, then kissed her spicy palm; she touched it, still wet from my lips, to my cheek.

I pulled up to the Child Development Center, sweaty and slightly frantic, forty-seven minutes late. The director, a woman everyone called Miss Linda, pulled me aside as soon as I stepped in the door. "I'm going to waive the late fee this time," she said, her voice low and tight. Normally it was $2 for every ten minutes after closing time. "I know how much is going on in your life. But you can't make a habit of this, Mrs. Parker." I had been late a few times in the last week, but by less than ten minutes. Nothing like this.

"I'm so sorry," I said. "Nori had to have another test, and I lost track of time. . . ." What a liar I had become. But I couldn't rightly tell her I had been delivering a wanted woman to her mountain hideout, could I?

"You should have called," she said. "Newton was very worried. He finally fell asleep in my office; he's sleeping there now." How she could look pressed and fresh after hours with small children was beyond my comprehension. Her short-sleeved pink blouse didn't have a wrinkle. Her makeup was immaculate. She and Samantha Walker would probably be friends. I felt like such a schlub as I followed her down the hallway, her low heels clicking on the waxed floor, my high-tops squeaking and scuffling.

The office was deeply air-conditioned and neat as a pin. Even the children's artwork on the wall was framed, behind glass. Noodle was the one wild thing in the room, hunched in the corner, his head resting on his knees. His hair had grown shaggy overnight, it seemed. I could see tear tracks on his grimy cheek. A grass stain streaked down one of his legs. His orange jelly shoes were coming apart, rubbery strands popping out of their woven grid.

"We're concerned about Newton," the director whispered. "He seems tired all the time. Has he been sleeping properly? Bathing? Eating decent meals? Consistency can make such a difference for children when there has been a family trauma. . . ."

"Noodle is doing just fine." I bent down and scooped him up. I smelled graham crackers on his breath, the tang of his unbrushed teeth beneath that. I smelled spilled apple juice, stiff on his shirt, the funk of his unwashed hair. I struggled down the hallway with him in my arms, pushed the front door open with my hip. I don't understand how kids get heavier when they're asleep—it's like their energy coalesces into wet sand.

Noodle woke when I stepped into the hot air. He let out a strangled shout and wriggled from my grip.

"It's okay, Noodle," I said. "We're going home now." I knew Miss Linda was watching us from inside the glass doors.

He blinked a few times, then sat down in the dirt. "You forgot me, Mama." His voice was shrill.

"I didn't forget you, Noodle," I said, my stomach withering into a ball. "How could I forget my boy? I just got stuck in traffic."

"You don't know anything, Mama!" he chided. "You don't know anything about boys."

"You're probably right," I said.

*A child said, What is the grass? fetching it to me with full hands;*
*How could I answer the child? I do not know what it is any*
  *more than he.*

"But I know I love you, and I know I wouldn't ever forget

you." Guilt pounded in my ears. Had I thought of Noodle while Sodaba was in my car?

"You forgot Nori!" he yelled, and ran toward the community garden, on the other side of an empty field between the building and the Student Family Housing complex.

"Noodle, the car's here," I called after him. "We can't walk; we need to drive home today."

He kept running. I raced after him, the smog and heat dry in my throat, pulling sweat and water from my pores until I was drenched. How could a six-year-old be so fast? The field was dead, crunchy beneath my feet, pitted with snake and gopher holes. The scent of sage and dirt and baked animal fur tumbled from the Box Springs Mountains.

"Noodle," I pleaded.

A golf cart from the campus Physical Plant appeared in the distance, careening down the dirt path that crisscrossed the field. Noodle didn't seem to see it; he continued to run in a haphazard way, arms and legs flopping.

"Noodle, stop!" I screamed. What if the golf cart didn't see him, either? What if it smashed into him? I imagined having two children in the hospital, two children I could barely bring myself to see. I ran so hard I thought I'd burn holes through the bottoms of my shoes. Just before the golf cart shot by, I caught up with Noodle and tackled him to the ground. The guy who cut the grass in our courtyard turned his head and waved at us as if he were part of a parade.

I scooped Noodle into my arms, the scent of dead grass sweet around us. He had a small abrasion on his forehead. It wasn't bleeding much, but it looked raw and embedded with dirt. "Are you okay?"

He nodded and curled into me, both of us panting. We

walked toward home, hand in hand, leaving Beulah in the parking lot at the Child Development Center, stopping only to steal a small watermelon from Pia's garden. As we plunged our hands into the wet spongy fruit, we tried not to look at our own withered plot, the crispy squash vines.

A woman was standing on our porch; I saw her as soon as we turned into the courtyard. She wore a navy blazer and knee-length skirt, a white blouse, sensible shoes, hose, brown hair pulled back into a bun. Standard government attire. She must have been boiling hot in those clothes. I checked to see if the car Naima mentioned was parked at the curb. It was, a man impassive behind the wheel. This woman must have been with them. My mouth, even full of melon, turned dry. I swallowed hard.

"Can I help you?" I asked as we drew nearer.

"Flannery Parker?" She didn't extend a hand, which was a good thing. I was sweaty, sticky, a mess. No one in their right mind would want to touch me.

"Yes," I said. Not the Yes from Julia's box. Not a Whitman Yes. A wary, resigned yes.

"Lorna Louis, Child Protective Services," she flashed an identification card. "You were told we would make an unannounced visit?"

"Shit," I said. Noodle looked like a street orphan; I was sure I didn't look any better. I hadn't cleaned the house in days. Could she have chosen a worse time to show up? "I'm sorry. I mean, welcome. I mean, please, come inside."


Lorna followed me into the house. With her there, every little speck of dirt, every piece of clothing on the floor, every dirty dish balanced on the arm of the couch, seemed magnified. Had those fingerprints always been smudged onto the door frames? Had that grime always been caked around the doorknobs and drawer handles? Had those cobwebs always been as abundant in the corners of the ceiling, those dust bunnies as plentiful in the corners of the floor? I watched her scan the pyramid of TVs, the heaps of stuff visible through the auction room door.

"It's not always such a mess in here," I told her. "We've been really busy. I haven't had much time to clean. . . ."

She made a little mmm hmm sound and scribbled in her notebook. I was gratified to see that a few strands of hair were springing out of her bun. Even she couldn't keep a handle on everything.

She peered behind the TVs.

"This is a fire hazard, you know." She pointed out all the plugs jammed into the multiple outlet. Wires in various shades of gray and beige and brown were tangled together and riddled with lint; some were frayed, their yellow and orange veins showing.

"I plan to sell all of these," I told her. "At my yard sales."

"I thought your yard sales were terminated," she said coolly. I wondered what else she knew. I followed her to the auction room. Samantha Walker's passport taunted me from the door. I could almost hear her say I should have left when I could have. I smacked the blue booklet as I walked into the room. It was a shambles. The linens pile had tipped over, knocking over the men's shirts pile, which in turn knocked over the women's lingerie. Toys were scattered all over the room—Noodle must have come in and unpacked a box or two when I wasn't looking.

"And this room?" she asked.

"This is my storage room," I said. "It's where I keep all of the items I win at auctions."

"Not Sotheby's, I imagine." She tapped a beige pair of maternity panties with her toe.

"Self-storage auctions," I told her. "It's how I get the stuff for my yard sales."

"Since you are no longer authorized to have yard sales, you no longer need to keep all of this in the house, am I correct? I might point out that all of this poses a fire hazard, as well. Not to mention a potential health hazard. Mice could set up shop in here. Cockroaches."

"I plan to sell it all on eBay," I said. It would take forever to sell the contents of the whole room. I hadn't checked my eBay account in days. There were probably several orders to fill.

"How much could you possibly get for this?" she asked, lifting the same large panties with her pump.

I flushed. I had never sold underwear on eBay before. "That would go with a set of maternity wear," I said.

"Listen," she said, tossing the panties across the room with a flick of her foot. "You need to clean this up. If this room isn't emptied by the next time I visit, it's not going to look good for you. You understand?"

I nodded. Julia's painting—which, after I dismantled the box, was four feet tall, eight feet across—looked almost mockingly festive on the wall.

"Either the stuff can stay, or your kids can stay," she said quietly, so Noodle wouldn't hear. "You choose."

My face turned so hot I thought it might crumble into ash. I followed her into the bedroom, blinking away tears. The beds were all unmade; the fitted Jetsons sheet was coming off of the twin mattress; the rest of the sheets were tangled together, strewn with dirty clothes. The slowly rotting zucchini, dotted with Band-Aids, lay smack in the middle of it all.

"This is where you all sleep?" she asked, obviously disgusted.

"The kids like to sleep with us," I told her. I could smell the sweat rise vinegary from my body. "Kids sleep with their parents all around the world."

"You clean out your storage room, you set up the kids' beds in there, it will look a hell of a lot better for you," she said. She looked at me as if I were a dimwit. "And get the vegetable off the bed. You're inviting pests."

"That's my sister!" Noodle yelled. He must have been behind us all the while. "She's not a pest. She's a uzini! And you're . . ." He took a deep breath. "You're a fucking duck!"

"Noodle!" I had never heard him swear before. His hands were balled into fists at his sides, his chin tilted up. He was radiant with defiance.

I turned to Lorna. "I'm sorry. He usually doesn't talk like that. We've all been under a lot of strain."

She kneeled down next to him. "What happened to your forehead, son?" She pointed to the small abrasion, still studded with bits of soil and grass.

He's not your son, I wanted to say. Instead I started to explain, "He . . ."

She turned to me. "I want to hear the story from him, if you don't mind."

Noodle lifted his chin even higher. I held my breath. *Don't make me sound like a monster, Noodle,* I tried to tell him with my eyes.

"My mama hugged me and we fell down." *Oh, good boy.* It could have sounded much worse.

"Do you often fall down when your mama hugs you?" she asked. Jerk.

He shook his head adamantly. "Only when a car hits us."

Lorna looked confused. "When a car hits your sister?"

"We were in the path of a golf cart," I said. "I was getting us out of the way."

She stood and smoothed her skirt over her thighs. "You're in the path of something else now, Mrs. Parker," she said. "I think you know what you need to do. You can expect another visit within the next couple of weeks."

"I'll be waiting," I told her. I almost extended my hand, but then thought better of it. Melon juice from the garden was still sticky on my palm. "You just caught us at a really bad time. It will get better around here, I promise."

"I'm going to hold you to that," she said. She looked exhausted. Some more of her bun had unraveled. I almost felt sorry for her.

╲╳╱ After she left, I pulled *Leaves of Grass* from my drawer to fortify myself. I pressed its gold cover to my chest, breathed in its wonderful dust, cracked it open and read

> *To cotton-field drudge or cleaner of privies I lean;*
> *On his right cheek I put the family kiss,*
> *And in my soul I swear I never will deny him.*

My mother had been the cleaner of privies in our house until she was too sick to do anything. She would kneel in front of the toilet with her bucket full of cleaning supplies, her arm moving like a piston; later, when she was going through chemo, she would kneel in front of the toilet in a different way. I wanted to put the family kiss on her cheek, on my dad's, on Shae's and Noodle's and Nori's. How could I deny any of them again?

After slipping the book back into the drawer, I embarked on a cleaning frenzy. First I scrubbed Noodle, then myself, then the laundry, then all the dishes, then all the floors, then all the cabinet fronts, then all the windows, then every single inch of the bathroom. I had never cleaned this much before in my life. I had to borrow cleaning products from Michael—all I had was laundry soap and dish soap and one nearly empty bottle of all-purpose spray. Cleaning had never been my thing. But that day it was all I could do. I felt like a wind-up toy, frantic, motored by some outside crank. Maybe it was my mom helping, spurring me along. Noodle helped, pushing a mop around, shaking a feather duster everywhere, spraying motes into the air. I tried to throw the zucchini away, but Noodle wouldn't let me. By the end of the day, my hands were red, my eyes were smarting, and the house was, if not spotless, at least cleaner than it had been since we moved in. Well, except for the auction room. The windows were freshly washed in there, the walls and door wiped down, but the floor was still in its normal jumbly state. I wasn't quite sure what to do with all the auction stuff. It would take a good chunk of time to sell and process all of it through eBay—much longer than a couple of weeks. It would never be gone before Lorna came back. Then I had an idea. I reached for the phone.

I buzzed all the yard-sale people who had been interested in private showings. I tried to track down people from the Return pile, who might miss the items from their seized storage units. I looked up the numbers of my auction friends. Whatever wasn't claimed or bought or traded within the next few days, I would take to Goodwill.

When the phone rang, I figured someone was returning a call.

"Flan's House of Junk," I answered. I was folding a thin plaid shirt, trying to straighten up the auction room before people showed up.

"Flan?" It was Shae. His voice was shaky. It sounded like he was crying. Something had happened. Something had happened to Nori.

"Shae . . ." I couldn't say anything else.

"Mama?" Noodle asked. I must have looked very pale. I wrapped my arm around him and pulled him close. His heartbeat pulsed against my forearm, light and gentle, like the glassy-winged sharpshooter rain.

"Nori . . ." Shae choked out.

"Oh my God." I dropped the shirt. The pile of men's clothes toppled over. I slumped against the wall. The smell of cleaning fluid burned my nose. The room heaved. Comets flashed in front of my eyes. This is it, I thought. This is the moment everything changes.

"We can bring her home, Flan. Tomorrow. She's going to be fine. We can bring her home." He started sobbing and laughing. I started sobbing and laughing. Noodle did, too.

I dropped the phone into a Tupperware bowl; I could hear Shae's voice echo inside the scuffed green plastic, but I didn't pick it back up. Instead I shouted "I love you! I love you, Shae!" loud enough so he could hear me. I grabbed Noodle even tighter and launched us backward, like a stage dive, into the waiting arms of shirts, the waiting laps of pants, the waiting softness of towels and blankets and purses, other people's stuff, other people's past, other people's sadness and hope cushioning our fall.

*Do you see O my brothers and sisters?*

*It is not chaos or death—it is form, union, plan—it is eternal life—it is Happiness.*

## part five

Shoulder your duds, and I will mine,

and let us hasten forth

It was a thrill to have Nori back home. She was excited, too, yelling "My TV!," "My chair!," "My bash tub!," "My Noodie!" as Shae carried her around the house. "Where's my trawberry cake, Mama?" she asked when we walked into the kitchen.

I had forgotten about the cake Shae said I would bake for her. I started to apologize, but Shae jumped in and said, "Mama has to bake another one, Nori girl. The first one got eaten by a crow." I wrapped my arms around him, grateful for his stories.

Nori laughed; she had figured out how to laugh carefully, but she quickly exhausted herself, anyway. Her eyes started to look glassy, her movements sluggish. We put her down for a nap in the middle of the futon. How reassuring to see her sleeping there, where she belonged.

Noodle stared at his sister before he grabbed the limp zucchini and ran to the kitchen door. Shae and I followed him and watched as he hurled the giant squash like a javelin into the trash can outside. It smashed against the metal side of the bin with a gooey splat. He turned around, beaming, triumphant. Shae and I applauded wildly.

"No more vegetable sister!" he whooped.

Shae rubbed his hand through his hair and said, "There's something else we can get rid of."

"For real?" I asked. I had been trying to get him to cut his hair for years.

He nodded. It was all I needed to know.

I set Shae up on a chair in the kitchen, newspapers spread over the floor below him. When I turned on the clippers, I didn't feel any sort of erotic buzz. Cutting his hair was like slicing bread or spreading peanut butter. Something simple and wholesome. It was gratifying, though, to watch his lanky locks drift down to the floor, onto the newsprint, the comics, the public notices.

When I cut Julia's hair, it made her look older. When I cut Shae's hair, it made him look younger. Younger and fresher. Soon his head was covered with just a fine velvety pelt, wonderful against my palm. The clipper might not have felt sexy, but his head sure did. I buried my nose in his hair and took a deep, lusty whiff. He reached an arm behind the chair and pulled me closer.

"Shake," Noodle said, delighted. "You look like a boy now!"


After the kids were asleep, I lay on the couch, Shae's newly shorn head resting against my thighs as he sat on the ground.

"I'm glad you're home," I whispered to him. The TVs, for a change, were off. The room felt blessedly quiet.

"Me, too," he said. We were still a little shy with each other, not quite sure how to touch. I let my hand drift down to his neck, dip inside the collar of his T-shirt, the skin of his back warm against my fingers. He swiveled his head around and kissed me on the lips. A soft kiss at first. A kiss that opened and deepened; a kiss that tasted like our seven years together, tangy with pain and love and fear and desire.

*How you settled your head athwart my hips, and gently turn'd over upon me,*

*And parted the shirt from my bosom-bone, and plunged your tongue to my barestript heart.*

A few hours after we went to bed, there was a banging at the door. It sounded like someone with a battering ram. I stumbled groggily to the living room, my heart racing. Who would be on our front porch at three in the morning? Some drunk student? A mass murderer? Pia, home from the Philippines, needing to talk? I flicked on the porch light and peered out the window. It was a fireman in a yellow coat and hat, maybe the same fireman who had raised the car off Nori. I wondered if I was dreaming.

"Open up," he shouted, banging some more.

I swung the door open. He almost fell inside. "What happened?" I asked, disoriented. As soon as I opened my mouth, I started to cough. "Did Nori get out?"

"There's a fire," he said. "You have to evacuate."

"All of us?" I asked.

"Now," he roared, and ran across the courtyard.

I stood there, stunned for a moment, in my tank top and boxers. Our porch was covered with ash. Black flakes of it fell, a soft, singed snow. I poked my head outside. The air was choked with smoke, but I could see red flames coursing down the Box Springs Mountains like lava. I didn't know fire could be that red. When I closed the door, I noticed that the front of my shirt was flecked gray with ash, as if someone had flicked a giant cigarette over me. One of the flecks burned all the way through; I could feel the prick of it on my belly. I ran into the bedroom and threw on the overhead light.

"Wake up," I said loudly, wriggling into my overalls. "We have to get out of here!"

"What's going on, Flan?" Shae squinted at me.

"There's a fire. We have to go."

Noodle shot up. "Oh my God. Mama!"

"It's going to be okay." I tried to sound calm. "We just have to go. Now."

I squatted down and lifted Nori from the bed. She somehow continued to sleep through the mayhem.

"I'll carry her," said Shae, clad only in boxers. Noodle was in a T-shirt with no underwear. I wanted to tell them both to put on some clothes, but it would take too much time. I slipped Nori into Shae's arms. He knew better how to keep her stable, how to avoid jostling her ribs when he moved. Her scratchy nightgown caused the hair on my arms to rise as I handed her over.

The courtyard was full of people in nightclothes and bare feet. Isobel and Nigel, I noticed, were wrapped in matching towels, their hair wet, as they ran to their respective cars.

"Where do we go?" I asked Michael. He was wearing pajama bottoms with kisses printed all over them; he carried a half-sleeping, disoriented Ravi.

"The Cesar Chavez Center," he said. "The fire guy said there's a shelter set up there."

It was only after we strapped Nori, still mostly asleep, into her car seat, and buckled our own seat belts that I realized I hadn't grabbed any of our stuff. Shae, somehow, had had the presence of mind to grab the diaper bag and Nori's antibiotics, but all of our family photos, all of my auction items, all of our clothes and dishes and everything else we owned were still inside. I thought of Julia's painting and my copy of *Leaves of Grass* and felt a jab of grief.

"Should we go back and grab some things?" I asked Shae as he turned the ignition. The street was full of cars, trying to get away. A couple of animals raced across the courtyard—they looked like dogs, but they could have been coyotes, flushed out of the mountains by the fire. There were blocks of homes between the foothills and our neighborhood, but the fire still seemed to be headed right toward us.

"They're not going to let us back in," he said.

"What about your dissertation?" I asked. That dissertation had been hanging over both of our heads for years. It had been our beacon, our albatross, the thing that both promised and kept us from our future.

"Let it burn," he said. Our tires squealed as we pulled away from the curb.

I don't know how the shelter had been set up so quickly. The basketball court at the community center was already filled with cots. Long rows of tables were full of things people with burning houses might need—toiletries, hospital scrubs and booties, bottles of water, boxes upon boxes of fried chicken dinners, bags of pretzels, bowls of apples. Counselors and chaplains and reporters were at the ready. A TV was set up in the corner of the gym, playing a Disney video, a cluster of kids around it. We staked out four cots in the center of the gym. Michael and Ravi set up camp near us.

"Can I look around, Papa?" Ravi asked. Michael nodded his assent. He looked as dazed as I felt.

"You can go, too, Noodle," Shae said, but Noodle shook his

head. He pulled a pillow closer to his belly with one hand and touched Nori's sleeping back with the other.

A firefighter suggested that we make lists of all the things we had left behind. "Not that you're necessarily going to lose anything," he said. "But it's a good idea to have a list, just in case."

A few volunteers passed out notebooks and pencils to everyone in the shelter. Noodle immediately began writing on his: *Turtul sharts, yelow hat, chaptr buks.* Nori carefully scribbled on hers, barely moving her arm, just her wrist, to draw arcs and squiggles. I stared at the blank paper.

Everything I owned was stuff in transit, stuff that used to belong to other people on its way to belonging to different other people.

I wrote down *photo albums* and *Leaves of Grass* and *Julia's painting*. That's it. Those were the only things left inside the house that I didn't want to lose, the only things I couldn't replace.

The gym was full of people I recognized from the park and my yard sales, but we were all too shell-shocked to do much socializing. A steady stream of disoriented people flowed into the gym, including Jorge, Isobel's husband. It was around three a.m., too early for him to be done with his shift; he must have heard about the fire on the radio. I watched his face as he noticed Isobel and Nigel sitting on a cot together, looking stunned, their hair still wet. They were both wearing scrubs now. He stormed toward them, bellowing in Spanish at the top of his lungs. Isobel stood up and yelled right back at him. Jorge yanked Nigel off the cot and threw several punches before a security guard pulled them apart and sent Jorge outside. Blood dripped from Nigel's nose. Isobel seemed unsure whether to help Nigel or chase after Jorge.

Shae leaned over and whispered "I have something to tell you, but you have to promise not to punch me, okay?"

"What," I whispered back. "You've been sleeping with Isobel, too?"

"No," he laughed. "Nothing like that."

"Spill it," I said. I wondered if anything could shock me anymore. I could still taste his tongue in my mouth, could still feel the trail of his hand on my skin.

"I haven't been working on my dissertation."

"Well *that's* no secret," I said, punching him in the shoulder.

"Hey, you promised not to punch me," he said. Several people looked over, including the security guard.

"Sorry," I dropped my voice again. "Actually, it looked like you were getting a lot of work done in the hospital."

"I wasn't working on my dissertation," he said. "I haven't been able to work on my dissertation for some time now."

"What were you working on, then?" I was flooded with curiosity. Maybe I had the potential to be surprised after all.

"Promise not to laugh?" I had never seen him so shy.

"I'll try. . . ."

"I've been writing soap operas," he said.

This was definitely not anything I could have expected. "People don't write soap operas," I said. "Soap operas are written by robots, aren't they? Or monkeys?"

Shae gave me a withering look.

"What about Baudrillard?" I asked.

"Baudrillard is an asshole," he said.

This was an improvement, at least.

Shae looked expectant, his cheeks flushed. "I sent out some samples to the networks a couple of weeks ago."

He was serious about this, then.

"ABC called me last week," he said.

"At the hospital?" It was nice to know that it could be a place for good news.

"I was waiting for the right moment to tell you," he said. "They want me to write a spec script."

"And they're going to pay you for it?" A faint buzz of excitement traveled up my legs.

"If they like the script, they are," he said.

Who knew all that TV watching could pay off? Of course I would believe it when I saw a check, but I felt a burble of hope. If he could earn some money, it would be my turn to go to school. Maybe UCR, maybe somewhere else. Possibly Reed up in Oregon, as I had originally planned. Or even Cleveland State. I wondered how awkward it might be to move in with my dad until we found our own place. Shae probably wouldn't be bound by geography; he could write anywhere. And if he had to write near a television studio, well, there were plenty of schools in New York and L.A.

He kept talking, but I didn't hear much after that. The whole room came into focus, like a high-resolution TV screen—the bleachers folded flat against the wall, the squeak of people's shoes on the shiny floor, the pervasive smell of fried chicken and smoke and bodies, the people curled on the cots, the lights on the scoreboard blinking Home, Home, Home.

I couldn't fall asleep surrounded by masses of people, some crying, some snoring, some whispering, some thrashing around. Every sound echoed off the towering walls. The kids finally drifted off around six in the morning. I was restless, eager to know what had happened to our house. Shae offered to stay with the kids, Ravi included, while Michael and I went to check out the damage.

Most of the complex looked fine, but when I pulled onto Avocado, I could see our street hadn't been as lucky. Our courtyard, in particular, looked as if it had been bombed. I wondered if the blocks of houses between us and the hills had all burned down.

The grass was charred like burnt coconut. The glassy-winged sharpshooter tree had burned to a twisted blackened crisp. I couldn't help but mourn the loss of the bugs, their crazy sticky spray. The picnic table looked barbecued. The air smelled like a cookout gone wrong.

Our house, our supposed firetrap, was the only one in the courtyard that hadn't been touched by the flames. The Suleimans' house was completely destroyed; only the foundation was left. Had Sodaba been able to see the fire from Mount Baldy? Had she been able to smell her life going up in flame? Not that her life wasn't on fire already; with all she had to deal with, a gutted house, especially such a spartan one, was almost incidental. Half of Isobel and Jorge's house was gone. Nigel's roof had burned and caved in. Pia and Michael's roof was riddled with holes. Other than the coating of ash on the porch and windowsills, our house appeared to be as good as new. All of the houses in the courtyard, even our unscathed one, were surrounded by yellow police tape. None of us were allowed to go inside.

"I think it's salvageable." Michael stared at his roof. "But we won't be able to live there for a while."

The university had told us they would put us up in the Farm House Motel until they could figure out where to house us. The little barn-shaped motel bungalows had been around since the fifties; it appeared from the outside that they hadn't been up-dated much since then. They weren't much smaller than our houses, but there was no grassy courtyard for the kids to play in, just a wide driveway dividing the two rows of rooms. I hoped we wouldn't have to stay there too long.

"It could be arson," Michael continued, blinking madly. "The neighborhoods between here and the mountains didn't burn, as far as I can tell."

I looked past the field at the back of the complex, and could see a row of houses standing, the hills smoking behind them.

"Maybe the fire leaped over here," I said.

"It's unlikely," he said.

"Who would want to burn these houses down?" I asked.

"Are you kidding?" he asked. "You saw the protestors. People are out for blood."

"You think someone wanted to kill Sodaba?" I tried to sound taken aback.

"Didn't you?" he asked, and I felt instantly naked.

"I didn't set the fire," I bristled, crossing my arms.

"I didn't say you did, Flan," he said. We stared at the space that used to hold their house. "I didn't see Sodaba last night. Do you think she got out in time?"

"I don't know," I said with a shiver of shame and pride. I hadn't told anyone I had helped Sodaba. If people thought she perished in the fire, she wouldn't have to go back to Afghanistan; she could enter the world as a different burqa-wearing woman. Or non-burqa-wearing woman. It might be easier for her to disappear if she were unveiled. I would have to phone Julia and tell her Sodaba might be free. I wished I could say the same for Raminullah.

Isobel walked up to us, sobbing. "What am I going to do?"

"You're going to have to face your actions, just like the rest of us," said Michael. Mr. Porno Tech was a moral philosopher all of a sudden.

"Jorge is going back to Guatemala," she said.

"Are you going to follow him?" I asked.

"I don't know. . . ." She sat down on the scorched ground.

I found myself almost admiring Isobel for her nerve. She wanted to kiss someone and she went ahead and did it, damn the impropriety. I wondered what it was like to cross that line. I knew Whitman would never judge anyone for touching someone else.

She was still sitting there when Michael and I left to return to the shelter.

The next morning I hooked an ash-filled Booty up to Beulah, broke through the yellow police tape by the kitchen door, and carried the contents of the auction room, armful by armful, strollerful by strollerful, out to the trailer. I made a few calls to the people on my auction list, my Return list. I drove to the park and began unloading the clothes and boxes and bags onto the grass. I posted a sign on a lightpost: FREE FOR FIRE VICTIMS AND ANYONE ELSE WHO NEEDS IT.

The normal park people—mostly moms with kids in strollers—began to filter into the playground. Everyone but the people in our courtyard had been told they could return to their homes. A lot of them stopped by my blankets.

"What a great idea," some of them said.

"Is this stuff really free?" others asked, picking up little T-shirts and pants that snapped along the bottom and bottle warmers and tangled mobiles.

A few people asked if they could bring their stuff out, too. Some said they had been meaning to get to Goodwill for ages; they already had giveaways bagged in their closets, the trunks of their cars.

"The more the merrier," I told them. It wasn't as if they'd be taking business from me. And it could be fun to share the experience after cornering the market for such a long time.

Over the course of the day, shell-shocked people streamed

into the park, strollers heaped with clothes, red wagons heaped with toys, arms heaped with casserole dishes and baking pans and bags of chips. It wasn't long before plates of food covered the picnic tables under the trees, and the grassy area was covered with blankets. Blankets full of nursing bras and wooden blocks and plastic groceries. Blankets full of chipped plates and model cars and bleached-out towels. Blankets full of the outgrown, the overlooked, the unwanted, the unmatching. Blankets full of the runoff of people's lives, much of which had come from my yard sales, now ready to enter the underground economy yet again. People snatched the items up left and right. I closed my eyes and listened to my nose. I smelled cotton, bread, dust, smoke, the dingy majesty of daily life. *Ever myself and my neighbors, refreshing and wicked and real.*

More and more people showed up—Shae and the kids and my fellow courtyard dwellers arrived from the shelter. Mr. and Mr. Chen from the auctions came after getting my phone message; they began to pick through the heaps, finding things for their junk store. I was glad to be able to help them out. It was a carnival, a revival. The C, slightly charred, blinked at us from the smoky hills—*See these people? See this place? See your whole amazing life?*

I was hoping nothing on anyone's blanket would catch my eye—I was trying to clean out our house, not restock it—but one thing jumped out at me. A red dress with spaghetti straps, rayon with a little sparkle in it. It was beautiful. I picked it up and the skirt unfurled, began to sway in the light breeze.

"Are you sure you want to get rid of this?" I asked the woman sitting behind the blanket, nursing her twins. "It's so nice."

"I doubt I'll ever fit in it again," she laughed. "Plus it's not good for nursing. I'll be doing this for a long time." I watched the two heads bobbing away at the vertical slits in her nursing shirt. She'd have to stock up on cabbage when those two weaned. "It will look great on you," she said. "It can be a sundress or a party dress, depending on what shoes you wear."

I hadn't worn a dress in years. I had never been a dress person. But this dress gave me that little wink of Yes inside.

"Wear it well," the woman said.


Someone had strung up blankets in a little grove of trees to use as a changing room—no mirrors, but at least people could tell if things fit. I went inside and took off my overalls. It was an especially hot day; it was a relief to have that denim bib off my chest. I don't think I ever let myself realize how heavy those overalls were.

I stood in my sweat-plastered shirt and underwear for a moment, enjoying the lightness of it. I slipped off the wet shirt. I took off my clammy bra, too. I knew some kid could come swing a blanket away and expose me to the world, but I didn't care. The air was sweet on my skin. *Wrenched and sweaty . . . calm and cool then my body becomes. . . .*

I eventually slid the dress over my head, let it pour down my body. It felt nice, almost as nice as wearing nothing at all. The skirt was swingy and spacious. The bodice was fitted but not tight. It breathed with me.

I left my feet bare; a red dress and red high-tops seemed a bit much. I wrapped my shoes and shirt and bra up inside my overalls and pushed through the heavy blankets out into the sunshine, into the buzzing heart of my neighborhood, changed.

I was sitting on the grass, picking away at my plate of samosas, chicken satay, ambrosia salad, and rice with pigeon peas, watching Nori take some tentative steps on the grass, Shae hovering over her, when someone crept behind me and placed their hands over my eyes. I would recognize the scent of that almond lotion anywhere.

"Pia!" I turned around and wrapped her up in my arms.

"Who is this woman in the sexy red dress?" she asked, pulling back to take me in.

"It's just me." I shrugged, pleased. "How are you?"

"Hanging in there," she sighed.

"I'm so sorry, Pia," I said. "And I'm so sorry about your house."

"It's just a house," she said. "Michael said there might be a spot opening for us on Kentucky Avenue. And of course, we'll have the Farm House in the meanwhile."

I couldn't imagine what life would be like once we moved into the motel, once we moved out of the motel, once we were living on different streets, possibly in different towns, depending on whether Shae really did decide to drop out.

"We'll have some barnyard dinners," said Pia.

"I don't think they have kitchens," I told her.

"It's remarkable what you can do with a coffeemaker these days," she said.

We sat together and watched Nori make more progress across

the grass, her little ribs taped under her pink shirt. She still had to take it easy, but she was excited to explore.

"Not too fast, sweetie," I called out. Shae looked at me as if to say he had it under control.

"She's doing well," said Pia.

"She's absofricking amazing." I sniffled and spooned a dollop of ambrosia into my friend's open mouth.


A lanky kid I didn't recognize walked toward my blanket.

"I think this is the one, Mom," he said over his shoulder. He turned to me, all green eyes and hormones. If I kissed him, I thought, his lips would taste like toothpaste; the inside of his mouth would be a sauna. "I think you have some of our stuff."

"And you are?" I asked.

"Dan Pastoreli."

His name set off lightbulbs somewhere deep inside my brain. "Dan, first painting, age four," I said. I rummaged through a box and found the construction paper. Flecks of paint tumbled to the ground like confetti as I handed it to him.

"Wow," he said, softly. "I remember this. First United Methodist preschool."

Noodle sidled over.

"Guess what, Noodle?" I said. "This is Dan. Remember his painting?"

"Art and ectoplasm," Noodle said excitedly. I was amazed he remembered the ART & ECT box. Dan looked at him, confused.

"You want to go on the slide with me?" Noodle asked Dan.

"I guess," he said, and Noodle, typically cautious around new people, took Dan by the hand and led him off to the playground.

"You must be Dan's mom," I said to the woman who was with him.

"That's how most people know me," she said with a rueful smile. *"Dan's mom."*

"Maybe someday we'll get our names back," I said, but at that moment, I could care less about my own name. Flan. Samantha. It didn't matter as long as I was Noodle's mom, Nori's mom.

As Dan's mom bent down and riffled through the Return box, sighing and laughing at its contents, I watched Noodle, who was afraid of heights, charge up to the top of the tallest slide in the park. I'm sure one hand had a death grip on the railing, but he waved furiously with the other.

"Hi Mama!" he called. He looked very proud of himself.

*Long have you timidly waded, holding a plank by the shore,*
*Now I will you to be a bold swimmer*

He sat down and came *whoosh*ing toward me, while Dan, his future teenage self, rose up the ladder behind him.

A man in a dark suit walked into the park as I did a final perusal of the potluck dishes, a floppy straw hat from Busch Gardens plunked on my head. The man looked out of place among the dwindling piles of old clothes, among my shaggy neighbors. I thought maybe he was a salesman, or a contractor who was going to oversee the fire restoration work. I didn't give him a second thought as I went to the bathroom. When I came outside, though, Pia shoved me into the stone wall.

"Pia," I laughed. "I always knew you wanted me." I left a sticky marshmallow kiss on her cheek and tried to get away.

Pia kept me pinned. "Shut up, Flan," she hissed. "I'm not kidding around. That guy is looking for you. You can't go back to the park."

My knees felt light. "The suit guy?"

"He's asking questions about you. It doesn't sound good."

"Shit." My pulse pounded in my throat. "Shit shit shit shit shit."

"What did you get yourself into while I was gone?"

I opened my mouth, but I couldn't find the words.

"Tell me in the car," she said. She looked around to make sure no one was watching, and hurried me over to the Fairlane. "Duck down!"

I crawled into the passenger door and balled myself up on the cluttered floor mat, my head by the stick shift. Michael had eaten at every fast-food place known to man while Pia was gone; the evidence was everywhere. I pictured Sodaba hiding in my backseat and felt a curious kinship with her.

I shared the story the best I could as we sped down the street, Pia looking repeatedly in the rearview mirror.

"You can't stay where they can find you," she told me, her jaw tight. "It's too dangerous. There's no due process anymore. If they take you in, they could keep you there." I thought of Raminullah. If they connected me with him, I could be in serious legal trouble.

"What about Shae and the kids?" I couldn't take off without them.

"I told them to meet us at the garden."

I wondered how she had the clarity to make such a plan. The garden was only a few blocks from the park, but with the concentric streets, it was like driving through a maze.

"Where will we go?" Bags from Del Taco and McDonald's

and Gus Jr. and Jack in the Box crumpled beneath me. A couple of petrified French fries poked into my legs.

"I don't know, sweetie," she said, turning to make sure no one was trailing us, "but you need to go. Soon."

The road beneath us changed, making the car bounce. I knew she had pulled onto the dirt path leading to the garden.

"Wait a second," she said after she stopped the car. "I have to make sure the coast is clear."

From my curled-up spot, I had a good look at her dark, rough knees as she stood right outside the car door. I wanted to rub lotion on them, to kiss them, to thank them for carrying her around.

The bags rustled around me; the smell of congealed ketchup filled the air when I shifted my weight.

"Okay." She bent down to talk to me. "You can get out. But be sure to hide in the corn stalks."

"Pia, what if this is nothing?" I said, as I unfolded myself from the floor and sat on the passenger's seat. "What if he just wants to ask me some simple questions? I might not be in any danger at all."

"You might not be," she said. "But I want you to take care of yourself, just in case you are. I don't want anything to happen to you."

I bit my lip, choked up.

"Besides," she said, winking a teary eye. "It's more exciting this way."

"Pia," I said. "I love you, but I'm not going into hiding for your entertainment."

"Think of it as *your* entertainment, then," she said.

"I think grief has made you a little loopy, my friend." I shook my head.

"Flan, you need a change," she said, ignoring my comment. "You've been in a rut for too long now."

I started to object, but she said, "This is your chance. It's not like you have a home here anymore, anyway." She bent back down, leaned into the car, and kissed me full on the lips.

The garden was in bad shape—everything seemed to have crisped and rotted overnight. The corn in Pia's plot was dusted with ash; every crevice was packed with black flakes, gray powder. I got out of the car and slipped into the vegetable patch, crouched down between some stalks, tried not to let the hem of my new dress pick up too much dirt. My feet were filthy. I could feel sweat peal down between my breasts, down the length of my spine, turning the flecks of ash on my skin into muddy runnels. The smell of rot, of sun-baked stems and leaves, engulfed me, heavy as humidity. I hoped the red of my dress wouldn't be too conspicuous among the pallid crops; maybe from a distance I'd look like a giant tomato, a huge sugared fruit. A ridiculous grown-up playing hide-and-seek.

Pia crouched down next to me. My quadriceps started to burn; my whole body was pulsing. I saw the ants crawling up her legs before I realized they were crawling up mine, too. I wasn't sure whether to laugh or scream.

"Maybe we should wait in the car," I said. "At least you have air-conditioning."

"Good plan," said Pia. "My car's here all the time. No one should suspect anything."

We scuttled back to the Fairlane and scrunched ourselves inside. The whole thing felt like a game, but she was right. I had to leave. I couldn't risk ending up in detention. I couldn't let myself become *the mother condemned for a witch and burnt with dry wood, and her children gazing on.* I had missed too much time with my family already. This could be our chance to break out of our patterns, fling ourselves into Whitman's great Unknown together.

Shae's confused face appeared in the window a few minutes later. "What the hell, Flan?"

Pia sat up, unlocked the doors and barked, "Get in the car!" She was obviously having fun with her role.

Noodle jumped in the backseat immediately.

"I hope you'll tell me what's going on," Shae said.

"Later," I said.

"Just get Nori inside," said Pia.

Pia's car didn't have a car seat in it, just a booster seat for Ravi. I hoped it would keep Nori secure. Shae strapped her in before he squeezed into the front seat next to me, pushing me closer to Pia.

"What do you guys need from your house?" Pia asked. "Just the essentials. I'll get it for you—you figure out where you're going."

"There's a yellow book in my underwear drawer," I told her. "And a photo album on the coffee table." I wanted Julia's painting, too, but it would take up too much space. I closed my eyes and tried to sear the swirl of color into my brain. "Go through the kitchen door. I've already broken the police tape there."

She nodded and said, "What would you need for a road trip, Shae?"

"Pia, what the hell?" His face was so red, it scared me.

"Flan will tell you," Pia said. Her voice was level, but her eyes were ablaze. "This is for real, Shae. What do you need?"

"Nori's antibiotics and ointment are in the diaper bag," he said, flustered. "I left it at the park."

"I'll be right back." Pia hopped out of the car. I slid over to the driver's seat. "If anyone comes by, just drive away."

"Grab the painting in the auction room for yourself," I called as she ran toward our house.

"Are you going to tell me what the fuck is going on?" Shae asked.

I took a deep breath. "I helped Sodaba escape."

"What?" he yelled.

"She was going to be sent back to Afghanistan if I didn't do something."

"She hit our daughter, Flan." Shae banged his head back against the headrest. "How could you?"

"They asked me to help, and Walt Whitman said the slave came to his door . . ."

"Walt Whitman?! What does Walt Whitman have to do with this?!"

Walt Whitman has everything to do with this, I wanted to tell him, but I just said, "We need to take off, Shae. I might not be in any trouble, but it would be best for us to lie low for a time, just in case."

A car pulled onto the dirt path in the distance. I held my breath until I saw it was an old Mustang, not the FBI guy. It drove past us; the woman inside waved.

"Couldn't you get in even more trouble by running away?" Shae's eyes were closed.

"They don't have to catch us," I said.

"Shit, Flan," Shae muttered.

Both of the kids started to cry quietly in the backseat. "I don't want you to go to jail, Mama," Noodle wailed.

"I'm not going to go to jail, sweetheart," I said, my pulse wild.

Pia eventually came running back with the diaper bag over one shoulder and a plastic bag in one hand. I rolled down the window to receive them.

"I grabbed that passport in case you could use a fake ID, Flan," she said.

I nodded. What had she gotten me into? What had I gotten myself into?

"And of course you should take my car. I'm sure they know your license plate number."

"What'll you do about a car?" I asked.

"Give me your keys," she said, and I fished them out of the diaper bag. "I'll use your car until Michael's brother gives us his old one. Now go. Get out of here." She gave me a quick kiss through the open window.

I shifted the car into drive, my hands jittery, hysteria rising in my throat. The corn stalks smacked together in our wake while Pia stood waving, spattered with dirt from her tires. She looked at home there in the garden, but she was right—I didn't belong at Student Family Housing anymore. *Faithful and friendly the arms that have help'd me.* What would I do without her?


"Do you have any fucking idea what you've gotten us into?" Shae asked as I pulled out of the Student Family Housing complex.

I looked in the rearview mirror. No one appeared to be fol-

lowing us. Noodle and Nori were completely silent in the backseat now. They both looked petrified.

"It's going to be okay, guys," I said to them. "It's going to be
fun."

"Fun." Shae scoffed. "Flan, how could you have helped that
woman?!"

"She's pregnant. . . ."

"She almost killed our daughter!"

Noodle let out a moan. Tears began to trickle down Nori's
cheeks again. She had perfected the art of crying without sound;
it was easier on her ribs.

"You weren't around to see the worst of it, Flan," Shae said,
his teeth clenched. "You didn't clean the hole in her chest."

"I know," I said softly. A hole bored itself into my own chest
at the thought of it.

I pulled onto the freeway. My muscles seemed to know what
to do even if the rest of me didn't.

"I think you should turn yourself in, Flan." His voice was
steady now. Resigned. "You should turn yourself in and deal with
the consequences."

"What if they send me to jail?" My face and hands started to
tingle. I hoped I wouldn't hyperventilate. The ridged gas pedal
felt loose under my bare foot.

"Then you go to jail." How could he sound that calm?

"No!" Noodle screamed.

"No, Mama," Nori cried.

I checked the rearview mirror. A yellow Volkswagen bug, two
minivans, one gold coupe.

"Sodaba has had such a hard life, Shae. She's lost a lot of babies. Three miscarriages, her translator told me. A stillbirth, too.
They think her husband's a terrorist. She doesn't want to go back

to Afghanistan. . . ." I wasn't sure if I was trying to defend her or myself. Maybe both of us.

"She wears a burqa in America but she doesn't want to go back to Afghanistan?" he scoffed. "I would think she couldn't wait to get back there."

"I don't understand it, either," I said. "But maybe I can get some answers." I pulled my cell phone out of my purse and dialed Naima's number, my hands shaking.

"Naima," I said when she answered. "I'm hitting the road. Some guy was asking questions about me."

"Oh, Flan." She sounded mournful. "Please be careful."

"Have you been in touch with Sodaba?"

"It is better if I am not," she said. "I shouldn't be talking to you right now, either."

"Just one more thing," I said. "Why does Sodaba wear a burqa?" I held the phone up so Shae could hear her answer, too.

"Sodaba is a woman of strong faith," she said firmly.

"But couldn't she just wear a headscarf, like you? The Taliban isn't roaming the streets of Riverside."

A beat-up Dodge Omni. A Ford Excursion. A blue sedan. No, a black sedan. Shit! "She wears a burqa because her sisters in Afghanistan have to wear them. She doesn't think she should be free if her sisters are not free." A chill ran down my legs. "One of her sisters was beaten when her veil slipped off her head. If she goes back, she will probably be beaten, too. If not worse."

The chill reached up through the rest of my body.

"I better go," I said. "Take good care of yourself, Naima." I barely knew Naima, but I felt as if I were saying my last good-bye to a close friend.

"You, too, Mrs. Flan," she said. "*Jazakh Allahu Khairan.* May Allah reward you for your deeds. And may your little girl prosper."

A silence fell over the car.

Green Cadillac Escalade. Gray Honda Civic. White CHP motorcycle. I held my breath as the officer pulled up next to us, then kept going.

"You know," Shae finally said, "there was an assumed identity subplot on *One Life to Live* this summer."

"Really?" I never imagined Shae's soap opera expertise having any sort of practical application in our lives.

"This woman wanted to be a counselor more than anything, but the school wouldn't let her graduate because she got too emotionally close to her patients."

"So she killed a counselor and assumed her identity?" I leaned into the steering wheel, my knuckle bones nearly bursting through my skin.

"Flan, God, don't be morbid. She fished a misspelled diploma out of the trash, changed her name, and started to practice."

"Did she get away with it?" I felt crazed.

"What do you think, Flan?"

I didn't answer.

"She was discredited," Shae said. "She had to deal with lawsuits. Public humiliation."

"Did she go to jail?"

"No, she blackmailed someone into marrying her." He stopped, knowing he sounded ridiculous. "Anyway," he said. "I know a thing or two about assumed identities. Just in case."

I reached out and squeezed Shae's leg. It didn't seem possible or even rational, but he was with me. This could be our adventure together. Our chance to taste Samantha Walker's life. To taste the world.

"Hey, there's the dinosaurs, guys," I pointed out to the kids. They always liked when we drove past the Jurupa Mountain Cultural Center. The scrubby hills that lined the freeway were dotted with large metal dinosaur sculptures—a blue stegosaurus with yellow spots, a green allosaurus, an orange triceratops. The newest addition, a rusty woolly mammoth, stood at the crest of one hill, its trunk held high, as if in welcome, or farewell.

"Bye Elphetump," Nori said softly, as if she knew we probably wouldn't pass that way again.

"Elephant," corrected Noodle. "Actually, its name is Woolly Mammoth." He said the name slowly so she could understand it.

"Bye, Worry Mamas," said Nori.

I smiled, wishing it was that easy to say good-bye to my own worries. I was going to be a Worry Mama for a long time. Maybe forever.

Purple Suzuki Samurai, red Toyota Camry, yellow Hyundai Sonata, white Mitsubishi Montero ...

One day a fossil would be found of my heart, a spiral of worry frozen inside.

We drove in silence, past the rundown apartment complexes and dirtbike courses along the 60 freeway, past the shiny car dealerships along the 15, past the shopping malls and housing developments along the 10. I saw three highway patrol cars and two dark blue sedans along the way, mixed in with the SUVs and beaters and work trucks, but none of them, thankfully, seemed to be interested in us. Shae kept his head pressed against the window, staring at banners for strip clubs and oak furniture and family fun parks.

"We can spend a few days in the mountains," I said, "and then we'll figure out where we should go."

"Nori is going to need follow-up care," he said. "She was supposed to have an appointment tomorrow."

"We can find another doctor," I said. "There are doctors all over the place."

"What if they need her records?"

"We can say they were lost in a fire. It's fire season. We were evacuated. People will believe us."

"Flan, I don't know. . . ."

"You know every test, every procedure, don't you?" I said. "You don't need a doctor to tell you what happened."

"I guess I could write it all down so I won't forget." He sighed, as if to remind me that he was the only one in the car with this information. I started to feel another wave of guilt, but then I looked at Nori, alert in the backseat. I reached back and touched her pudgy little thigh. She smiled at me in the rearview mirror.

"I can't believe we're doing this." Shae closed his eyes. "You're lucky I'm so exhausted—I never would have agreed to this after a good night's sleep."

"Yes you would have." I punched him gently in the arm. "You owe me, you know."

"I'm well aware of how much I owe you, Flan." He grabbed my hand and pulled it to his lips.

As I turned off the freeway onto Mountain Avenue, I fished around for the passport in the plastic bag Pia had packed. I wanted to get another look at my potential alter ego. My hand found a piece of cardboard instead. I pulled it out of the bag—it was the strip that said FLAN in big brown and orange letters, the one that had been thumbtacked near the passport. Pia must have grabbed everything from my auction door. I rubbed my fingertips over the name before I rolled down the window and let the stiff rectangle fly. I watched it tumble backward through the air, smack against someone's front grill, disappear from sight. If the FBI guy was following me, he could nab me for littering, too. For throwing my old self to the wind.

We hit the curvy mountain road. I rolled down the windows to smell the sage in the air at the lower altitudes, the pine when we got higher.

"So where are we going again?" Shae asked.

"My mountain lair," I said.

"A lair?" Noodle started to cry.

Nori reached over and patted his arm. "Da bue," she consoled. She must have recognized the road, the trees.

"The blue house?" Noodle asked, voice quavery.

"We won't have to go on the ski lift, Noodle," I said. "Don't worry."

"What blue house?" asked Shae.

I started to tell him about Julia and watched his face register everything from confusion to curiosity to sadness. We had kept so much from each other.

When we pulled into the clearing, Julia was sitting on her front steps, cradling a mug in her hands. More of her hair had grown back; now it was a longer thistle thatch, this time sporting a bright orange tint. She was back in her paint-spattered overalls.

She got up and walked toward the car. "I guess you're going to keep showing up on my doorstep." She didn't seem upset about this. She didn't necessarily seem happy about it, either.

"This is my husband," I told Julia.

Shae reached across me. "Shake," he said. Maybe taking on assumed names wouldn't be such a bad idea after all. He was bound to end up with something better.

"Julia," she said, sizing him up. The sun rays on her chest shimmered as she shook his hand. Then she saw Nori in the backseat. "Hey, you," she said. "You're all in one piece."

"She's doing great," Shae said as Nori mugged for Julia.

"I'm in one piece, too," Noodle piped up.

"That you are, kind sir." Julia bowed to him.

"Is Sodaba still here?" It occurred to me that I should have called first to ask. If Sodaba were around, Julia's house would be the worst place for us to hide.

"The Zen Center is offering refuge," she said. "But for her

safety and theirs, they're going to move her to a center up north soon."

I realized I hadn't told Julia about the fire yet. "Sodaba's house burned down. There's a chance the FBI will think she's dead."

"We still need to be careful," she said. "A woman in a burqa is a moving target."

"Do you think the Center could hook us up, too?" I asked. "We're sort of on the lam." The words were a bit thrilling, like something Samantha Walker might say.

"Hiding one person is hard enough," she said. "Hiding a whole family is another story entirely. Besides, I think I've used up all my sanctuary points. But you can come in for a spell."

The five of us packed into her tiny kitchen, our bodies almost as tight as crayons in a box. Julia made some tea, sliced some apples, put some ginger snaps on a plate while we told her what had happened.

"So, you're running away, huh?" she asked, tray in hand, as we adjourned to the living room. "What did you bring with you?"

"Nothing, really," I said. "We had to take off fast."

"We have Nori's medicine," said Shae.

"Everything else is still at home?" She set the tray down. The kids dove for the cookies as if they hadn't eaten in weeks.

"Everything," I said. "I wish I could have grabbed your painting. Maybe you could go down to my house and get it—I hate to think of it getting lost."

"Don't worry about that," she said. "I'll paint you a new one."

The thought made me absurdly happy.

"Right now," she said, "we have more practical matters to think about."

She looked at my dirty bare feet. "My feet are bigger than yours," she said, "but I have some flip-flops you can wear."

"That would be great," I said. I wouldn't be able to go many places without shoes.

"I have some old sweaters you can bring. Blankets. Pillows. And I could pack some snacks."

"Thank you," said Shae, his face serious, humbled, while he trailed after Nori. I think the reality of what I had gotten us into finally hit him.

"Do you have money?" Julia asked.

"A little." I had about $150 in my wallet. I had fallen into the habit of carrying a lot of cash; they only accept cash at auctions, and I wanted to be able to go to one at a moment's notice. We had a few more hundred in our bank account, but we'd probably need to be careful about that. If we really were being followed, our bank activity might be monitored.

"I could give you a few bucks," she said. "And a tent. You could use a tent for camping. Then you wouldn't have to spend as much money."

She bundled several care packages together and helped us load them into the car. The flip-flops felt weird against my soles, like dull tongues. The thongs burned between my toes.

"I can't thank you enough," I told Julia as I got into the car, on the passenger's side. Shae had already strapped in the kids and claimed the driver's seat.

"Just stay safe." She leaned through the open window to give me a last hug, her woody tea breath sweeping across my face. Then she saw *Leaves of Grass* slipping out of the plastic bag.

"Oh, wow," she said, picking up the book. "This is incredible."

"It was my mom's."

She flipped open the book. "Eighteen eighty-two," she said. "This was printed during Whitman's lifetime. Do you have any idea how much this is worth?"

I shrugged. I had always thought of it as priceless.

"I have a friend with a rare-book store in Pasadena," she said, handing the book back. "He's a Whitman nut. You should let him see this. If you can take the time, of course."

She pulled a purple marker from her bib pocket and wrote the address on the back of my hand. Then she turned my hand over and wrote "YES" on my palm. I may not have had her painting, but at least I had that. I could feel the word throb and smear against the dashboard as we drove away.

Old Town Pasadena was hopping with restaurants and galleries and funky boutiques when we got there an hour later, hopping with people full of vim and purchasing power, people wearing new clothes, nice shoes, striding down the streets like they owned them. In downtown Riverside, people moseyed. People wore marked-down suits and yard-sale clothes. People always seemed a bit out of place among the old restored buildings. I loved that. I *was* that. The thought that I might not see Riverside again made me unexpectedly sad.

Jake's Rare Books was located between a Tibetan café and a yarn shop.

Shae dropped me off at the curb. He wanted to bring the kids to visit Ada, whose retirement home was only a few miles away. We made plans for him to pick me up in an hour. I stood on the unfamiliar street and watched my family take off in my friend's car.

A bell squawked when I opened the door to the bookstore, but otherwise the place was deeply quiet. It smelled like a self-storage unit inside. A rarified self-storage unit, stripped of all body scent, leaving the musty, almost singed smell of yellowed pages and binding glue.

*I breathe the fragrance myself, and know it and like it.*

"Can I help you?" A man walked toward me from the back of the store, and I gasped a little. Long white beard and hair. Narrow face. Intelligent eyes. A rough weave to the shirt, open at the throat.

"Walt?" I must have said it out loud.

He bowed a little. " *'I am the poet of the body, / And I am the poet of the soul.'* "

I couldn't believe it. Walt Whitman. Right in front of me. In the flesh! I was struck dumb. He stood before me and smiled and said, " *'I dote on myself—there is that lot of me, and all so luscious.'* " Those last words came with a laugh, a sweep of the arms.

I finished the stanza for him, " *'Each moment and whatever happens thrills me with joy.'* " The wet wool smell of his hair filled my head. I was tempted to reach into his shirt, put my palm against his beating heart.

"What a delight. Another Whitman fan!" The man extended his hand, and my fantasy came crashing down around me. "Jake Chalmers."

It took me a few breaths to find my voice. I hoped he wouldn't sense my disappointment. "Flan," I said, shaking his hand. "Julia sent me."

"Julia!" His face broke open with pleasure. "What color hair is she sporting these days?"

"Bright orange," I said.

"Perfect." His teeth were long and slightly yellow. "And why did the lovely Julia send you here?"

"She thought you would like to see this." I pulled the book out of my bag and set it gently on the counter. My hands shook a little.

"Is this what I think it is?" His voice dropped with reverence. He grabbed a pair of white gloves from a drawer and slipped them on before he picked up the book.

"I've been looking for this," he said excitedly as he scanned the first few pages. "This is the first printing of the third edition."

"What's so special about it?" I asked.

"What's so special?" he asked, incredulous. "The pages are half an inch larger in both dimensions than the more common reprints of that year, for starters."

Half an inch didn't seem like such a big deal to me, but he was thrilled.

"Not to mention the fact that this was the first edition in which he gave a title to 'Song of Myself.' "

I felt dizzy. "Really?"

He opened the book to page twenty-nine, where "Song of Myself" began. "Whitman hadn't titled it in the previous editions."

Jake ran a gloved finger over my mother's underlines, picking up traces of her graphite in the cloth.

"These markings will detract from the value, but they can be erased."

I wanted to snatch the book back.

" 'I celebrate myself,' " he read out loud.

I closed my eyes and joined in with him for the next two lines " 'And what I assume you shall assume, / For every atom belonging to me as good belongs to you.' "

"This book belongs to me," I said softly, my eyes still closed. Why had I come here? Why was I letting this Whitman wannabe fondle these pages?

"I can offer you ten thousand dollars," he said, and my eyes flew open. "I could have offered more if it hadn't been for the markings."

"My mother made those markings," I said. "They're all she left behind." I reached out and touched the dark valleys, the pale hills, on the page.

"She left you behind," he said. His words were quiet, but they hit me like an anvil. My eyes went hazy.

"She didn't mean to," I whispered. "She was sick. I was only seven. . . ."

"No," he said, his voice gentle. "I meant she left herself here." He lightly touched the inside of my wrist, the map of blue veins. My blood her underline. My body her book.

"Take your time"—he handed the book to me—"loafe and invite your soul."

I found a sagging armchair in one of the corners of the labyrinthine store and collapsed into it, the book in my sparkly red lap. The chair's mustardy fabric was the same color as the cover. If I left the book on the seat, it would have almost disappeared into the upholstery, camouflaged.

I let the book fall open:

*I teach straying from me—yet who can stray from me?*
*I follow you, whoever you are, from the present hour;*
*My words itch at your ears till you understand them.*

I sat for a few minutes and let the words sink in before I walked up to the counter, legs wobbly.

"It's yours," I told Jake. Whitman's voice would still follow me, still itch at my ear, long after my mother's book was out of my possession. I would have to pick up a newer copy of the book, maybe a *Song of Myself* pocket edition like the one Julia had in her studio.

"Are you sure?" he asked.

I nodded, choked up. I kissed the cover long and hard before I set it down, breathing in its dust, its sharp mineral tang one last time.

*This is the touch of my lips to yours . . .*
*this is the murmur of yearning.*

Jake handed me a check made out to Cash for $10,000, clipped to a blank notebook. "Now you can write your own Song," he said. Walt Whitman's eyes sparkled from his face.

I stepped out into the sunlight to wait for Shae. The check simmered inside my pocket. I tried to read the menu on the window of the Tibetan café next door but none of the words made any sense to my shocked brain. Tea made with butter? Noodles made from glass? Dumplings named *momo*? Then I glanced at the map of Tibet, and a memory of my mother came flooding back.

I was sitting on her lap not too long before her last hospitalization. She was so weak, I was scared I would crush her, but she insisted I stay there. I pulled the globe from the side table onto my own lap. The metal base of it carved a circle into my thighs, but I loved the feel of the bumpy mountains, the smooth oceans, as the candy-colored world twirled and slowed under my finger. My mom told me that every place I touched, I was sure to visit some day. Tibet. Alaska. Venezuela. Some places, like Zaire and Yugoslavia, that don't even exist anymore, at least not by the same name. She turned the globe so North America faced us, and pointed to Ohio. Her fingertip obliterated the entire state.

"I'm stuck here," she said, "but you're not, honey. The whole world is open to you. I hope you'll see most of it."

She gave the globe a spin. I wonder if she was thinking of Whitman as the countries blurred before our eyes:

*My left hand hooking you round the waist,*
*My right hand pointing to landscapes of continents, and a*
*    plain public road.*

*Not I, not any one else can travel that road for you.*
*You must travel it for yourself.*

When Shae returned, I flashed the check through the car window. He rolled the window down. "Holy crap, Flan. There's your bail money."

"Ha ha," I said. He grinned and scooched over to the passenger seat when I opened the driver's side door. I had forgotten how good he looked with his shorn hair. I ran my hand over it again after I sat down in the driver's seat.

"What's the notebook for?" he asked.

"It's so I can *sound my barbaric yawp over the roofs of the world.*"

The kids started yelping like dogs in the backseat. I could smell the nursing home on their skin. My stomach lurched.

"You didn't tell Ada what was going on, did you?" I asked.

"I told her I was hired to write for a soap opera in New York. She was over the moon. I said I might be too busy to stay in touch for a while."

"We better get busy then," I said, filled with relief. I pulled away from the curb, the kids still barking and howling at the moon. I noticed Shae had thrown all of the fast-food bags away. I knew I'd have to pay more attention to the ways he said Yes to our family.

"So what do we do now?" Shae was still staring at the check.

"Well," I said, taking a deep breath. "Seems to me we have two choices. A: We can go back to Riverside and wait for the FBI to come pounding on our motel door. B: We can travel the country and give the FBI a wide variety of motel doors to choose from."

"Flan." Shae rubbed his palm over his forehead.

"I don't know about you," I said, "but B sounds like a lot more fun to me."

"We could always leave the country." He sounded tired.

"I'm the only one with a passport," I reminded him. "And it's not even mine."

He sighed and looked out the window.

"We have a C option, too," I said. The C on the hills behind our house—our house that wasn't our house anymore—flashed into my mind. "C for Cleveland. We could visit my dad."

Nori started to sing the "C is for Cookie" song from Sesame Street in a gravelly monster voice. "Dats good enuh for me," she growled, and it was. It was good enough for me just being with my family, wherever we might end up.

"I may wake up tomorrow and realize this is all a big mistake," Shae said.

"Me too," I said.

"We might have to turn around and go back," he said.

"I'm willing to take that chance." I pointed the car toward the freeway. The freeway that led to New York and New Orleans, Moab and Seattle, Miami and Fargo and Dallas and Philadelphia and every place in between. The freeway that led to Cleveland, with its combustible river, my aging father, my childhood home full of ghosts.

*See ever so far, there is limitless space outside of that.*

Cars of all colors and sizes surrounded us; people of all colors and sizes filled them. I tried to imagine what each person would keep inside a self-storage unit—Plexiglas chandeliers and kiddy pools and bedpans and military uniforms and yearbooks full of embarrassing pictures. Boxes with people's names on the side, boxes marked IMPORTANT, boxes marked FRAGILE. Stuff and stuff and more stuff.

What would happen if every door of every storage unit rolled up all at once, if all the boxes shot open, if everyone's longing came rushing out? The longing that lived inside our belongings, that lived inside us. Think of the sound that would make—a sustained, operatic Yes. I could hear it loud and clear over the hum of the traffic. The zeroes on the check added their open mouths to the chorus; my yapping kids, my sighing husband, did, too. We were all part of the song. We would find our way, whatever direction we might choose. Whitman all but promised it at the end of "Song of Myself":

> *Failing to fetch me at first keep encouraged,*
> *Missing me one place search another,*
> *I stop some where waiting for you.*

My new notebook vibrated on the seat between me and Shae. I thought of all the blank pages beneath its mottled cover. That's where Whitman waited for me, I realized as we hurtled down the freeway: that empty space where his voice and mine could meet. A place where I could try to store my story, my self. His poem was the flashlight I'd use to peer inward, the flashlight I'd use to usher forth my own dark pencil marks. I knew he wouldn't mind if I borrowed his opening line.

# Acknowledgments

ᏅᎤᎾMy gratitude is large. I have multitudes of people to thank:

Walt Whitman, first of all, for giving me such gorgeous and expansive words to play with.

My parents, for continuing to be my most vocal cheerleaders.

My sister, Elizabeth, and her family, for sharing the book's decisive moment (and so much more) with me.

Arielle Eckstut and Anika Streitfeld, for being the agent and editor of my dreams. I am so lucky to work with both of you brilliant women and am still in awe over the timing of it all. I also want to thank everyone at the Levine/Greenberg Agency and Random House for believing in me and my work.

Stacy Miller, for introducing me to the world of self-storage auctions.

David Boyns, for helping me with Shae's dissertation topic.

Chris Baty, for creating National Novel Writing Month. I may have never written *Self Storage* without that crazy November marathon.

All the wonderful people who read early drafts of the novel— both family (Matt McGunigle; Arlene, Buzz, Elizabeth and Magdalene Brandeis; Patricia O'Donnell) and friends (Jeannie Bernstein; Cindy Bokma; Andi Buchanan; Laraine Herring; Catherine Kineavy; Caroline Leavitt; Renee Sedliar; Victoria Zackheim)—for your invaluable suggestions and encouragement. Special thanks to Barbara Kingsolver for not being afraid to say I had a long road ahead of me and then taking me by the hand and pointing me in the right direction. Your guidance is a blessing.

I can't thank all of my friends and family members enough for your undying love and support. If I named every one of you, I could fill another book. I hope you know how much I love you all. I am also deeply grateful for my Family Voices crew, my poetry group, the Women Creating Peace Collective, CODEPINK, Women in Black, writermamas, MYWG, Readerville, independent booksellers, public libraries (especially Riverside Public Library), the UCLA Writers Program, UCR Extension, Antioch University, the University of Redlands and all of my students for inspiring and sustaining me, not to mention Bucksworth and Old Brown Shoe for serenading me while I write.

Finally, I want to thank my husband, Matt, and our kids, Arin and Hannah, for being the true source of Yes in my life.

*For every atom belonging to me, as good belongs to you.*

꧁꧂

Walt Whitman's "Song of Myself" first appeared in the 1855 edition of *Leaves of Grass,* but the poem wasn't named until the third edition of the book was published in 1882. Whitman continued to revise "Song of Myself" until his death in 1892. The following are Flan's favorite sections of the poem, taken from an edition published in 1900.

# Excerpts from "Song of Myself"

1

I celebrate myself, and sing myself,
And what I assume you shall assume,
For every atom belonging to me as good belongs to you.

I loafe and invite my soul,
I lean and loafe at my ease observing a spear of summer grass.

My tongue, every atom of my blood, form'd from this soil, this air,
Born here of parents born here from parents the same, and their
       parents the same,
I, now thirty-seven years old in perfect health begin,
Hoping to cease not till death.

Creeds and schools in abeyance,
Retiring back a while sufficed at what they are, but never forgotten,
I harbor for good or bad, I permit to speak at every hazard,
Nature without check with original energy.

2

Houses and rooms are full of perfumes, the shelves are crowded with
       perfumes,
I breathe the fragrance myself and know it and like it,
The distillation would intoxicate me also, but I shall not let it.

The atmosphere is not a perfume, it has no taste of the
       distillation, it is odorless,
It is for my mouth forever, I am in love with it,
I will go to the bank by the wood and become undisguised and naked,
I am mad for it to be in contact with me.

The smoke of my own breath,
Echoes, ripples, buzz'd whispers, love-root, silk-thread, crotch and
  vine,
My respiration and inspiration, the beating of my heart, the passing
  of blood and air through my lungs,
The sniff of green leaves and dry leaves, and of the shore and
  dark-color'd sea-rocks, and of hay in the barn,
The sound of the belch'd words of my voice loos'd to the eddies of
  the wind,
A few light kisses, a few embraces, a reaching around of arms,
The play of shine and shade on the trees as the supple boughs wag,
The delight alone or in the rush of the streets, or along the fields
  and hill-sides,
The feeling of health, the full-noon trill, the song of me rising
  from bed and meeting the sun.


Have you reckon'd a thousand acres much? have you reckon'd the earth
  much?
Have you practis'd so long to learn to read?
Have you felt so proud to get at the meaning of poems?


Stop this day and night with me and you shall possess the origin of
  all poems,
You shall possess the good of the earth and sun, (there are millions
  of suns left,)
You shall no longer take things at second or third hand, nor look
  through the eyes of the dead, nor feed on the spectres in
  books,
You shall not look through my eyes either, nor take things from me,
You shall listen to all sides and filter them from your self.


6

A child said *What is the grass?* fetching it to me with full hands;
How could I answer the child? I do not know what it is any more
  than he.

I guess it must be the flag of my disposition, out of hopeful green
    stuff woven.

Or I guess it is the handkerchief of the Lord,
A scented gift and remembrancer designedly dropt,
Bearing the owner's name someway in the corners, that we may see
    and remark, and say *Whose?*

Or I guess the grass is itself a child, the produced babe of the
    vegetation.

Or I guess it is a uniform hieroglyphic,
And it means, Sprouting alike in broad zones and narrow zones,
Growing among black folks as among white,
Kanuck, Tuckahoe, Congressman, Cuff, I give them the same, I
    receive them the same.

And now it seems to me the beautiful uncut hair of graves.

Tenderly will I use you curling grass,
It may be you transpire from the breasts of young men,
It may be if I had known them I would have loved them,
It may be you are from old people, or from offspring taken soon out
    of their mothers' laps,
And here you are the mothers' laps.

This grass is very dark to be from the white heads of old mothers,
Darker than the colorless beards of old men,
Dark to come from under the faint red roofs of mouths.

O I perceive after all so many uttering tongues,
And I perceive they do not come from the roofs of mouths for
    nothing.

I wish I could translate the hints about the dead young men and
    women,

And the hints about old men and mothers, and the offspring taken
    soon out of their laps.

What do you think has become of the young and old men?
And what do you think has become of the women and children?

They are alive and well somewhere,
The smallest sprout shows there is really no death,
And if ever there was it led forward life, and does not wait at the
    end to arrest it,
And ceas'd the moment life appear'd.

All goes onward and outward, nothing collapses,
And to die is different from what any one supposed, and luckier.

    16
I am of old and young, of the foolish as much as the wise,
Regardless of others, ever regardful of others,
Maternal as well as paternal, a child as well as a man,
Stuff'd with the stuff that is coarse and stuff'd with the stuff
    that is fine,
One of the Nation of many nations, the smallest the same and the
    largest the same,
A Southerner soon as a Northerner, a planter nonchalant and
    hospitable down by the Oconee I live,
A Yankee bound my own way ready for trade, my joints the limberest
    joints on earth and the sternest joints on earth,
A Kentuckian walking the vale of the Elkhorn in my deer-skin
    leggings, a Louisianian or Georgian,
A boatman over lakes or bays or along coasts, a Hoosier, Badger,
    Buckeye;
At home on Kanadian snow-shoes or up in the bush, or with
    fishermen off Newfoundland,
At home in the fleet of ice-boats, sailing with the rest and tacking,
At home on the hills of Vermont or in the woods of Maine, or the
    Texan ranch,

Comrade of Californians, comrade of free North-Westerners, (loving
  their big proportions,)
Comrade of raftsmen and coalmen, comrade of all who shake hands
  and welcome to drink and meat,
A learner with the simplest, a teacher of the thoughtfullest,
A novice beginning yet experient of myriads of seasons,
Of every hue and caste am I, of every rank and religion,
A farmer, mechanic, artist, gentleman, sailor, quaker,
Prisoner, fancy-man, rowdy, lawyer, physician, priest.

I resist any thing better than my own diversity,
Breathe the air but leave plenty after me,
And am not stuck up, and am in my place.

(The moth and the fish-eggs are in their place,
The bright suns I see and the dark suns I cannot see are in their place,
The palpable is in its place and the impalpable is in its place.)


19
This is the meal equally set, this the meat for natural hunger,
It is for the wicked just the same as the righteous, I make appointments
  with all,
I will not have a single person slighted or left away,
The kept-woman, sponger, thief, are hereby invited;
The heavy-lipp'd slave is invited, the venerealee is invited;
There shall be no difference between them and the rest.

This is the press of a bashful hand, this the float and odor of hair,
This the touch of my lips to yours, this the murmur of yearning,
This the far-off depth and height reflecting my own face,
This the thoughtful merge of myself, and the outlet again.

Do you guess I have some intricate purpose?
Well I have, for the Fourth-month showers have, and the mica on the
  side of a rock has.

Do you take it I would astonish?
Does the daylight astonish? does the early redstart twittering
    through the woods?
Do I astonish more than they?

This hour I tell things in confidence,
I might not tell everybody, but I will tell you.

21

I am the poet of the Body and I am the poet of the Soul,
The pleasures of heaven are with me and the pains of hell are with me,
The first I graft and increase upon myself, the latter I translate
    into a new tongue.

I am the poet of the woman the same as the man,
And I say it is as great to be a woman as to be a man,
And I say there is nothing greater than the mother of men.

I chant the chant of dilation or pride,
We have had ducking and deprecating about enough,
I show that size is only development.

Have you outstript the rest? are you the President?
It is a trifle, they will more than arrive there every one, and
    still pass on.

I am he that walks with the tender and growing night,
I call to the earth and sea half-held by the night.

Press close bare-bosom'd night—press close magnetic nourishing
    night!
Night of south winds—night of the large few stars!
Still nodding night—mad naked summer night.

Smile O voluptuous cool-breath'd earth!
Earth of the slumbering and liquid trees!

Earth of departed sunset—earth of the mountains misty-topt!
Earth of the vitreous pour of the full moon just tinged with blue!
Earth of shine and dark mottling the tide of the river!
Earth of the limpid gray of clouds brighter and clearer for my sake!
Far-swooping elbow'd earth—rich apple-blossom'd earth!
Smile, for your lover comes.

Prodigal, you have given me love—therefore I to you give love!
O unspeakable passionate love.

24

Walt Whitman, a kosmos, of Manhattan the son,
Turbulent, fleshy, sensual, eating, drinking and breeding,
No sentimentalist, no stander above men and women or apart from
    them,
No more modest than immodest.

Unscrew the locks from the doors!
Unscrew the doors themselves from their jambs!

Whoever degrades another degrades me,
And whatever is done or said returns at last to me.

Through me the afflatus surging and surging, through me the current
    and index.

I speak the pass-word primeval, I give the sign of democracy,
By God! I will accept nothing which all cannot have their
    counterpart of on the same terms.

Through me many long dumb voices,
Voices of the interminable generations of prisoners and slaves,
Voices of the diseas'd and despairing and of thieves and dwarfs,
Voices of cycles of preparation and accretion,
And of the threads that connect the stars, and of wombs and of the
    father-stuff,

And of the rights of them the others are down upon,
Of the deform'd, trivial, flat, foolish, despised,
Fog in the air, beetles rolling balls of dung.

Through me forbidden voices,
Voices of sexes and lusts, voices veil'd and I remove the veil,
Voices indecent by me clarified and transfigur'd.

I do not press my fingers across my mouth,
I keep as delicate around the bowels as around the head and heart,
Copulation is no more rank to me than death is.

I believe in the flesh and the appetites,
Seeing, hearing, feeling, are miracles, and each part and tag of me
    is a miracle.

Divine am I inside and out, and I make holy whatever I touch or am
    touch'd from,
The scent of these arm-pits aroma finer than prayer,
This head more than churches, bibles, and all the creeds.

If I worship one thing more than another it shall be the spread of
    my own body, or any part of it,
Translucent mould of me it shall be you!
Shaded ledges and rests it shall be you!
Firm masculine colter it shall be you!
Whatever goes to the tilth of me it shall be you!
You my rich blood! your milky stream pale strippings of my life!
Breast that presses against other breasts it shall be you!
My brain it shall be your occult convolutions!
Root of wash'd sweet-flag! timorous pond-snipe! nest of guarded
    duplicate eggs! it shall be you!
Mix'd tussled hay of head, beard, brawn, it shall be you!
Trickling sap of maple, fibre of manly wheat, it shall be you!
Sun so generous it shall be you!
Vapors lighting and shading my face it shall be you!

You sweaty brooks and dews it shall be you!
Winds whose soft-tickling genitals rub against me it shall be you!
Broad muscular fields, branches of live oak, loving lounger in my
     winding paths, it shall be you!
Hands I have taken, face I have kiss'd, mortal I have ever touch'd,
     it shall be you.

I dote on myself, there is that lot of me and all so luscious,
Each moment and whatever happens thrills me with joy,
I cannot tell how my ankles bend, nor whence the cause of my faintest
     wish,
Nor the cause of the friendship I emit, nor the cause of the
     friendship I take again.

That I walk up my stoop, I pause to consider if it really be,
A morning-glory at my window satisfies me more than the
     metaphysics of books.

To behold the day-break!
The little light fades the immense and diaphanous shadows,
The air tastes good to my palate.

Hefts of the moving world at innocent gambols silently rising,
     freshly exuding,
Scooting obliquely high and low.

Something I cannot see puts upward libidinous prongs,
Seas of bright juice suffuse heaven.

The earth by the sky staid with, the daily close of their junction,
The heav'd challenge from the east that moment over my head,
The mocking taunt, See then whether you shall be master!

     28
Is this then a touch? quivering me to a new identity,
Flames and ether making a rush for my veins,

Treacherous tip of me reaching and crowding to help them,
My flesh and blood playing out lightning to strike what is hardly
    different from myself,
On all sides prurient provokers stiffening my limbs,
Straining the udder of my heart for its withheld drip,
Behaving licentious toward me, taking no denial,
Depriving me of my best as for a purpose,
Unbuttoning my clothes, holding me by the bare waist,
Deluding my confusion with the calm of the sunlight and pasture-
    fields,
Immodestly sliding the fellow-senses away,
They bribed to swap off with touch and go and graze at the edges
    of me,
No consideration, no regard for my draining strength or my anger,
Fetching the rest of the herd around to enjoy them a while,
Then all uniting to stand on a headland and worry me.

The sentries desert every other part of me,
They have left me helpless to a red marauder,
They all come to the headland to witness and assist against me.

I am given up by traitors,
I talk wildly, I have lost my wits, I and nobody else am the
    greatest traitor,
I went myself first to the headland, my own hands carried me there.

You villain touch! what are you doing? my breath is tight in its throat,
Unclench your floodgates, you are too much for me.

38
Enough! enough! enough!
Somehow I have been stunn'd. Stand back!
Give me a little time beyond my cuff'd head, slumbers, dreams,
    gaping,
I discover myself on the verge of a usual mistake.

That I could forget the mockers and insults!
That I could forget the trickling tears and the blows of the
    bludgeons and hammers!
That I could look with a separate look on my own crucifixion and
    bloody crowning.

I remember now,
I resume the overstaid fraction,
The grave of rock multiplies what has been confided to it, or to any
    graves,
Corpses rise, gashes heal, fastenings roll from me.

I troop forth replenish'd with supreme power, one of an average
    unending procession,
Inland and sea-coast we go, and pass all boundary lines,
Our swift ordinances on their way over the whole earth,
The blossoms we wear in our hats the growth of thousands of years.

Eleves, I salute you! come forward!
Continue your annotations, continue your questionings.

44
It is time to explain myself—let us stand up.

What is known I strip away,
I launch all men and women forward with me into the Unknown.

The clock indicates the moment—but what does eternity indicate?

We have thus far exhausted trillions of winters and summers,
There are trillions ahead, and trillions ahead of them.

Births have brought us richness and variety,
And other births will bring us richness and variety.

I do not call one greater and one smaller,
That which fills its period and place is equal to any.

Were mankind murderous or jealous upon you, my brother, my sister?
I am sorry for you, they are not murderous or jealous upon me,
All has been gentle with me, I keep no account with lamentation,
(What have I to do with lamentation?)

I am an acme of things accomplish'd, and I an encloser of things to be.

My feet strike an apex of the apices of the stairs,
On every step bunches of ages, and larger bunches between the
    steps,
All below duly travel'd, and still I mount and mount.

Rise after rise bow the phantoms behind me,
Afar down I see the huge first Nothing, I know I was even there,
I waited unseen and always, and slept through the lethargic mist,
And took my time, and took no hurt from the fetid carbon.

Long I was hugg'd close—long and long.

Immense have been the preparations for me,
Faithful and friendly the arms that have help'd me.

Cycles ferried my cradle, rowing and rowing like cheerful boatmen,
For room to me stars kept aside in their own rings,
They sent influences to look after what was to hold me.

Before I was born out of my mother generations guided me,
My embryo has never been torpid, nothing could overlay it.

For it the nebula cohered to an orb,
The long slow strata piled to rest it on,
Vast vegetables gave it sustenance,
Monstrous sauroids transported it in their mouths and deposited it
    with care.

All forces have been steadily employ'd to complete and delight me,
Now on this spot I stand with my robust soul.

46

I know I have the best of time and space, and was never measured and
   never will be measured.

I tramp a perpetual journey, (come listen all!)
My signs are a rain-proof coat, good shoes, and a staff cut from the
   woods,
No friend of mine takes his ease in my chair,
I have no chair, no church, no philosophy,
I lead no man to a dinner-table, library, exchange,
But each man and each woman of you I lead upon a knoll,
My left hand hooking you round the waist,
My right hand pointing to landscapes of continents and the public
   road.

Not I, not any one else can travel that road for you,
You must travel it for yourself.

It is not far, it is within reach,
Perhaps you have been on it since you were born and did not know,
Perhaps it is everywhere on water and on land.
Shoulder your duds dear son, and I will mine, and let us hasten forth,
Wonderful cities and free nations we shall fetch as we go.

If you tire, give me both burdens, and rest the chuff of your hand
   on my hip,
And in due time you shall repay the same service to me,
For after we start we never lie by again.

This day before dawn I ascended a hill and look'd at the crowded
   heaven,
And I said to my spirit *When we become the enfolders of those orbs,*
   *and the pleasure and knowledge of every thing in them, shall we*
   *be fill'd and satisfied then?*
And my spirit said *No, we but level that lift to pass and continue*
   *beyond.*

You are also asking me questions and I hear you,
I answer that I cannot answer, you must find out for yourself.

Sit a while dear son,
Here are biscuits to eat and here is milk to drink,
But as soon as you sleep and renew yourself in sweet clothes, I kiss you
    with a good-by kiss and open the gate for your egress hence.

Long enough have you dream'd contemptible dreams,
Now I wash the gum from your eyes,
You must habit yourself to the dazzle of the light and of every
    moment of your life.

Long have you timidly waded holding a plank by the shore,
Now I will you to be a bold swimmer,
To jump off in the midst of the sea, rise again, nod to me, shout,
    and laughingly dash with your hair.

51
The past and present wilt—I have fill'd them, emptied them.
And proceed to fill my next fold of the future.

Listener up there! what have you to confide to me?
Look in my face while I snuff the sidle of evening,
(Talk honestly, no one else hears you, and I stay only a minute longer.)

Do I contradict myself?
Very well then I contradict myself,
(I am large, I contain multitudes.)

I concentrate toward them that are nigh, I wait on the door-slab.

Who has done his day's work? who will soonest be through with his
    supper?
Who wishes to walk with me?

Will you speak before I am gone? will you prove already too late?

52

The spotted hawk swoops by and accuses me, he complains of my gab
    and my loitering.

I too am not a bit tamed, I too am untranslatable,
I sound my barbaric yawp over the roofs of the world.

The last scud of day holds back for me,
It flings my likeness after the rest and true as any on the shadow'd
    wilds,
It coaxes me to the vapor and the dusk.

I depart as air, I shake my white locks at the runaway sun,
I effuse my flesh in eddies, and drift it in lacy jags.

I bequeath myself to the dirt to grow from the grass I love,
If you want me again look for me under your boot-soles.

You will hardly know who I am or what I mean,
But I shall be good health to you nevertheless,
And filter and fibre your blood.

Failing to fetch me at first keep encouraged,
Missing me one place search another,
I stop somewhere waiting for you.

# SELF
# STORAGE

# Gayle Brandeis

A READER'S GUIDE

# A Conversation with Gayle Brandeis

Laraine Herring, author of Lost Fathers: How Women Can Heal from Adolescent Father Loss and Writing Begins with the Breath: Embodying Your Authentic Voice interviewed Gayle Brandeis about the novel Self Storage. Gayle and Laraine attended an MFA program together at the Antioch University in Los Angeles and have remained close friends and writing companions.

**Laraine Herring:** You've said that fiction allows us to slip into others' skins—to see through different eyes. How is the process of creating that other perspective different for the writer than for the reader?

**Gayle Brandeis:** Readers have the luxury of jumping directly into the story, slipping it on like a magic jacket. The writer, on the other hand, has to make sure that the stitching is correct, that the cloth has integrity, and that it won't come apart at the seams. It's a huge responsibility, writing about another culture—you want it to ring true, to have an authentic foundation. It takes a lot of humility and chutzpah all at once. Then again, all fiction does.

You probably remember my agony over writing *The Book of Dead Birds* when we were at Antioch. I struggled so much with my right to write Ava's story, my right as a white woman to deign to explore the life of a woman whose mother was Korean and whose father was African-American. Ava wouldn't leave me alone, though—she wouldn't let me walk away from the story, and I had to build up my courage and disappear into the work as fully as I could. And ultimately I found that I had much more in common with Ava than I realized. In *Self Storage,* I hoped to convey our common humanity through Sodaba, even though it can quite literally be veiled by our differences on the surface. I wanted to get down to the beating human heart we all share.

**LH:** What lessons has your work taught you?

**GB:** My writing is constantly teaching me lessons. One lesson I keep relearning is the importance of getting out of my own way. Each story has its own rhythm, its own flow, and if I try to control its unfolding, it will often end up stilted and unsatisfying. Writing has taught me to trust the moment, trust the creative process. It has taught me to not take myself too seriously (but at the same time, to take the work itself seriously.) It has taught me to be open—to not judge characters (including real ones!). To be receptive to inspiration wherever it wants to come from. To not be afraid of the dark. To take risks. To pay attention to life. To have fun!

**LH:** After a novel is finished, are you ever surprised to discover what you're *really* writing about? Is that different from what you thought you were writing about? I'm thinking not so much about particular plot points, but about deeper emotional truths of a writing project.

**GB:** Oh my goodness, yes. And the truth is often much smaller and more intimate than I lead myself to believe. Sometimes I'm convinced that a book is about some big concept, but it turns out to be more about a quiet moment between two characters. *Self Storage* started out almost as a thesis about the *self*—I wanted to explore what the self means in the context of our culture today. Later I realized that the book was much more about the characters' desire for and fear of connection. It operated on a much more human scale than I had imagined. I love how stories find their way into their own truest heart, almost in spite of the author's intention; my writing is definitely smarter than I am!

**LH:** Our mentor at Antioch, Alma Villanueva, stressed the importance of dreams in fiction writing. Have dreams ever played a role in your writing process?

**GB:** A fever dream changed the whole course of *The Book of Dead Birds;* I had been writing in the third person because it felt safer. I could be an observer, not claim to live inside Ava's skin. Then I came down with strep throat and had intense fever dreams in which I became Ava. When the fever broke, I realized Ava needed to tell the story in her own voice. I'm not sure I would have made that shift without that dream; it was the shift that brought the book to life for me.

Writing dreams aren't always that productive, though. Once I dreamed I was in a movie theater. On the screen was a close-up of a giant book I had never seen before. I read each page, and then a giant hand would turn to the next page. I read the whole novel that way, completely engrossed. I woke up thinking that all I had to do was transcribe the dream, and the novel on the screen would be mine. Unfortunately, by the time I sat down to write, I couldn't remember a single word of it.

**LH:** Let's shift to *Self Storage* now. I think there's something unusual about a culture that has to rent space to store "stuff" that doesn't fit at home. Do you think the plethora of self-storage units across the country is indicative of something larger at work in the fabric of America?

**GB:** In 2003, when I was on a book tour for *The Book of Dead Birds*, I met a woman on an airplane who told me she supplemented her income by going to self-storage auctions and selling her winnings at yard sales. Though "self storage" signs had piqued my interest for years, I had never heard of self-storage auctions before. I actually wasn't supposed to be on that plane to begin with: I took an earlier flight to be home with my family; my mother-in-law's husband, Jack, had just been diagnosed with brain cancer. He died a few days later. I dedicated the book to his memory—I wouldn't have known about self-storage auctions if I hadn't changed flights. Of course, I'd rather have Jack in the world than the book.

The ubiquity of self-storage establishments does speak volumes about our consumer culture. I imagine it's indicative of a deeper hunger—we keep trying to fill a hole inside ourselves with stuff, but those calories are empty. We buy more and more until we don't have room for it, but we're still hungry, so we keep buying, as if the next purchase is what will make us whole.

**LH:** Did you attend any auctions at self-storage centers? If so, what prevailing feelings did you notice at the auctions?

**GB:** I attended a couple of auctions as I was writing the book, and then a couple more before the book came out so I could pick up some boxes to open at readings. I really wanted to share that moment of discovery with the audience. I invited anyone who asked a question to come choose something from the box to bring home, and people were very excited to come claim their treasure.

The auctions are quite congenial, sometimes even raucous—a real sense of community develops among the bidders. There is such anticipation when the metal door is lifted—what gold mine or trash heap waits inside? At the same time, a sense of sadness permeates the whole enterprise. The lots up for auction hold the evidence, the remnants of people's lives—people who most likely have fallen upon hard times—and it can make the bidders feel like vultures circling a carcass. I started to feel a bit sick about what I was doing at my readings. I had to stop bringing boxes to my events. I've held onto the items that seem most personally significant—homemade Christmas ornaments, photos of children, et cetera—and I'm going to try to track down the original owners so I can return them.

**LH:** Flan's husband, Shae, spends most of the novel on the couch watching soap operas. Flan's frustration with him is an underlying tension throughout the novel. How did you, as the author, find empathy with his character?

**GB:** I think we all have a couch-potato side to ourselves, a side that just wants to give in to entropy. I remember when you and I shared a beach house during our Antioch residencies, our friend Peggy once called me a house cat because of how I would lounge around and read and not necessarily be "doing" things all the time. So I can relate in a way to Shae (although I think that Shae's lounging comes from fear, from feeling stuck, not from a desire to luxuriate). I also wanted to give Shae a chance to redeem himself, to get up off the couch—and thank goodness he did!

**LH:** The heat seemed almost to be a character in the novel. You live in the desert in California. I spent twenty-five years in the Phoenix desert. It's hard to really describe the heat, the pervasive, unrelenting sunlight and dryness that exists most of the year in these regions. As you were writing, did you consciously think about how weather can oppress?

**GB:** I realized recently that I keep writing about heat. *The Book of Dead Birds* takes place in the summer in the desert; *Self Storage* takes place in the summer in the (irrigated) desert. I am currently writing a novel set during the summer pear harvest in the Sacramento Delta. I wasn't thinking consciously of how oppressive the summer heat can be in Riverside, but I'm sure it seeped in subconsciously as I wrote *Self Storage*. Perhaps my next novel should take place in the snow!

**LH:** *Self Storage* strikes me in many ways as a commentary on the changing social structure of America, and I think you use Whitman in part as an anchor throughout the text to pull us back to the struggle between individual identity and community identity. I think about how many people live behind gates, or behind block walls, especially here in the west—how many people don't know their neighbors and don't know how to create community. Were you thinking in any way about the end of the "rugged individual" archetype in American society in favor of a more sustainable, community-based lifestyle? Is America waking up?

GB: I very much like this interpretation. I think our cultural focus on the individual and self-reliance can be inspiring in terms of people wanting to find their own voice and trust their own vision, but it can also be very isolating. Such a focus makes it easy for us to forget how interconnected we are; we can forget to reach out to a larger community that can nourish us. I set *Self Storage* in family student housing at the University of California at Riverside because I loved the sense of community when my family lived there in the early 1990s. We would have communal meals and share child care, just like in the book; no one had much money, but everyone had plenty to give.

I first encountered Whitman in my junior year of high school. I was very shy and cautious at the time, but there was a part of me that longed for the freedom of Whitman's long breathless lines. I loved how he connected with absolutely *everything*, how open he was to experience, to the world. He gave me a sense of possibility that blew my mind.

I do think America is waking up. We're realizing that we need to take more responsibility for our planet—reduce our carbon footprints, eat locally when possible, recycle, et cetera. It's very cool to see these issues enter mainstream public awareness and discourse. People are asking more questions now—of the government and the media—which is such a relief after so many years of fear-induced public silence. More of us are beginning to realize that things need to change, and—as Gandhi said—that we must be the change we wish to see in the world. I hope *Self Storage* reminds people that through tolerance and compassion, we can begin to achieve real change.

# Reading Group Questions and Topics for Discussion

1. How does the excerpt from the Marge Piercy poem that serves as the epigraph to the novel set the stage for what follows? Why do you think the author chose this particular passage?

2. At self-storage auctions, Flan bids on objects that used to belong to other people, and, in many cases, were important to those people. How do objects inform our sense of identity? Do you believe some part of our selves is stored within the ephemera of our lives?

3. Do you have any experience with self-storage facilities? Did the novel change your impression of secondhand goods?

4. When Flan first meets Julia, she fantasizes about kissing her. Later, she has other fantasies about sexual encounters involving women and men with whom she comes into contact. Are these feelings the result of Flan's frustration with her relationship with Shae, or is something else happening?

5. Is Flan right to help Sodaba? Can you imagine other ways of

helping her than the ways Flan chooses? What would you do in Flan's position?

6. How does education—both formal and otherwise—affect the characters in *Self Storage*?

7. Flan and her family experience communal living of a sort in their family student housing neighborhood. How do their living arrangements impact the events of the novel? Have you ever experienced a similar sense of community?

8. Are Shae and Flan responsible parents? Do they become better parents over the course of the story?

9. What role does motherhood play in the novel? Who are the strongest maternal figures? The most surprising?

10. Were you familiar with the work of Walt Whitman before reading *Self Storage*? If so, did the excerpts here—and the role Whitman plays in Flan's life—change your impression of him? If you were not familiar with Whitman's poetry, are you inclined to read more of it now?

11. When Flan finds a piece of paper with "yes" written on it inside a box, it leads her on a quest to discover the source of "yes" in her life. Is her quest successful? What is the source of "yes" in your own life? Have you ever thought of the word in this way?

12. *Self Storage* takes place in the year following the 9/11 attacks. How has America changed since that day? How does the novel reflect that change?

13. When Flan decides to sell her copy of *Leaves of Grass,* do you think that means that she has moved beyond her need for Whitman, that she is free of him? If not, how might Whitman continue to play a role in Flan's life?

14. At the end of the novel, Flan fears that she is about to be arrested and perhaps "disappeared" by the government for her role in spiriting Sodaba to safety. Are her fears justified, or does running away represent an opportunity for Flan to change her life? Do you view this ending as hopeful, or ominous?

GAYLE BRANDEIS is the author of the novel *The Book of Dead Birds*, which won Barbara Kingsolver's Bellwether Prize for Fiction in Support of a Literature of Social Change; *Fruitflesh: Seeds of Inspiration for Women Who Write;* and *Dictionary Poems*. She lives in Riverside, California, with her husband and two children.

## About the Type

This book was set in Minion, a 1990 Adobe Originals typeface by Robert Slimbach. Minion is inspired by classical, old style typefaces of the late Renaissance, a period of elegant, beautiful, and highly readable type designs. Created primarily for text setting, Minion combines the aesthetic and functional qualities that make text type highly readable with the versatility of digital technology.